The
Locksmith

JULIAN
POULTER

Chapter 1

The outskirts of London 1880.
One year after the Zulu wars.

The sun rose over the rough cobbles, narrow sideways, and crumbling houses trying to bring fresh light and hope, but to little avail. Day by day, night by night, life carried on in the hardest, but also simplest, form in the village. It seemed not one wall or brick was not battered or broken in some way. However, the people there were, on the whole, good natured and would take each day as it comes, working hard in life, be it for their masters or husbands or the land itself. Every day was about survival for the individual and for the family, food and money being the most important things, and yet these were the things lacking the most. Of course, there were some people who did not have such concerns, where most pleasures were in abundance. Alas, that was not the case for Jonathan and his family. Jonathan's mother and father were part of the many and not the few.

It was on these very cobbles where Jonathan could be seen walking towards his family's house;

a soft and gentle lad in hard yet picturesque country surroundings, standing no taller than four and a half foot. He was not ten minutes away upon realizing that he must quicken his pace. His father ruled the household and his family with an iron fist, along with an iron heart. Step by step, heart beating faster, he was getting closer to home, dashing across roads, jumping over half broken wooden fences, until he finally reached his destination.

Just as he opened the front door, his father in a rage yelled out, 'You're late! Again!'

'Sorry, Father,' replied Jonathan as he entered the house.

Jonathan's father, 'Edward', was a large, stout man, not long out of Queen Victoria's army; the Duke of Cambridge 17th own Lancers to be precise, arguably one of the toughest regiments around at this time, or so Edward would make you believe. True or not, those red coats had done their bit for Queen and Country, whilst fighting at Rorke's Drift just one year prior. But the scars of war are not always easy to perceive with the naked eye.

Ever since returning from that god-forsaken war, Edward had not remained how he was before, not that he was the most pleasant of men beforehand, at any rate. It was as if he'd left for Africa a pig of a man and returned as a wild boar. It seemed worse still that he had all the reason in the world to be happy, or at least contented in that of his wife Sarah. No job was too hard for her, and a smile almost always remained when her son was close. She'd put a brave face on and try not to upset her husband in any shape or form. Deep down, in her heart, she wished a Zulu spear could have pierced her husband's body on the hot sands of a faraway continent. Edward would constantly recount tale after tale of the horrors and ugliness of what he'd been through, and of course, being nothing more than a liar and a coward with a strong arm, he would often be the hero in his tales.

Every story he gave only contained a slight element that held any weight of fact. In truth, he was often more of a hindrance to his fellow soldiers and comrades as opposed to being a help, let alone being a hero. Over the past twelve months as a civilian, it seemed that he'd started to believe his own lies. Sarah was not in need of a hero. All she wanted was the man she once knew. She was fully aware from other sources that Edward was not highly disturbed and suffering inside from his war days, but she'd dared not say anything to question him. It was hard for her to hear his stories of taking on ten, even twenty, Zulus single-handed or saving a hospital from a fire, at the same time knowing that they were just that: stories.

May as well have been the myths and legends of the snake-haired Medusa or centaurs and minotaurs, or even the winged horse Pegasus. At least *they* had been made up for mostly wholesome reasons, or fairy tale and folklore. Six thousand years ago, the stories told by Greek elders circling campfires of Gods and beasts held more fact than what Edward would often portray. They were not just lies; they desecrated the true heroic deeds that *had* happened in war by another's hand.

Sarah tried to be supportive, understanding, and would listen and help where she could, but 'it wasn't an easy task with such a horrible man. Most of her replies would be, 'Yes dear', whilst thinking to herself *'Oh, why lord, if he was grossly outnumbered, why oh why could he not have been taken?'*. Many a decent solider and honourable man lost his life in that war, which made it all the more of an injustice that Edward had lived.

The mean eyes of Edward glared at Jonathan as he breathlessly stood in the entrance to his house, shaking from the frantic run home.

'Go and get my food, you little shit. Your mother's at work!' he yelled. Obediently, Jonathan did as 'he was told. From the kitchen he gathered a crusty bread roll and a couple slices of ham, accompanied by a bottle of beer. With a single tear rolling down his face, he handed over the plate to his father. He snatched his son's efforts and sat in his chair in the corner of the room.

'Get on with the rest of your work!' he ordered.

The reply from Jonathan was just two words; the most commonly used words in his vocabulary, which were simply: 'Yes, Father.'

There were plenty of other places that would have been even worse for this young fellow, especially being only twelve years old. The streets, the workhouse. Jonathan always tried his best in life, just like his mother, and no reason could warrant the behaviour of Edward to his loving family. War has worsened him, but he had always been a vile man, especially to the ones he loved, or at least reported to love.

The hours passed as the early evening darkness slowly drew in, and the highlight of Jonathan's day approached. Sarah was one of the few decent people he had in his life, and it was always a joy to see her. Looking at the clock on the old oak mantelpiece, watching the second-hand tick by, the door opened right on time as Jonathan rushed into the warm embrace of her arms.

'Oh, love, let me get inside the house properly,' she said with her usual smile.

As she closed the door behind her, she attempted to strike up conversation with her husband, asking about his day. But it seemed as if her attempts fell on deaf ears, as it did almost every day. She seldom complained and took the hand that God dealt her in this life.

'You could at least say hello, dear,' she said to Edward.

A deep voice yelled in reply from the chair, 'Hello! Satisfied now?'

With a deep breath of sadness, she carried on as usual. She would have been surprised by any other response, but it would have been a nice surprise and one fitting a happy husband and wife.

Jonathan tried to respect his father and knew he should, even for the sake of his mother, but any good feeling he had towards his father was always a little hollow, void of love and harmony. It was real but also forced, as if it was going against his nature to love and respect his father. What love he lacked from his father, his mother made up for. Many other people had it worse in these times.

The days rolled on, every day the same as the last. Work and sleep with little time for anything else. Survival was the key. Sundays were always the nicest of days for Jonathan. With the exception of the normal routine chores, and church, of course, he had the whole day to do with as he pleased. He'd often see his best friend, Thomas, a lad of similar stature and position to himself. They'd known each other most of their lives. Without being an extra burden to his mother, Jonathan would often talk, play, and enjoy the company of his friend.

On a Sunday in mid-Autumn, Thomas and Jonathan sat on a rough stone wall, as they often did, talking about everything and nothing, having a break from their very important cup and ball competition, whilst guzzling down a rare treat; a litre of lemonade, given to them by the owner of the corner shop.

'Didn't even cost us a penny!' said Thomas with a smile on his face, licking his lips.

'Good job, too. We haven't *got* a penny,' replied Jonathan.

Jonathan, with his harmless but mischievous nature, suggested they take a trip up to the farmlands, no less than a mile away, to explore the woods and the fields and, if 'they were lucky enough, pick some berries. Thomas quickly agreed and added, 'We could shoot a couple rabbits and have them for tea. I can shoot, and I've seen you do it once before.'

Jonathan paused and figured it was not just a good idea but also a fun one.

In the excitement, Thomas realised they did not have a gun. 'I could make a rabbit trap,' he said.

Jonathan had made rabbit traps in the past, and even though it was fun, he was still contemplating the idea of shooting.

'I know where there is a gun,' said Jonathan with a cheeky smile.

Thomas tilted his head.. 'Where … where?'

'My father's rifle,' replied Jonathan. 'I know exactly where it is'. The look of happiness and excitement on Thomas' face quickly turned to one of confusion.

'Oh, I don't know …' he said. Thomas knew all about Jonathan's father and what kind of a man he was.

'It'll be fine,' Jonathan said. 'I can get it and put it back without him even knowing.'

The mood in the air changed as a gust of wind howled for what seemed like minutes, as if it was some kind of warning from a higher power. Thomas agreed, albeit with some hesitation, and the two boys hatched a plan that on the following Sunday they would get the rifle and go shooting. With a good feeling, the friends parted ways knowing that a little adventure would await them in just seven days' time. Jonathan, almost skipping back home, was lost in thought about how he would get the rifle. He had all week to think of something.

The next day was the same as any other, same old chores, same old father and, luckily, same old mother. Jonathan was wishing the days away; all he could think about was the next time he'd be with his friend. Monday turned into Tuesday, Tuesday turned into Wednesday, and before he knew it, it was the weekend. Saturday night 'was bitterly cold and dark, and Jonathan was in his bed thinking about the next morning. He knew he would have to tell a lie to his father in order to get him out of the house. It was not a comforting thought, even though it wasn't technically evil or cruel. Just a little naughty at the very most. He could hardly sleep with the thought of the next day but knew he needed his strength. The wind set in as the night carried on, but the dark brown branches of the tree in the garden bashing against the window did not wake Jonathan up. He was fast asleep and dreaming of better times.

6.30am, the morning had come with a fresh, cool, damp mist. Jonathan happily got up and started making breakfast for his mother and father with what little food they had in the kitchen. With his eagerness, he was bashing and clattering away with the pots and pans.

Sarah greeted him and asked to help. 'Come on, darling, we shall do it together,' she said.

The horrid voice that they had both come to accept yelled from the bedroom, 'Keep it down in there, bitch!' Sarah took a deep, slow breath and, with a forced smile, carried on in almost silence. Even Jonathan knew at his young age that his mum was trying so hard to be brave and make the best of it for the sake of him. They were each other's strength.

Time ticked slowly by. Jonathan was just waiting for the church bells to start their weekly cheerful ring, knowing that was the time to feign an illness to avoid going. Sarah was just about to gather his Sunday best when Edward suddenly announced he would not be attending church.

'Oh, come on dear,' said Sarah. 'It's only once a week.'

Edward, with his usual and almost constant frown, replied, 'Go, take the lad. I have some business to attend to.'

Now, this was not uncommon for Edward, however, the vast majority of the time, his 'business' consisted of being in the tavern with people he probably had more in common with than his own family. Sarah always pretended to be disheartened at the absence of her husband at church. Long gone were the days when she would try to persuade him with any effort to do anything with her.

Jonathan paused for a moment at the thought of his father going down the pub.

'How long will he be?' thought Jonathan. *'Can I still get the rifle and carry on with my plan? Will Father*

let me stay here alone?'. He needn't have worried too much as Edward had little care for his son.

'Please yourself,' said Sarah. 'Jonathan and I will go and do our duty.'

This was the hardest part for Jonathan, lying to his mother. 'I'm sorry, Mother, I didn't sleep too good at all. Can I stay at home? I promise I'll go next Sunday.'

Sarah was happy to grant her son's wishes and knew that his well-being was more important than church.

The large brass bells from the old stone church steeple rang out over the land, as the villagers from the area started to make their way, some to ask for forgiveness, some to ask for their prayers to be granted, and some who felt it was their duty to attend.

Sarah, looking as lovely and gentle as ever in her clean white cotton dress, left the house in order to join her fellow church-goers.

At home, Jonathan had just fifteen minutes to get his father out the house. But he knew he couldn't say anything to hurry his father along. Not one word would make a difference. Jonathan started praying to finally be alone, whispering to himself,

'Please Lord, please make him leave.'

Within a minute, there was a knock at the door. 'I'll get that, Father,' said Jonathan.

'You leave it be!' he snarled.

Upon pulling the door open, young Thomas was standing, dead still in the frame, with a fearful expression on his face

'Oh ... Oh, hello, I've come to see Jonathan, sir.'

With a movement of his head towards his son, Edward gestured Thomas to come in without a reply or a welcome of any sort. Thomas slowly and delicately entered the front room, cautiously sliding in between Edward and the door frame.

'Thank you, sir,' he said, but the response was a single grunt. Edward reached over to grab his stained flat cap from a rusty hook, making Thomas twitch, slamming the door behind him, with no goodbye. It was to be a blessing that there was the lack of concern regarding his son.

'You're ten minutes early.'

'Never mind,' replied Thomas, 'That was sure a close one, though.'

The two boys stared out of the cracked glass window, eyes on Edward getting smaller and smaller as he walked away and slowly out of sight. Jonathan turned and made his way through a narrow hall towards his parents' bedroom, gingerly opening the door. Knowing they had the house to themselves, his heart was still beating ten to the dozen.

As the door creaked open, Jonathan saw, on the wall above his parents' bed, the rifle. A smile spread across his face. Hanging there in all its splendour, a Martini–Henry looking almost as good as new. Having to stand on the bed in order to reach it, he stretched out as far as he could, his fingertips running along the barrel until they reached the lock of the gun to unhook it from the wall. Returning to the front room of the house, rifle dangling from his shoulder, Jonathan received a hard tap on the arm from his friend.

'Well done,' said Thomas, 'And did you remember the bullets?'

'Well, of course I did. What clot would forget that?' replied Jonathan with a cheeky grin. Thomas, knowing his friend very well indeed, was fully expecting the next sentence to come from Jonathan's mouth.

'Hang on, I'll just get them, and yes, I did forget … Clever-dick'. With a laugh from Thomas, Jonathan dashed off, only to return a moment later, clutching a handful of bullets.

'I'd say we have two hours. Let's go,' said Jonathan as the two left the house with much merriment and excitement, filled with anticipation in their hearts.

Chapter 2

Hard rain began to fall from the heavens as Jonathan and Thomas began their walk up to the farmlands. The rain did not seem to bother them for one instant. It was always a welcoming sight for them being away from their homes. Although only one mile away, it seemed like they'd left their troubles far behind. They were on their own and they could do whatever they wanted. Thomas had a thousand thoughts in his head about what they would do when they got there. They could build a shelter in the woods to protect them from the rain and then cook freshly shot rabbit and sit back, feeling like a king with a full stomach. The possibilities were endless, or so he thought. With each step they took, another raindrop seemed to fall.

'Tis good in a way, this rain, you know,' said Jonathan.

'How's that?' replied his friend.

'Look around, hardly anyone can see us.'

With the combination of church and the bad weather, there was hardly anyone about to set sight on the two boys, and that was just what they wanted.

As they left the crooked village houses behind them, they slowly got closer and closer to the wet and fresh green fields of Mr Pitwick's farm. Farmer Pitwick was a kind, meek, and humble man. Even though the boys would normally be delighted by his presence, on this occasion, they'd rather not see him. He didn't seem to have a bad bone in his body, and yet he wasn't the sort of man they would want to cross.

'We're almost there,' said Jonathan, 'Just around this lane.'

The lane curved round, and the two boys found themselves at the edge of an English wood. Trees of all shapes and sizes stood before them. Old oaks with branches like dead man's hands, birch trees perfect for making arrows, pines to climb, and willows to hid in.

'Let's go and find a ghost, or a monster, or a snake,' said Thomas. The boys climbed over a small wooden fence and jumped down onto the leafy floor, twigs snapping as they landed.

'I'm going to be Robin Hood and will kill the Sheriff's men and rescue Maid Marian,' said Thomas.

'I'm going to be like David Livingstone,' replied Jonathan.

A confused look fell on Thomas' face.

'You know? He's that bloke who found that river in that other country somewhere ... the Nile or something,' continued Jonathan.

With his face showing a modicum of interest, Thomas replied,

'Ahh, I see ... did he find a ghost? In the Nile? How do you know his name?'

Jonathan smiled, 'No ghost. We have a book about him. Only got two books in the house and one is all about him.'

Thomas quickly responded, 'Books? Now who's the clever-dick!'

The boys laughed and worked their way through the woods. Running and dodging trees all around them, this was the place they were happiest. Berries to pick, old oak trees to climb, chestnuts to find, insects to discover, badger sets to detect, and streams to follow and wade in.

Before they knew it, as the minutes flowed away in the passages of time, they found themselves in a clearing just as the rain seemed to stop. With just another few steps forward, they were in a lush green field, grass reaching up past their ankles. The boys laid down on the grass, ignoring how damp it made their clothes.

'Don't think we'll have much luck with rabbits today,' muttered Jonathan.

Not being one for giving up an opportunity to fire the rifle, Thomas replied, 'No matter, we can still shoot. I challenge you to a competition. Loser owes a shilling.'

Neither of the friends had a shilling to hand, but the challenge was accepted nonetheless. Deep down in their heart of hearts, they knew nothing would come of it. Instead of being indebted a coin, the loser would simply be the butt of several jokes. A price worth paying.

Not fifty yards in front of them stood a deep green hedge, covered in brambles as thick as your wrist, as it rang along the edge of a field. This was to be the backdrop for their target.

"There you are,' said Thomas as his little bony finger pointed towards the hedge.

'That's our target? That huge hedge? Now, I know you think I'm a bad shot, but even my own grandma could hit that, and she's dead," Jonathan said in a baffled tone.

'No, you fool … these,' said Thomas as he raised his hand to show Jonathan three sticks he had picked up earlier from the woods. Jonathan smiled in agreement and reached into his left pocket to grab his mother-of-pearl pocketknife to cut away at the ends of the sticks to form a sharp point.

'It'll be like playing cricket,' said Thomas, 'Course … instead of a ball, we'll use a bullet,'

'If we hit the damn thing, that is,' replied Jonathan.

Within a few dozen cuts and slices from the knife, the sticks resembled short spears. Jonathan sat down in the damp grass and placed the rifle beside him. He wiped his brow of sweat as Thomas walked towards the hedge to plunge the would-be stumps into the ground. With Jonathan's whittling skills and the ground being somewhat damp, the sticks punctured the soil like a knife going through warm butter.

With the excitement of seeing the target in front of him, just as Thomas was walking back, there was a temptation to pick up the rifle and take aim straight away.

However, even at the tender age of twelve, Jonathan knew to never point a gun at anyone, whether it was loaded or not. He waited patiently for his friend to return.

As the two boys stood almost shoulder to shoulder, the sun was behind them.

Perfect for a little shooting. Jonathan, being kind, offered his friend the first shot. Thomas, who had never fired a rifle before, was curious and yet slightly anxious and declined the offer.

'Oh ... Oh, you can go first, if that's all right,' He stuttered.

Jonathan lowered the lever beneath the stock of the rifle, causing the breech to lower, exposing the chamber. One bullet in, lever closed, and now it was ready to fire.

Jonathan raised the gun to his shoulder, took aim, and squeezed the trigger. BANG! The noise was so loud it made their ears ring, and, followed be the kick from the butt of the gone, the combination took both of them by surprise as the rifle jerked back violently. With shocked laughter, they waited a few seconds for the smoke to clear. Through the smoke, they slowly saw the target still standing in one piece. Not even a single scratch on the sticks.

'You must have bashed the sights on a tree or something earlier,' Thomas said as way of explanation.

Jonathan, having some knowledge of guns, albeit limited knowledge, knew it would just take a few shots to get used to it. He admired his friends words and meaning though. Or perhaps Thomas was readying his future excuse, just in case he were to miss as well. It mattered not either way, both were very competitive and wanted to win, however, the winner would always be the both of them through their friendship. The fun came first and the winner would simply get a pat on the back.

Jonathan handed over the gun.

'Can you load it for me please?' he asked.

Jonathan did so at once. Thomas copied how Jonathan had stood and held the firearm. BANG! Hearts beating as fast as a steam train, They looked through the gunpowder mist and saw history repeating itself. Not one splinter cracked off the sticks.

'Maybe we could get closer?' Thomas suggested.

Laughing, Jonathan replied, 'If you like,' deep down rather liking that suggestion. A few paces forward and the fifty yards turned to thirty.

The boys took it in turns, each trying to destroy the stick target with an explosive and exciting conclusion. Jonathan's second shot was a miss, as the bullet zipped within an inch of the post, soon followed by Thomas doing the same.

'Maybe we could get closer again?'

With a frown, Jonathan replied, 'No way, closer again would be for girls."

As the words flew from his mouth, he reached into his pocket and felt that they only had three bullets left. Thinking to himself maybe it would be better to follow his friends suggestion after all. To save his pride, he reluctantly agreed, but also content that he was doing it to help Thomas as well as himself.

A few more paces forward, the boys were close to twenty yards away from what seemed an ever-elusive target. Jonathan loaded another bullet into the rifle, took aim, and held his breath whilst pulling the trigger. The familiar loud crack from the gun was instantly followed by the comforting sound of wood snapping. It was a direct hit as the wood shattered into a dozen pieces.

'Gor!' said Thomas with a smile on his face, 'Well done!'

'Course, it's all in the timing and wrists is all. You either have it or you don't,' Jonathan said with a cheeky glint to his eyes. Thomas knowing his friend very well knew he was having a jest and agreed to go along with his good natured arrogance.

Two sticks left of the target and only two bullets remaining. Thomas raised the gun and was swiftly interrupted by Jonathan.

'Would you like to get closer again? Another few yards and we could throw stones at the sodding thing."

'Shut up,' said Thomas, and with that, he pulled the trigger and 'SNAP!', one of the two remaining sticks splintered into pieces, shards of wood flying left, right, and centre. Laughter filled the air. With a pat on the back, Jonathan congratulated Thomas. Two sticks down and one remaining.

'To tell you the truth, I was aiming for the other one,' he confessed.

As the last bullet was loaded into the rifle, the smell of cordite left the barrel and filled the senses. The final shot of the morning's fun was taken, and with that, the mock-up cricket stumps were no more. That welcoming sound of the snap and crack of wood being hit, as the lead bullet penetrated fast was most pleasing to the boys.

Jonathan, being the winner, had the great joyous duty of thinking of a forfeit for Thomas. What could it be? The possibilities of horrid yet harmless things ran through his mind. Picking up a slug, sticking your hand in a cow pat, allowing a spider to crawl over the face, running around the field with your trousers pulled down. After much thought, one idea sprung to mind.

'Your forfeit …" Commanded Jonathan, 'will be to run and jump over the bramble hedge.'

'That's not fair,' said Thomas. 'You had one extra shot than me.'

Jonathan could not argue with that fact, so he suggested they both do it together. They both glanced at the sheer size of the brambles, with their razor-sharp barbs sticking out long like daggers. With the rifle safely tied to Jonathan's back with strong leather string, they readied themselves. At the same time, they both sprinted side by side towards the hedge that stood in front of them, following the same path as the bullets. They approached the threatening brambles and leaped into the air, high and long, hurdling themselves over and landing with a thud into the damp mud on the other side.

Mr Pitwick's farm was somewhat large, almost thirty acres in total. Consisting of several fields, lanes, and paths and woodland, the boys were still well away from prying eyes. But they knew time was up for the morning and they had to return home.

Not wanting to return the way they came ,they decided to take a slightly longer route home and follow the field they now found themselves in.

'It's only an extra ten minutes or so,' said Jonathan as they walked across the bright green field, talking about their shooting game almost non-stop.

Suddenly, Thomas stopped, squinting his eyes and placing his hand on his forehead to stop the glare of the sun. 'What's that?' he asked.

'I don't see anything,' replied Jonathan.

With a firm point from Thomas' raised finger, he hastily said, 'There … over there.'

Jonathan focused in and, with a squint, saw a strange black mound in the distance.

'What on earth is that?' questioned Thomas.

'I have no idea,' Jonathan replied.

They decided to go and investigate. 'Probably just couple of hay bales,' said Jonathan.

'Could be. Could also be a pile of sheep dung,' replied Thomas.

The two friends started walking towards the unknown, strange dark mound that lay in front of them until it was only about one hundred yards from their gaze. As they got closer and closer, they slowly saw a tail along the grass, long and whispery, then a head with a curled ear sticking stiff in the air. As they got within touching distance, they saw it was a large dark black horse, as motionless as a stone statue.

'Strange place for a horse to sleep,' said Thomas. 'He should be in the stables or something.'

'Go and touch it,' dared Jonathan.

'Have you ever seen a horse wake up suddenly? I'm not going do that and get a kick, thank you.'

Both of them wanted to see the horse wake up, but were not prepared to do the waking themselves.

Jonathan slowly and quietly walked around to the underside of the horse, keeping a close eye on those strong muscular legs, waiting to scarper at the hint of any twitch from them. Jonathan noticed the horse's eyes were wide open, along with the mouth, it's long, pink, fleshy tongue hanging out. Startled, he took a swift step back.

'It's dead' he said in a high tone. Thomas followed in Jonathan's footsteps to see the eyes and mouth for himself. Unsure if the creature really was dead, he took two paces forward and tapped it on the belly. No movement came from the horse, not even a slight jerk or tremble. Both boys were rather anxious at the sight that lay before them. It us a somewhat miserable vision indeed. This magnificent animal, once strong and happy, now lay, a carcass of meat. 'Neither of them had ever seen such a big powerful beast dead before. Within a few moments, a look of horrid realisation fell on Thomas' face.

'We killed it!' he said in a panicked voice. 'We must have shot it earlier!'

With his jaw dropping, Jonathan looked over towards the hedge where they had come from and saw that this dead horse was indeed in the line of their shooting.

His head shaking and heart pounding, an uncomfortable heat flooded his body, and he stuttered, 'No ... no, couldn't have ... I mean ... I don't know, did we?'

'What are we going to do?' said Thomas as a tear fell down his cheek.

Both boys were upset, worried, and very unsure of their next move. They both sat down on the grass to collect their thoughts and tried to regain a little calm.

Silence filled the air.

The first thought that sprung to both their minds was the easiest of options. To forget about the whole incident and never tell anyone. But they knew that the risk would be high. A horse was worth a huge amount of money, far more than any of them had seen in their entire lives. But it wasn't just the monitory value that was the only concern. They knew Farmer Pitwick well and had a rather strong fondness for the man.

'We could say it was an accident,' said Thomas, and that would not have been a lie.

'Mr Pitwick isn't just gonna leave it and let us get away with murder, though,' replied Jonathan. Both boys felt terrible at the thought of murder. What would their parents say?

Thomas could have very easily just passed the buck over and laid all blame on Jonathan. Deep down, Jonathan knew this. A lesser friend would have done just that. But that was not the case with these two. They were side by side, brothers in arms, and they went through hardships together. Whatever their next move, they decided they would stick together no matter the repercussions that would follow.

After much deliberation and soul-searching, Jonathan decided to come clean and tell his parents what had happened. He knew he would certainly get a telling off and most probably a smack around the ear, but he also knew that it was simply an accident. He has known far worse things to have happened to other people and heard stories far more cruel than this particular escapade. An hour or so of raised voices and a sore head from his father's firm hand would be better than keeping it a secret forever more.

'No point in both of us getting into trouble,' said Jonathan. 'I'm going to go home and tell mother.'

'What about your father?' replied Thomas.

Jonathan's plan was to tell his mum everything and leave it up to her. God willing she "wouldn't tell her husband and all would be forgotten in due course. Coming clean with everything now may make up for the lie he'd told earlier about feeling unwell. All could be rectified within twenty minutes, or so he thought. Get back, put the rifle back on the wall, tell mother, and that' was it. But a simple plan with simple deeds does not always follow through as easily as one expects.

Knowing that his friend's home life wasn't quite as nice and simple as his own, Thomas offered to return to Jonathan's house with him. Thomas' home life was far from perfect, but it was rather nicer than his friend's.

Jonathan appreciated the offer and saw it was one of kindness and brotherhood, however he instantly declined. He'd rather do this alone and take any punishment that were to befall him. Not only that, it would also save any embarrassment. Edward's wicked ways would not be held back or restricted if others were present. If Sarah was upset, Jonathan would not like to see her be like that in front of his friend. Sarah had a lot of pride and would be torn between letting her emotions out there and then or bottling them up and keeping them to herself. Jonathan would not knowingly put her in that position. This would be a private affair; a son talking to his mother in confidence, where both could say exactly what they wanted.

Jonathan took charge of the situation and suggested they both return to their homes. Fearful as ever and managing to hold back the tears, almost as an order, he told Thomas to go and said everything would be all right.

'I'll see you next week,' he said as he waved off Thomas.

'Maybe not for shooting, though,' he replied, thinking that the cup and ball game they often played in the yard was suddenly more appealing.

The boys parted ways as they left the field, walking down the hill towards the village. As his friend walked off, Jonathan, with his head down, walked rather slowly, thinking to himself, *'It'll be all right'*, repeating the same words in his head over and over again, while thinking of all the things he would say to his mother to downplay the accident. The list grew longer in his head. Anything to soften the blow. *'Tis only an animal', it didn't suffer, it was an accident, I didn't break Father's gun, and we didn't get hurt'.*

By the time he got within fifty yards from his home, a wave of calm and solace came over him like a breath of fresh but warm air. His heart seemed to slow a little. He had almost convinced himself that it really would be all right. With a smile, he said to himself, 'By teatime tonight, all will be said and done.'

With the rifle still held tightly over his shoulder, he turned the last corner of his lane to reach his house. He stopped just outside and, with one final exhale, he reached for the door and opened it.

As the wooden door creaked open slowly, there before his eyes was not an empty room where he could quickly dash to return the rifle back to its rightful place, nor was it Sarah. It was the last thing he wanted to see. His father, standing still and tall, with a look in his eyes that even Jonathan had never witnessed before.

Chapter 3

Jonathan's bright eyes widened as his mouth dropped and his heart sank.

'Close that fucking door!' Edward said angrily in a deep, menacing voice.

'Yes, sir,' replied Jonathan. As the door was pushed closed, it knocked the corner of the rifle butt that was still hanging on his shoulder by the sling. A stillness filled the air in the front room, the atmosphere dense and unsettling. Jonathan stood like a statue, almost like a soldier standing to attention. He dared not speak, fright replacing any thought of words. Edward took a few steps towards his son, standing within half an inch of his face, almost nose to nose. Jonathan would like nothing more than to take a step back, even just at least to escape his father's disgusting breath, but he did not dare.

Edward ordered his son to stand against the grey stone wall that stood on the other side of the room. Jonathan did so at once, eyes locked onto at his father's glare as he took what felt like a walk of shame. Jonathan had seen the contorted and bitter face of Edward many a time in the past, but it had never looked like this – possessed almost. Edward paced back and forth across the room, not saying anything at all, stopping every now and then to look at Jonathan. His eyes were black as if a demon was inside.

This was to be no simple lecture or telling off, more so a hard lesson to be learnt and never forgotten. It was to be hard-etched into the mind, as if a stone mason were engraving a marble tablet on one's tomb.

'You will hand over my rifle that you stole from me, now!' Edward commanded. Upon receiving it, he hit Jonathan across his forehead with the hard steal barrel, forcing him to fall to his knees. A tidal wave of anger and hatefulness flew from Edward's mouth. Towering over his son, spit flew from his mouth as the vile words exploded.

'Stand up!' yelled Edward.

Jonathan was scared but knew the best thing was to follow whatever his father said.

'Why did you steel my gun? What did you do with it?'

It seemed the more Edward yelled, the more enraged he became.

'I...I' stuttered Jonathan.

'What makes you think you can just take this? I fought for our country with this very weapon, and you take it as if it were a toy!'

Edward grabbed his son by the lapels of his shirt and threw him like a ragdoll across the room, knocking him into the table.

Rising to his feet again with tears rolling down his face, Jonathan brushed himself off. His father 'didn't even know about the horse yet.

'I'm waiting for an explanation!'

Jonathan took a few seconds to compose himself and explain. 'We didn't steal it, Father, we just wanted to fire it in the field, up the road.'

'We? Who is 'we'?'

Jonathan was about to say his friend's name but stopped himself at the last minute. 'A friend of mine, Father, that's all.'

Most fathers might at least have taken some sort of interest in their son's friend, but that was not the case here. Jonathan knew his father did not care about anything concerning Thomas.

Edward lifted the rifle, pointing it directly at Jonathan, the barrel staring at him at close range as if death itself was looking.

'You want to be tough like your old man, do you? "You think in your tiny mind you can handle my firearm?'

As it happened, Edward could not have been further from the truth. He was not tough at all, just appeared to be, especially in front of children, and Jonathan, for his age, could handle the rifle surprisingly well, and better than most.

'I'm sorry, Father … I really am, It won't happen ever again,' cried Jonathan. After yet another whack, his words fell on deaf and ignorant ears.

Jonathan was curled up in the corner of the room, blood trickling down the side of his face.

'You stay there like a dog!' yelled Edward as he left to put the rifle back on the wall in the other room.

The doorknob turned, and Sarah came in with the usual smile on her face, humming with her soft, feminine voice. But her smile was soon to be replaced with horror when she saw her son cowering in the corner, arms clutching his knees as they were held to his chest. The little face of Jonathan was hardly recognisable, tears and blood covered it like a blanket of moisture. She rushed over and knelt down beside him.

'Oh, my son, what happened here? What on earth happened? You can tell me'. Sarah placed her hand on Jonathan's arm to try to help him up. But before she could apply any strength, a larger hand was on top of hers, squeezing and pulling by force.

Sarah turned and looked up at her husband. 'What happened here?'

'Don't question me, bitch!'

'I said, what happened here?'

Jonathan was about to speak, but before he could utter a single word, Edward told his wife about the rifle being taken.

Sarah paused. 'And that's why you beat him?'

Questioning Edward did not help the situation but it was a question that had to be asked and hopefully answered.

'You left our son like this because he took your … your bloody rifle?'

Full of determination, she reached for Jonathan, leading him to the other side of the room, away from her overbearing husband, holding his hand and standing close by, like a lioness protecting their cub.

Jonathan's sad eyes looked up at his mother. 'There ... there is something else,' he muttered.

Kneeling down, Sarah in a calm and civilized voice, said,

'What is it dear? I promise you, it's all right. You can say anything, as long as it's the truth'.

'We ... I mean, I ... I killed a horse.'

'What!' screamed Edward.

'I ... I think I killed a horse, Father, up at Mr Pitwick's farm,' he said with his head down, full of shame.

Before Jonathan could continue, Edward took a step forward, but was stopped in his tracks by Sarah raising her arm.

'You stop there! And we will listen to our son!' Sarah firmly said.

Surprisingly, Edward did just that and stopped, but the anger was still raging inside him and his veins were ready to burst from his head.

'Now, come dear, please tell us more,' said Sarah as she looked warmly at Jonathan. After a few moments of silence, which appeared to be a stand-off between Jonathan's mouth, heart, and brain, he slowly told his parents what had happened in more detail. He explained everything. Lying about why he couldn't go to church, taking the gun, shooting in the field, and killing the horse. Jonathan was in the epicentre of two emotions: terror at what would follow his confession and relief, as if a large weight had been lifted from his shoulders.

'It was an accident though, I promise, it was an accident, I didn't mean to,' he repeated like a mantra.

Sarah knew that any act of misjudgement or error from her son would be an accident, no matter how careless or foolish it was. As Sarah stood, she felt the rough hands of Edward on her shoulders. As he closed his grip, he pulled her and threw her over to one side by force, sending her ten feet across the room.

'You little shit!' yelled Edward. 'Do you know how much a horse will cost us!'

A horse to Jonathan's family would have been equal to about three months of their wage. Edward could only think about the deceitful and monitory side of the story, without putting any thought to anything else. His tunnel vision was a good match to his narrow mind.

His hand began to clench as his fingers curled up tight to make a solid fist. 'Stand up!' he demanded, but Jonathan was too frightened and could not move an inch. The only motion he made was the trembling of fear, and his heart beat faster than a bolt of lightning. Jonathan was forcefully brought to his feet and pinned to the wall, his father slamming him hard against the stone. Edward, his eyes and heart as black as coal, took a swing and launched a vicious attack on his son.

Blow after blow, the fist came hard and fast at him. The first punch was to the left eyebrow, splitting it open. The second was to mouth, and the third to the side of his head.

But the attack did not stop there. Jonathan's cries came to nothing as he pleaded with his father to stop. Edward appeared to be possessed.

He threw Jonathan's weak and bloodied body across the other side of the room towards the wooden table. He crashed into it, breaking one of the legs, causing the table to crack and contort. The contents on the table flew in the air as Jonathan landed hard. He could hardly move and lay still in a semi-conscious state with a ringing in his ears. Pewter cups and plates lay smashed, and cutlery carpeted the floor around him.

Hearing the thuds and cries, Sarah could not take any more of this callousness and cruelty. In order to protect her son, she launched her own attack on her husband, running towards his back. Upon hearing her footsteps, Edward quickly turned to face Sarah.

'You come at me, you whore!' he yelled. His tempter did not seem to wane, even after unleashing his vileness on his son.

Edward grabbed his wife, stopping her in her tracks, and pulled her down to the wooden floorboards, tearing the top of her best white Sunday dress as he did so.

After just a few moments, as the ringing in his ears began to fade away and the focus came back to his eyes, his eyes witnessed an act that horrified him. The blurred vision came clear as he saw his father sat astride is mother, arm raised and dropping hard, followed by the sound of bone against bone. Again and again, he saw the fist rain down on his mother.

Without thinking, allowing a protective instinct to take over, Jonathan rushed over as fast as he could to help save his mother. With a single strike to the side of the stomach, Jonathan hit his father as hard as he possibly could. Surely a twelve-year-old could not do anything to stop the barbaric assault? With much surprise, the blows from Edward stopped with immediate effect. Edward turned and looked up to see Jonathan standing still as if in shock and astonishment. The frantic efforts of violence had ceased as Edward held his side and fell back and away from Sarah.

Sarah was battered and bruised, but alive and conscious. Jonathan gently placed his arm around her back and helped her sit up.

'Mother, are you all right?' he said in a tearful tone.

'Oh ... Jonathan, I ... I will be,' she replied slowly with a cough and a look of terror in her eyes.

She looked down at her son's hand and was startled at what she saw. In the grasp of his hand was a knife, blade covered and dripping with fresh, glistening blood.

'Oh, Jonathan!' she gasped.

He looked down and saw his hand holding the bloodied kitchen knife. It fell to the floor as he rapidly loosened his tight grip of the handle.

'I ... I ... he stuttered. 'I ... I didn't mean to.'

Jonathan looked round and saw his father lying on his back on the dark wooden floor, hand still clutching his side. Jonathan crawled over on his hands and knees. He moved closer and saw the dirty white shirt slowly begin to change colour to blood red. The bright, crimson colour 'slowly spread over Edward's chest and stomach, like a full ink pot that had just been tipped over. No words or a sound came from any of them.

He placed his thin pale hand on his father's damp stomach and watched his chest's heavy breaths. The whiteness of his palm changed to an oily red as his father's blood covered it, filling the contours of his skin. Up and down, up and down his chest moved, and then slower and slower, until the final exhale left Edward's body as his hand dropped to the side and his head tilted to the side, lifeless.

Edward's cold, dead, nightmarish wide eyes met Jonathan's. A stare with a gaze as if it were looking not at you, but through to your very soul. It would be a vision he would never forget, but one he would spend years trying to cast to the back of his mind, only to fade as time drifted on.

Time did not seem to follow on and roll forward as it should do; it seemed to stand still as if time itself were trapped in a void of emptiness. Jonathan edged his way to the corner of the room, not daring to stand, to distance himself from the body, his sad and fearful eyes fixed on it, as if it would suddenly rise and attack again. Sarah, still in a state of nervous tension, could hardly believe what lay in front of her. Seeing her brute of a husband lying dead, blood flowing from his motionless body and dripping over the floor, like tar on a new pavement, like claret combining itself with the dirty oak boards.

Her motherly instinct yet again kicked in and she knew she had to take care of her son. She slid towards the body to check if he really was gone from this life. The confirmation was clear within a few seconds. No pulse, no heartbeat, and enough blood to fill a sink.

Jonathan rose to his feet, his legs shaking.

'I'm sorry ... I'... didn't ... I ...' he said whilst shaking his head and trying to wipe away tears.

In her heart, Sarah wanted nothing more than to hug her son as tight and lovingly as she could and reassure him that everything would be all right. But she didn't not have the mental strength". She wasn't angry at Jonathan, more so at the dreadful events that, through no fault of their own, had been forced upon them.

Before she could reach out with a warm embrace, Jonathan, still in dismay and still shaking his head, stepped backwards towards the front door. One step back, then two, then three, getting closer to the door, whilst repeating the same words again and again and again.

'I ... I ... didn't mean to.'

He turned his body and bolted out the door.

'Jonathan!' she cried. Even in her weakened state, she managed to leap to her feet to try to run after him. Being a mother, and a good mother at that, the feeling of helping her son easily overpowering her own pain. With much effort, with her injuries as they were, she wasn't as fast as Jonathan. Despite trying to keep up, she was too late. As she pulled open the door that an instant earlier had been slammed shut, she looked up the gravel road that stood beside her humble house and saw Jonathan in the distance running away as fast as his little legs could carry him.

One more yelling cry. 'Jonathan!' But it was to no avail. She knew that he would probably not have turned around and that he was almost out of earshot at any rate. Jonathan either didn't hear her or chose to ignore her cries.

Chapter 4

Jonathan sat on a grey stone wall, his legs dangling down, not managing to touch the ground. He was full of pain, physically and emotionally. Whilst clutching the feeling of being as hollow as a mountain cave. He wiped his face with his shirt to try and restore a little norm to his appearance. He was full of guilt and sorrow. *How did things go so wrong in such a short period of time?* he thought to himself. He could not understand it. He felt strongly in his mind that he was now and would be forever one of the worst things a man could be: a murderer. Murderer of beast and human, and not just any human, his own father. He knew deep down that he didn't possess evilness and that they were both accidents. Nonetheless, life had been extinguished by his very own hands. It mattered not that there were many extenuating circumstances, or that maybe his father who fell to his final sleep was not full of innocence.

Jonathan heard voices in the distance. Just normal muttering and chit-chat by other villagers going about their usual day-to-day business. He hopped down to the other side of the wall, trying to avoid the unwanted gaze from others. Hiding there, squatting, his eyes inching over the wall to keep lookout, pupils shifting left and right like a pendulum, he was convinced the world was after him. His mind was split into two opposing thoughts.

'Everyone is after you, boy, you're going to prison, and you will hang and you deserve everything you get!" one side was saying.

Sharply followed by, 'You didn't mean to, it was in self-defence, and you were protecting your mother. You're a good boy and you did the right thing.'

Jonathan had no one to turn to. The two pillars in his life were Sarah and Thomas. But he couldn't turn to either of them, not now. He decided, either wrongly or rightly, the only thing to do was to run away, get as far away from this place as he could. What once was a place called home with relative comfort, now would be a place to avoid and forget about, a task that filled his heart with sorrow and dread. He was already missing his mother but knew he could not return to her.

He did not know where to go, for he had no family or friends in other places. Where to go? It did not seem to matter in the least. Anywhere but his current location; anywhere he would be free from arrest and prison and the hangman's tight noose. Jonathan noticed the coast was clear and stood, only to look up and see a post pointing east, adjacent to the road. The tall white iron poll had

'LONDON' marked on it. He had never been to London before but thought to himself that place was just as good as any other.

Whilst looking left and right for any threat that he thought may come for him, be it a lynch mob or baying crowd out for justice or a policeman, he jumped over the wall and onto the dirt road. With a deep breath and a stretch of his narrow shoulders, he started his long walk towards the large city, without having any substantial knowledge of the place at all. He did not know how long it would take to get there, but what was at the forefront of his mind was nothing more than to get away and flee.

Along the tapering road he walked, with a good pace to start off with, looking around every second, head not keeping still for a moment. Left, right, and behind, like a buzzard hunting its prey.

Cutting across a field that lay on the outskirts of his village, he was free from danger. Much of the concern did not leave him yet though, as he knew he still had a long way to go, and with a heavy heart in the knowledge that every step was a step further away from his loving mother and his home.

The sign for London said 'forty-four miles'. But this information was utterly useless to the young lad, for he had no knowledge or concept of distance. Forty or so miles could be an hour's hike or it could be many many more. Even so, he set London as his destination. He had heard of the city before and knew it was much larger than his village, but this was to be the extent of his limited comprehension.

He would have to stay away from roads, at least for now. *There are far fewer people in the grasslands*, he thought, and the greenery was also a welcoming sight. To see the fields and trees surrounding him gave him a little solace, as it rekindled happier times with his friend Thomas.

Crossing field after field, fence after fence, and gate after gate, he did not know what time it was. But still his legs kept moving him forward, on and on, working like a strong plough horse.

It was getting dark, as the sun gave up its day's light in exchange for the glow of the moon, complemented by the clear sky filled with diamond-like stars. For he did not rest, even now. The unknown place of London was the only thing he could think of.

Night time slowly turned into daytime, with the sun rising to greet the world again, as Jonathan continued his long and arduous journey, still alone, still tired, and at this stage very hungry indeed. With the lonesome exception of a mouth full of water from a stream he had come across earlier, nothing had touched his lips apart from the fresh air.

As the following day continued, minute by minute ticked by, just as Jonathan's footsteps took each step, and he still had his primary focus of getting to what would possibly be his new home. After what would have been almost thirty hours of walking, his footsteps slowly turned to a lumber, dragging and scraping his shoes along the ground like a prisoner trawling a thirty-pound iron ball and chain.

His bones and muscles, as well as his mind, were near to giving up as he knocked his head back as if in a dizzy daze. His legs buckling and eyes blurring, he collapsed, dropping as if earth's gravity had pulled him down to the ground with force.

The sun was shining bright above him, bearing down with its power. As he looked directly into the sun's core, eyes closing from sheer exhaustion, Jonathan calmly and peacefully passed out with a single thought in his head, which took hold in the image of his mother.

Sarah was at home, sat in her small, humble garden in her long dark blue working dress, which was adorned with soil. Soil from what should have been a place of peace and harmony. Her garden was no more than forty square feet and surrounded by a short stone wall. A place of privacy and beauty as it held a few dozen flowers of various shapes, sizes, and colours. But instead of planting seeds or burying bulbs, the latest edition to the earth was Edward's stiff corpse.

Sarah sat down on her pine wooden garden bench, staring at the hand-crafted grave that now was to be a permanent fixture. She did not know if she was doing the right thing, but she felt like she did not have much choice or say in the matter. She could not and would not go to the police and tell them what her own son had done. Jonathan was now the only thing she had of true value in this world.

It would have been very different if the taking of life was from evil intent, but she knew it was not. Ill judged and cruel actions does not always come from ill-judged and cruel intention of will. The vast majority of cases concerning murder are with unfavourable and dire minds, but it was certainly not the case here and she was well aware of that.

She held some relief knowing that she was doing it for herself and for her son.

However, the relief was sporadically interrupted with the knowledge that this was unconsecrated ground. Being a Christian, this was somewhat important to her, and even more as this was her own husband, even if he had been a vile man and deserving of all that had happened.

Sarah was in a most strange state. Feeling a sense of loss from her son and husband, she felt guilty that, deep down, she was glad of Edward's passing, just not so glad about the manner in which it happened. The whole ordeal had been a trial to say the least.

To ease her strange state and to try to clear at least some of her moral sense, she decided to visit Mr Pitwick to rectify some of the damage that had been done. It was not an easy act to do. She knew that paying back the farmer and clearing her debt would be an almost impossible task, but it had to be done, nonetheless. Whatever it would take, she would do it, working her hands to the bone for month after month through a harsh and unrelenting winter if needs be.

Sarah changed her current dress for another, washed her face, and brushed her hair in order to look somewhat presentable to Mr Pitwick, as she knew she had news that no farmer would want to hear. He was a nice, kind man, but not knowing him well, she was not sure what his reaction would be from hearing about what her son had done.

After a short walk from her house, she approached Mr Pitwick's large old farmhouse that had been stood there for at least two hundred years. With a deep breath and a moment to compose herself, she knocked three times softly on the large oak door that was filled with black iron nail heads, more befitting an old church or castle.

After about thirty seconds, but what felt like thirty minutes, Sarah's heart beat as fast and strong as ever as the large door opened.

'Good day, Mr Pitwick,' she said quietly.

'Oh, hello my dear. Sarah, isn't it?' he replied manner. She nodded politely.

'If you pardon the intrusion, I have a matter of some importance to discuss with you, if it pleases you, sir.'

With a small laugh and smile, he said,

'Well of course, of course, and not so much of the 'sir', if you don't mind. I work for a living. Come on in.'

Sarah entered the warm, welcoming home of the farmhouse as the door closed behind her.

The setting was very comfortable and homely, as Sarah and Mr Pitwick sat down round his large kitchen table, oval in shape and covered with a red and white chequered cloth. The table was overwhelmed with jars of jam, two loaves of brown crusty bread, and some tea in an old but pristine pale green teapot.

'I was just about to have a quick bite. Would you care to join me? We have plenty here, thanks to the wife."

Sarah would have liked nothing more than to tuck in and enjoy the rare treat of jam. Even though she was very tempted, she managed to fight the strong urge and say no. She would not dare ask for food, knowing the words that were about to flow from her mouth and fall upon his ears. Mr Pitwick pushed a cup towards her and filled it with tea.

'Now come come, you must at least have a cup of tea,' he said. Sarah smiled, as she had not asked, but was also very happy to accept it.

'Thank you,' she said as she took a slow sip, although she was not in the mood to fully enjoy it. After just one sip, she wanted to tell Mr Pitwick all about his horse and what she could do to rectify it.

He noticed something was troubling her. He also had noticed a few markings on Sarah's face. Three bruises and two cuts, one being somewhat deep. Mr Pitwick would have liked to have known the source of the markings that lay on her fine face, but he could tell that she had something to say. He thought it best to wait and allow her to elaborate if it pleased. After all, it could be for a whole host of reasons, and he was not one to assume or jump to any erroneous conclusion. Being the gentleman he was, he was willing to allow Sarah to talk in her own time and in her own way.

'Not that it isn't a pleasure having you here, my dear, but what brings you to my house? You said you have something of importance to tell me? Sounds very grand indeed.'

Sarah found it hard to begin talking, her pretty mouth opening slightly and then closing again without any sound leaving it.

'Now, now,' said Mr Pitwick. 'If you have something to say, you must say it. Surely it can't be that bad.'

His voice and face being very warm indeed, it was hard for Sarah *not* to talk. She started telling him all about Jonathan being in his field two days prior.

'Is that all, Sarah? Your boy walking in my fields is hardly a matter of importance. Little lads do it all the time; a pest maybe, but no harm.'

'I wish it was just that, Mr Pitwick, but there is something else far worse than a simple trespass.'

Mr Pitwick leaned forward across the table and towards Sarah with interest, but still with his usual calmness and friendliness.

'Come on now, out with it,' he said. Sarah paused for a slow breath.

'My son, Jonathan ...''

'Yes, I know the boy. Good lad, he is, a decent type.'

'Well … yes, he is … he really is' said Sarah.

'Sarah, I am a very tolerant man, but I will not want to ask you for a third time,' he said, but still in his friendly way.

Sarah pulled herself together and came out with the full truth about the horse.

'Two days ago … my … my son shot and killed one of your horses.' Mr Pitwick was taken back for a moment. Before he could reply, Sarah quickly followed in a desperate tone, 'I promise you, it was an accident, and I will repay you for your loss. I really am so sorry. I will pay my debt as soon as I can, you have my word.'

He learned back in his chair, scratching his head with a confused look on his face. Going over it again and again in his head, he tried to understand what Sarah had just said. He had a harsh frown upon his brow as the wrinkles contorted and buckled. It was not with displeasure, though, merely through deep thought.

After a minute or two, he shook his head slowly.

'I believe you are mistaken, my dear. I have not had a horse shot for a long time.'

"But you must have done,' she replied with a somewhat forceful tone.

Mr Pitwick tried to recall a shooting, but nothing like that came to the forefront of his mind.

'In the last three months, I have only had one creature die, Sarah. It *was* a horse and it was in the same field you are talking about, but it was not shot.'

Sarah, with a baffled look, questioned the farmer. 'Are you absolutely sure of this?'

Mr Pitwick calmly said, 'More than sure. I am certain. It's as true as the fact that we are sat here now.'

Sarah still possessed a confused look, although it began to hold a slight relief. With much interest, she listened carefully to what he was saying.

He continued 'It as very upsetting indeed but also expected. Black Bessy, the wife called him, was very old and ill. I can assure you with great certainty. He was not shot. It wasn't even his heart that gave way, it was his stomach and age; age that claims us all in the end.'

She followed his words with a large smile. Relief and warmth filled her inside, like a hot cup of coco on a cold winter's night. An instant later, the pleasant feeling of a weight being lifted was soon to be taken away, as she realised all that had happened was over a misunderstanding and nothing more. The joyful feeling and knowledge of her son's innocence was eliminated within a moment at the thought of Jonathan's whereabouts and what he had done to his father, or rather what he had been made to do.

'Oh, Jonathan,' she said softly to herself.

Mr Pitwick noticed a change in her face as her expression was not what he had expected.

'My correction of your assumption has not pleased you?' he said.

She quickly restored the smile on her face, with a forced smile that held little meaning. Reassuring Mr Pitwick, she replied, 'Oh … yes, oh of course it has, thank you.'

'Jonathan is all right, isn't he?' Everything well at home?'

With the same forced smile, she told the kind Mr Pitwick everything was all right, normal, and as it should be. She did not like telling a lie, it was against her morals, and especially to this fine man, but she knew on this rare occasion it was the best and only thing to do.

If Mr Pitwick knew of Sarah's dilemma and what had happened, he possibly would have helped and shared her burden. He held a fondness for her and her son and did not carry the same warmth for her husband. But it was a risk and not one Sarah was willing to take.

Sarah stood up from the table and went to thank him by offering a gentle but very meaningful hug.

Mr Pitwick happily accepted the embrace. He knew of Sarah's husband and his unpleasant ways and could tell that something wasn't quite right. But being a decent man and not nosey in the slightest, all he could do was offer his help whenever it was needed.

'If you say so, but I'll always be here if and when you should need me,' he said

'Now you must get going if there is nothing else. If Mrs Pitwick sees us hugging, especially a pretty lady such as you, I won't get any super tonight, and that will never do.'

Sarah smiled and laughed and thanked him again as she left the farmhouse. The world would be a better place if more of his ilk were present.

Chapter 5

After what seemed like an eternity and endless walking, a very tired Jonathan found himself in London. He was staggering like a drunkard, exhausted, and on the brink of what felt like death. He was thin and weak, his clothes in tatters. Although they were not in the best state to begin with, after what he had just been through, they resembled torn and dirty rags. However, he had achieved what he'd set out to do. He had finally reached his destination. He was past the thought of the implications of his actions. The only thing running through his veins now was survival.

He was in his own little world, eyes half closed as he walked, almost oblivious to everything around him, walking slow, as if in a daze, similar to a zombie bumping into many a person as he brushed against them. Not one victim of his apparent clumsiness or distress seemed to care, most of them just carrying out their normal hectic day just as though it was any other and seeing a starving boy was the norm in these parts.

As chance would have it, Jonathan found salvation. Drinkable water sprung up into the air and curved down again from a large white marble fountain. Before even noticing his new surroundings, paying attention to nothing and no one, he cupped his dirty hands in the fresh water and took mouthful after mouthful, drinking so fast, he was gasping as he drank. Almost ten handfuls of water filled his belly, the last handful covering his face as he wiped some of the dirt off. Life had returned to him. He was still very tired and hungry, but the grasp of death's overshadowing hand had been taken away to find another poor soul for the afterlife instead.

Jonathan sat down on the two short white steps that circled the life-saving fountain and his jaw dropped. It was a world he'd never seen before.

A thousand voices in a thousand accents flowed through the streets.

Almost everyone seemed to be in a hurry. People of all appearances, colours, and creeds filled the streets. Men with large bellies in yellow and green striped waistcoats; gentlemen in black top hats and capes; working men, market traders and shop keepers; ladies with long flowing dresses in all colours with small umbrellas under their arms; servants in black and white dresses shopping for their masters; men riding penny-farthings, horses, and cartridges zipping up and down; children; young, old, rich, and poor of all kinds surrounded Jonathan. The place was a zoo, where people replace animals, with the exception of horses.

It was a loud and busy place to say the least. In his previous state it was like he had been deaf to it as he'd first entered the street. With the much-needed help from the water and rest, he slowly but surely looked around in amazement.

Quite frightened and not having a single clue as what to do next, little Jonathan just sat down still and gazed at his new environment. He realised he was in the middle of some sort of a market street, stretching down almost as far as his eyes could see. The street was long, flanked by rows of shops of all sizes, along with many other places of businesses. He took a slow but deep breath and rested for a moment.

As he looked around the busy street, full of commotion and activity, he was fascinated by the trade that was going on all around him. It was quite a phenomenon to his young eyes. It seemed that anything, no matter how exotic, could be found here. As long as you had the money, there appeared to be no limit as to the purchase of wares and commodities. This new world seemed more hectic than anything else he had witnessed before.

Oyster girls in white dresses yelled, 'Oysters! Oysters! Fresh oysters, three for a penny!'

Silk traders covered in colourful long robes spouting, 'Smooth silk! Just feel the quality, sir, five shillings a yard!'

Paper boys in white shirts and waistcoats bawling, 'Extra, extra, read all about it! Come on, sir, tis only a halfpenny!'

Coffee sellers flaunting their raw beans called out, 'Coffee! Beautiful coffee, only five shillings!'

Bread makers in their flour-covered aprons shouted, 'Soft and tasty bread! A bargain! Grab some now!'

Amateur medicine men enticed the crowds with pitches of miracle elixir's. Young boys were shining shoes and polishing boots to make them glisten black.

There were tinkers, their carts filled with tools for mending anything from wooden chairs to pots and pans, knife grinders offering their services to housewives, cleavers at markets and pen knives to office workers, milkmaids carrying heavy yokes over their shoulders, walking up and down, trying to sell a pint here and there. Most common were the 'costermongers;' these rather important souls sold everything food- and drink-related, mostly fruit and veg, though they were also butchers and fishmongers.

Hardly anything was wasted here. Every leftover was used and utilized in some manner. Scraps were used to feed cats, dogs, and chickens or to help fertilize the garden. Even the servants sold on leftovers for pig food. These people were called 'the wash' hence the term 'hogwash' that we have today.

As Jonathan watched the world around him, he was in pain. It was a pain he had experienced many times in the past and was almost natural to him, but never quite as strong as now. It was the pain of hunger and it needed to be remedied as soon as possible.

With his stomach empty, void of even a crumb, and rumbling like a distant thunderstorm, he decided he would find some food. Finding the food was not the problem; he was surrounded by all the food in the world. Finding the money to get the food was another matter. He knew his pockets were vacant of coins of any denomination, but he slid his hands in, nonetheless.

'You never know,' he thought. *'Might find a penny somewhere in the corner'.*

However, he did know, and his hand returned only holding a small piece of fluff. He blew it away and sighed, deep in thought.

After a few moments, Jonathan gave in to temptation. The want and desire to steal some food from a market stall was ever-growing. His first inclination knew it was wrong, however, this was through necessity and not merely greed.

He looked around for what an unwilling victim, the target of his needs. There were many options. The apple seller to his right, the bread maker to his left, or maybe even the sweetshop that stood just thirty feet behind him.

He had never stolen anything in his life. Once in a while, during warm summers past, he had gone scrumping for the occasional apple or pear in orchards with Thomas. The orchard owner had certainly believed that it was a most serious crime and worthy of harsh punishment and strict discipline. However, even Jonathan was aware that man was in the vast minority in holding such a belief, and was only worthy of a slap on the wrist at most. Even though he was somewhat naive as to the ways of the streets, he knew he couldn't just saunter up to a street stall or shop counter and merely take what he wished. There would have to be some sort of tactic or diversion, maybe even a slight-of-hand like a conjurer on the stage.

The victim of his ill-gotten gains was to be the bread-maker. Largely because it was the closest to him, moreover it had the delicious smell of warm fresh baked bread drifting in the air as if deliberately taking aim for his nostrils. It was as inviting and tempting as Eve in the garden of Eden biting into that infamous apple.

Jonathan was just about to make his move as he stood up to make his way towards the street baker just a few yards away from him. He had not taken more than two steps when he saw another child, even young and smaller than himself, approach the baker. Jonathan paused and watched as the child looked left and right, to then reach out over the stall and grab a bread roll without paying. Within what seemed like less than a second, the baker's assistant latched onto the thin, pale wrist of the boy, forcing him to drop the roll, then smacked him hard around his face.

'Get out of 'ere, you little rat!' he snarled.

The would-be thief ran off down the street, crying and holding the side of his very red face.

Jonathan's jaw dropped, partly because it was quite a shock to see such a small lad be struck so hard by someone literately twice his size. But also because he realised it would not be so easy to just swipe some food.

He realised that these street traders would probably be used to many a child, and adult for that matter, doing the same crime.

'Probably happens every hour,' he said to himself.

But it was worth the risk, even if he were to get a smack around the face and had to flee the scene. He needed some food, and he needed it now.

He went for the same stall and was not put off in any way by the baker's assistant, who appeared to have the eyes and reflexes of a hawk. Though any other stall worker would not necessarily be easier pickings, he thought. All the traders in the area were probably of equal skill in catching people with criminal inclinations. This was what they did, all day every day, and were well of verse to the natural desperation of what many feel in such a large place.

Jonathan readied himself for his second attempt. With his heartbeat racing faster than a speeding bullet, he was shaking inside but had the appearance of a calm boy on the outside. Quietly and full of false confidence, he approached the baker's stall. It was only twenty paces, however it felt like two thousand.

He stood at the stall, casually looking around at the array of currant buns, bread rolls, and loafs on offer. Either side of him, towering over like two large pillars, were other customers. Some were merely looking, some were buying, and others were haggling, trying to get a shilling or even just a halfpenny off the asking price.

With the baker and his assistant busy dealing with the crowds, Jonathan managed to snatch two round glazed buns and a small brown roll. He quickly but smoothly placed them in his pocket and then did something very wise indeed. His natural reaction would be to run, but he knew that would be a clear indication of guilt and would certainly draw unwanted attention. He stood there, pockets full, still looking around just for a moment or two, waiting for the dreaded words from someone, anyone, saying, 'Oi, thief!'

But they never came. No sound and no commotion, other than the normal bustle of shoppers and traders.

He slowly turned around and walked away, back to the fountain steps, but sat on the other side, just in case the baker spotted him. He brought the first buns to his lips and felt like a king, chomping away at it with bite after bite, smiling as each mouthful tasted better than the last. It was the most delicious bun he had ever tasted.

Whilst eating, he noticed two pigeons, walking close and bobbing their little grey heads back and forth as they do, searching for leftovers of anything edible. Jonathan looked one in the eye.

'You're not having any of this,' he said in a muffled tone, his mouth as full as could be, his cheeks bulging like a hamster storing his food.

The bun was devoured in a flash, soon to be followed by the second.

Not one crumb fell to the ground as he made sure to lick his fingers every other moment. Even the odd blackcurrant did not escape him or into the gutter to be snatched up by a rat or any other pest.

He leaned back against the cold marble pillar of the fountain, tilting his head back to enjoy the feeling of a satisfied stomach as the daytime sun shone down. His eyes were almost closing from the combination of the sun's glare, exhaustion, and a full stomach. His head dropped forward and then recoiled back as if trying to fight against sleep. His body forcing itself to stay awake. He forced his eyes wide open, as wide as they could go for a few seconds, straining them, almost hurting himself. He blinked and saw a rather interesting looking character standing on the other side of the street, about five foot tall; not a child, but not quite an adult either.

The stranger had a cheeky and likeable face and was dressed in dark and dirty trousers, a white scruffy vest, a brown leather waistcoat, patterned with old holes, and a black flat cap with creases all over it, as if it had been scrunched up a thousand times in its lifetime. The stranger's eyes were staring at Jonathan. His eyes fixated on him as he stood there leaning against a wall, chewing a long piece of liquorice. It had occurred to Jonathan to run away. But the unknown fellow from across the road did not seem to be a threat and was certainly not a policeman, but it was still rather unnerving to him to be watched in this way. This was no glance in a crowd, but more like a long stare with nothing distracting the line of rather uncomfortable sight.

'Maybe I've been found out with the bread?' he thought to himself. Even so, running away would not have been a practical solution at this precise moment in time, for he did not have the energy to walk away at speed, let alone run.

The stranger walked across the road and approached Jonathan, standing in front of him and looking down.

'Oi, you all right, are ya, kid?'

Jonathan looked up and said, 'Err yes ... yes ... I'm all right, thank you.'

The boy sat down on the step, leaned back with his hands behind his head, and stretched his legs out in a very casual and relaxed manner.

'Don't mind me saying, but you look as good as a tramp's vest. You a street kid, are ya?'

Jonathan paused in his reply for he knew he was not a so-called 'street kid', but on the other hand, he gathered that he now possibly was.

'I've been walking for three days to get here,' said Jonathan

'Do ya know where ere is exactly?'

With a slight shake of his head, Jonathan replied, 'London."

'Ha, well yeah, you got that right, kid. London Town it is, but you're in Whitechapel if you wanna be precise.'

Jonathan said nothing, as 'Whitechapel' meant nothing to him. If the stranger were to say that they were in Edinburgh, his reaction would have been much the same.

The stranger did not ask where Jonathan came from or why he had walked to London. He simply leaned sideways closer to him and held his hand out to introduce himself.

'The name's Jim ... Jim Shepard, but people call me 'Wooly'.

With his little arm out across his torso, Jonathan's hand met Wooly's and shook it. He introduced himself as 'Jonathan White'.

'Why do people call you Wooly?' questioned Jonathan.

'Gor, you fick or somefing? Jim Shepard ...'

Wooly's head rose a little and gestured with his hand rotating, waiting for the origin of his nickname would sink in. Jonathan sat there none the wiser and looked somewhat confused as an awkward silence hovered between them. The strained silence was only present for about five seconds, but it felt like five minutes as it can easily do in awkward times.

Wooly's patience ran out very quickly. 'Shepard ... got it?'

Jonathan's confusion did not fade away. Nothing was obvious to him, especially being so tired and in an alien world. He was not in the mood or right frame of mind for guessing games. He said nothing and simply shook his head.

Wooly explained. 'Shepard ... sheep ... wool. Wooly. Got it now?'

Jonathan nodded with the smallest of smiles but was not overly impressed.

After just a few minutes, Jonathan felt relatively comfortable with this boy. It could have been Wooly's confidence, accompanied by his cheeky face, or just the fact that Jonathan was tired and rather desperate, his wits not sharp at all, but he felt protected by being close to Wooly.

Being kind and maybe a little naïve, he reached into his pocket and pulled out the last bread roll he had pinched earlier. He broke it in two and offered Wooly half. The boy was taken back for a second by the generous gift, but took it without a second thought.

'Ere, you're all right you are, No one gives nuffink away for free,'

Jonathan smiled .

Wooly continued. 'By the way, was nice that, real smooth, when you dodged this bread,' and then in a high-spirited way, he said, 'Always nicer when it's free, ain't it.'

Even though Jonathan could tell Wooly was pleased, it did not help much at all, as his head dropped in shame and the guilt began to rise up inside him.

Wooly laughed and quickly reassured him, 'Ah chin up, kid, it was done well. Ya waited till there was a crowd and everyfing. Couldn't have done better myself. Ya should be proud.'

'I should?' questioned Jonathan, the feeling of guilt slowly edging away from him.

Wooly put his arm round him and made him feel that it wasn't just all right but something he really should be proud of and that was it a great achievement.

Jonathan was no fool, but he was young and impressionable and took Wooly's words on board. After all, he was the first friendly face he had seen since arriving in London.

'Ya got a place to stay?' asked Wooly Jonathan shook his head. 'Well, ya have now, if ya wanna, that is ... follow me.'

With his hands in his pockets, Wooly started to walk off with a happy and cocky stride, knowing Jonathan would soon follow. He was not ten steps away when he was joined by Jonathan as they both walked off down the street side by side.

Jonathan was happy to have a new friend, or at least what appeared to be a new friend.

Chapter 6

Whilst Jonathan and Wooly walked down the long market street, there were dozens of new sights for Jonathan to look upon, passing by just a few engrossing offerings that this area in Whitechapel had to provide; places of business and entertainers to amuse the public, most of which he had never seen, much like everything else here. It seemed everywhere he looked there would be someone trying to make some money in some shape or form for their daily crust. The street seemed to get even more crowded than when he'd first arrived. There was much for Jonathan to explore.

Little flower girls weaving in between street performers of all kinds. Fire eaters, jugglers, pavement chalk artists, and musicians casting out their talents from street corners. The so-called talents of these 'musicians' were often questioned by members of the public, as well as Jonathan. For some, the noise from the bands and singers was an uplifting sound and a pleasant distraction from other sounds of the street, with its non-stop clatter of horse's hooves on the cobbles or people yelling and shouting. Whilst for others it was just another source of annoyance.

Exploring, at least for now, would have to be put on hold, for Jonathan was at the mercy of Wooly's lead, accompanied with the fact that all he wanted was to arrive at Wooly's house and have a chance to rest. Given the choice of sleep verses all the other pleasures in this world, be them money, a mother's touch, food, or any other worldly treasures, the one that would have trumped all of those would be shut-eye and a chance to dream.

Not wanting to appear rude or a pain, Jonathan did not ask how far the walk would be.

'I do hope it isn't far. Please be close, please … please,' he thought to himself. What made it all the more of a task was that Wooly was not a dawdler. He had a strong, confident walk that shifted with vigour. He walked as if he owned Whitechapel itself and appeared to be afraid of nothing and no one. He was pleased in his own little world as he often was and did not think about much else, including the fact that his one stride was almost two for Jonathan. Still, Jonathan managed to keep up, matching his steps one for one, albeit with some awkwardness to his gait.

As they continued to walk fast with purpose, a tall man with a big bushy beard bumped into Wooly's shoulder with relative force, making them both stumble back a little.

'Oi!' said Wooly.

The man and Wooly turned around to face each other. 'Watch where you're going, will you!' shouted the man.

'But you bumped into me ... see, in a civ'lized world, ya say sorry, or if you wanna be more precise ... sorry, *sir*,' he replied as he cheekily took a bow and removed his cap.

Angrily, the man stepped forward in a confronting stance. 'Who you saying ain't civ'lized? I'll break your jaw!'

Scared, Jonathan felt an instant chill as he took half a step closer to Wooly. Wooly held his hand and took a step back, pulling Jonathan with him to create some distance and said, 'Piss off, will ya!'

The man, with a bitter look on his face, turned around and walked off, continuing on his journey. Wooly watched and waited a few seconds to double-check the man was indeed walking away, with the comfort of knowing that there would not be a surprise attack.

'Gotta watch out for guys like him. This place is full of them,' said Wooly.

Jonathan, whilst still holding Wooly's hand, said, 'Gosh, Mr Wooly, were you scared?'

He answered with a sniff and a laugh, 'Nah, course not.'

'I would be if a big man like that wanted to hurt me.'

'Listen, kid, you gotta stand your ground if you're gonna survive 'ere. And quit calling me Mr Wooly'.

Jonathan nodded in agreement. Wooly was feeling very powerful. He had a new apprentice for a long time and felt important sharing his wisdom to impress another. It did not occur to him that it did not take much to impress the child.

A moment later, they were passing an apple seller, but it was not a stall as such with a table laden with fruit like the rest. It was a lady standing behind three waiste-high oak barrels, two of which were full to the brim with fresh red and green apples, which were finely balanced on top, almost spilling over the edge of the rim.

Without any sudden movements and walking just as they were before, Wooly looked left without turning his head and noticed the apple seller turn around to put some paperwork in her back pocket. Her back was not turned for more than three seconds when he reached out and grabbed an apple from the top of the pile as they walked past. Their steps had not slowed down, not even a little. The act was smooth as if nothing had happened. Jonathan looked back at the lady selling her apples, totally oblivious to what had just taken place.

Wooly took a bite and then gave the rest to Jonathan. 'See, kid, ain't just about being tough. Ya gotta be smart, too.'

Jonathan was very impressed as he then took a bite of the apple. 'Thank you, Mr ...'

He looked at Jonathan to interrupt him with nothing more than a stare and raised eyebrows.

'Thank you, Wooly,' continued Jonathan.

He felt quite at ease with Wooly at this stage and was happy to ask how far his house was. What followed was a reply that rang like music to his little ears.

'Don't worry, kid, ten minutes and we'll be there and you can have a kip.'

They walked to the end of market street, only then to turn off, nipping through side roads and alleyways. The roads seemed to get narrower as they went on. Jonathan was more lost now than he ever was. It mattered not though. He was in Wooly's hands, quite literately being guided left and right and on again through passageways.

"Just round the corner and we're home. Two minutes,' said Wooly.

His words showed themselves to be true, as two minutes later, they were at the entrance to an alley. It was long and thin, with tall, black brick walls on either side and ropes adorned with white linen hanging up high, stretching from one side to another.

It was about six o'clock, the sun still shining in the blue sky, but with the alley being so long and narrow and flanked by dark bricks, you could have easily been mistaken for it being dusk.

Halfway down the alleyway, they turned left and up two flights of crooked wooden stairs. Every tread had to be taken with extreme caution for every other one was almost rotten. At first glance, it looked safe enough, but behind the first layer of hardened knotty wood, deep inside lay woodworm, mould, and dry rot, making each step hang by a thread. Each step they took, even whilst trying to be light on their feet, made the wood bend and buckle with a dubious sound of stretching.

With the ominous creeks from the stairs, they finally reached Wooly's front door.

'Ere we are,' he said happily.

Wooly knocked on his own door, but not with the usual 'knock knock' you would expect. This knocking had a particular rhythm to it, almost musical in tone, like some sort of secret code. Within an instant, the door was opened wide by a young girl the same size and age as Jonathan, give or take an inch and a month. The boys entered, and Wooly quickly shut the door behind him.

Jonathan found himself in a large attic room, walled with red bricks that he could easily see due to much of the plaster being broken off. To the far side of the room stood a fireplace surrounded by pots and pans. Opposite was a low slanting ceiling that reached halfway across the room. There was not one window, but the place was spacious and held enough candles to fill a cargo ship.

Round the edges of the room lay small single beds, each one covered in rags and blankets, whilst in the centre of the room, he observed a long wooden table, one on the planks missing down the middle, encircled with six chairs.

'Home sweet home,' Wooly said whilst raising his arms. 'Ain't much, and it certainly ain't no Buck House, but it's ours.'

Jonathan looked around and nodded with a smile. In his previous life, even coming from very humble beginnings as he did, he would have been somewhat disappointed with what he was now faced with. But that emotion was a luxury he could ill afford.

His smile was mostly due to politeness, for he would never say what he actually thought out loud, especially seeing how proud Wooly seemed of this place. He was however relieved to be off the street, and he certainly appreciated Wooly's help and very kind offer. Wooly showed Jonathan one of the wooden beds in the corner. Jonathan looked down at the blankets and the pillow and thought it was a very inviting sight.

'There ya go, kid, get some sleep. Lots to chat about in the mornin', and you can meet the rest of us then, too'.

'Oh thank you, thank you so much.'

He lay in bed for the first time in nearly four days. As he was on his back, looking up at the timber rafters through all the gaps in the plaster, he was at peace and quite comfortable. His tired body would have gladly put up with almost anything right then, as long as it meant laying down. He lay there still when a smile came to his face with a single thought in his head. A pleasant picture appeared in his mind of his loving mother.

He would have had a dozen wonderful thoughts, as well as strong concerns for her well-being, wondering how on earth she could be coping alone after all that had taken place. But before there was time for his mind to drift, his eyes began to get very heavy and he fell asleep.

Chapter 7

Whilst Jonathan was lying down, cosy, in relative comfort, and in a sleep deeper than the ocean, Sarah was about to do the same, just fifty miles away. With each of them not knowing where the other was, that fifty miles might as well have been five hundred.

She sat on the edge of her bed, which over the last few days had become more spacious and lonely. She wasn't in mourning over the passing of her husband, his death being a relief in a sense. It was the manner of his passing that hurt her as she worried for hers on. She knew that taking another's life was something that would lay heavy on a heart, but even more so on a pure and innocent heart.

Not that she had personal first-hand experience of such an act, but she had been close to people who had. Her own son being the culprit made it all the worse. She blamed herself for what had happened. The trauma of her young son having such a burden was unfair and not right.

Every morning whilst brushing her hair and looking in the mirror, she would tell the reflection staring back, '*I* should have done it. *I* should have killed Edward. Blood should be on *my* hands and not my sons!'

If anybody who cared about Sarah knew what had happened, they would have told her to stop being ridiculous and that she and her son were not guilty of any wrongdoing. Their just hands had been forced to react in unjust ways. However, grief caused doubt and unwise thoughts in her wise and level head.

Over the years, the marital bed was not often a place of good feeling and comfort as what it should have been for her, whether it was due to Edward's mood, his unloving verbal outbursts, or his lack of physical love, void of even attempted seduction and lacking even a single kiss.

The extent of which consisted of once a week rolling over on top of her, spreading her legs wide apart for him to pump away for a short time, only to then finish, roll back and sleep. He would always sleep on his side, facing away from her.

Never offering a new and exciting pleasure. Not only was the lack of his offers but also the negative reaction from Sarah's offers.

Whenever she took attempt to do anything that may please, the reaction was always pushed away and dismissed.

All the more of a shame, as Sarah was highly sexed and would not only be willing, but would enjoy other carnal pleasures to share and relish in making her man happy. But Edward would have none of it. His entire act would start and finish in less than a minute, as he delighted in his wife laying still only to be a vessel for his seed.

Other wives had it much worse though, as Sarah found out through gossip from her female acquaintances. Edward being the owner of a manhood of very small proportion in length and girth meant there was no pain. The only feeling she had when her husband was on top was his pelvis bashing hers for five or six strokes. In the fifteen years they had been man and wife, she had only considered leaving once. That consideration was soon expelled with the truth that she couldn't. Her life would have been much worse off without him, and, unfortunately, he knew it.

Although the bed was now, in part, a more comfortable place, the feeling of being alone in it did not feel right. She knew that the absence of a man was preferable to a vile man, but with the life she had grown accustomed to, it still felt very strange to her.

She sat in her bed with a tear rolling down her soft, pale face, a bad habit of hers of late, but a habit that would have come to many a person given the same circumstances. She was now alone and only with her thoughts. She would often think before sleeping, *'If I'd known fifteen years ago what I know now, I would have never said those sacred words "I do" on that sacred ground.*

These thoughts were soon replaced as she knew that her husband being gone from this world was now irrelevant, and she took away the bitterness of her marriage because one thing had come from it that made it all worth it. But that one thing was not with her anymore, but she hoped and prayed that would be rectified in time, and the sooner the better.

She wiped her sad eyes, then lay down as she tucked herself in and strived for sleep, for a chance to say goodbye to another day. Never far from her thoughts was what she could do about her so-called "missing" husband. Talk would soon get around of his absence. Sarah did not have anybody close enough to her to talk to about it. She would gladly take the blame and go to prison in Jonathan's stead. It was an option she had on the table, but an option she did not feel fully content or at ease with but would take if necessary. She felt terrible that she could not protect her son from her husband in times past, but if she were to take the blame for his demise, that would in some way make up for it and restore her balance of decency and virtue.

She closed her eyes to finally sleep, whilst trying to clear her mind of harsh thoughts in the hope they'd be replaced with pleasant dreams. Just as her eyelids fell, there was a loud knock at her front door. She chose to ignore it, in the hope that whoever it was would soon leave. From her bed, she lay still, and silence followed for a moment.

'They've gone,' she said to herself, but still waited with bated breath just a few more seconds to be sure.

The silence was shattered with three more knocks, slightly harder and louder than before.

Sarah sat up and realised she could not be in hiding for ever and hiding would only make things worse. With a deep huff, she got out of bed to button up her nightdress from breast to neck. In her bare feet, she made her way from the soft and warmth of her sheepskin rug that lay under the bed, to the cold wooden planks on the floor in the front room.

Standing still in the middle of the room, debating if she should really answer it, she shook her head to shake and said quietly,

'Come on, girl, stop being stupid, you can do it, just answer it.'

She took three paces forward and was in touching distance of the door. Just as her hand was reaching for the handle, the knocks came again, although this time the sound resembled thuds and bangs. Bangs hard enough to make the wooden door rattle. Her hand hovered over the handle, paused but shaking.

Then her fears cleared suddenly, as if taken away in a second as she said to herself, 'I can handle whatever is on the other side of that door. I've dealt with worse.'

Whether it was the police, the hangman, a vigilante gang ready to tear her to pieces, or even the bloodied ghost of Edward himself, she would face it and take whatever was coming. With her heart booming out of her chest and a cautious look upon her face, she slowly edged the door open and peaked round.

What stood before her eyes was a surprise, and a very welcome one at that. The figure was no threat of violence, nor was it the ghost soaked in blood, levitating motionless and silent that had haunted her dreams in recent nights.

It was the Reverend Muckleberry, locally known by many as 'Muckles', although to his face it was either 'Rev' or Mr Muckleberry. He was not a close friend to Sarah, as it were, but he stood much more than a mere acquaintance. With the rare exception of a few inhabitants of the village, he was admired and greatly cherished by many of the local population. He was tall and thin and possessed a warm and friendly glow. His appearance was always impeccable, the only dirt on him stuck to the underside of his shoes. His eyes were an interesting mix of wisdom and strength yet held a sublime vulnerability to them. A very decent man indeed with a heart as pure as silk.

He smiled and lifted his hat. 'Dear lady.'

'Oh … Mr Muckleberry, many apologies for my delay. Had I' known it was you at the door, I would have come much quicker,' she replied.

A few people would have taken liberties with Mr Muckleberry, him being a soft touch. However, Sarah was not that way inclined for she would never confuse kindness for weakness.

Being brought up in the early part of the nineteenth century, he had a past even more arduous and difficult than what Sarah and her kind. He certainly had many a tale to tell, but being a gentleman, he would not boast about deeds of courage and bravery and seldom spoke of such, especially to a lady, unless he was encouragingly pushed. He did not wish to impress or win over anyone of the opposite sex to as he was already very happily married. 'Just as well, as Mr Muckleberry, having more years to his name than most, was now beyond the age at which one can change one's personality and transformation of character.

Being in the paramount position he was in, in addition to his charm, he was well known by the vast majority of people in the local area due to his work for the church and his desire to do nothing other than to help his people, or his 'flock' as he commonly referred to them.

'Please ... please come in,' offered Sarah with a welcoming smile.

Mr Muckleberry entered her house and stood in the front room, removing his hat to hold it down by his side. He took notice that Sarah was in nothing other than her nightdress.

'My dear, it is I that must offer apologies if I have disturbed your sleep.'

Not being late in the evening it was an easy assumption of his that she would still be up and awake.

'I trust you are not ill?' he asked.

'Lord no, not at all, I was just resting is all. I wasn't even in bed,' she lied.

'Of course this was a lie but a lie worth it,' she thought. Anything not to make him feel guily or a burden, as she knew he would with the knowledge of interrupting her sleep.

Sarah, as with many other people, did not have much in the way of make-up or nice clothes, with the exception of her Sunday best, which, thanks to the brutality of her late husband, lay torn, but luckily not beyond repair from the seamstress' needle, at the bottom of her wardrobe. But she was proud and usually tried her best with the little she did have. Self-respect was certainly not lacking, and being a lady and acting as such came naturally and happily to her.

'Please excuse my appearance,' she said, her cheeks burning.

'There is nothing to excuse, my dear. Even in a nightdress you are most radiant. It matters not, as long as you are comfortable. I can leave if you wish and return at more pleasing hour," He said.

'No … no, please don't,' she requested.

With Mr Muckleberry being the man he was, Sarah did not mind wearing her nightdress in his company. Furthermore, her night attire reached down to her ankles, the only flesh showing from her arms.

'Well, firstly, I do beg your pardon for my somewhat erratic banging on your door. I pray to the Lord it did not give you a fright,' he said.

Not wanting to lie to a vicar twice within such a short period of time, Sarah didn't reply but conveyed her pretence of ease with a large smile and a short shake of the head.

'To say I have been rather concerned for you, my dear, would be an understatement," the vicar began. "I usually see you every day, walking on your way to work, but this is the first time I have set sight upon you in many days ... and there are rumours afoot bearing unsavoury undertones for your well-being,' he said.

'Oh ... wanton gossip is all. As you can see for yourself, I am alive and well,' she replied.

'I'm glad to not only hear it but see it for myself and have the proof standing before my very eyes,' he said with some relief. 'And the family are all well I trust? How is your Jonathan and your Edward?' he continued.

Sarah was forced to lie again, although this particular lie came with some ease because she knew it was for her son's safety.

'Oh ... the boy is doing very well thank you. He is up north at the moment staying with his aunty.'

Mr Muckleberry smiled at hearing the news. 'And Edward?' he asked.

The next words from Sarah's lips came effortlessly. 'Ah ... he's ... around, close at hand. Thank you.'

With Edward being buried in the back garden, this was technically not a lie. If Sarah told a lie again and again to a vicar, it would certainly hurt her inside, down to her very soul.

He again smiled and was satisfied. He did not pursue Edward's well-being for he had met him a few times and did not care for the man. With them being in different circles and having different tastes in friends and so on, it was the norm for Mr Muckleberry to go sometimes a month or two and not see Edward.

'Forgive my questioning, but I assure you it comes from a wholesome heart. I am not one to take much note of gossip, but I would not be able to rest without checking, you understand,' he said reassuringly.

The village they lived in was quite small, the population count at no more than three hundred. Half-truths and gossip were commonplace, and private affairs would often become public, as would almost anything out of the ordinary. The gossip varied from decent tales to not so decent tales that flowed from varied mouths. Some being caring with genuine concern, with others being nothing but nosiness who relished in bad news as long as it did not affect them personally.

Some of the locals had become aware of Edward's disappearance within just twenty-four hours after the last sight of him. At least it was still just gossip.

Even though Sarah was not in the mood and not in the least interested in entertaining guests, she was more than willing to make an exception for Mr Muckleberry and play the host.

'Would you care for a cup of tea?' she offered.

'You are most kind, but sadly I must decline. I have taken up enough of your time, and I do have other matters to attend to,' he replied.

With a short bow, Mr Muckleberry showed his gratitude to Sarah, then placed his hat back on his head. He walked to the door and pulled it open.

'I believe I have a bottle of whiskey in the cupboard. Please have a tot if you wish ... for the walk home,' proposed Sarah.

Mr Muckleberry stopped immediately, with such suddenness it was if he had just walked into a solid brick wall. "

'Well ... well, perhaps just a tot, merely for medicinal purposes of course ... though would be rather pleasant.'

From her cupboard, Sarah pulled out a bottle of a thirty year-old single malt scotch whiskey and a small glass with a chip on the edge of the rim. The bottle was only half full and was possibly one of the most expensive items she owned.

'Allow me,' she said as she poured the water of life into the glass, continuing with a friendly warning of the sharp jagged chip and this whiskey being a little stronger than others.

'God himself created this, and as a servant of his Lordship, it is my duty to evaluate his work,' he said as he drank the whiskey in one go.

"Pon my soul, well done, Lord. Another miracle you have given humanity,' he continued. For the first time in quite a few days, Sarah laughed as she took back possession of her now empty glass.

'Many thanks indeed, Sarah, and the next time I am in your presence, I shall reciprocate your kind offering. Perhaps not in church though. The best I can offer you there is wine, and only a sip at that.'

Sarah smiled and laughed again.

'Good evening, dear lady, this old man is off to bother another soul. I trust I shall see you soon,' he said as he walked out the door and into the dark evening.

'Thank you, Rev. Most certainly, good evening and thank you again,' she replied and then closed the door. Deep down, she wanted to say the kind words of 'thank you' a half dozen times. The meeting did not last more than ten minutes but it meant a great deal to her.

Chapter 8

Jonathan was jerked awake, his deep sleep broken by a shake of his wooden bed. A foot was tapping three times on one of the bed legs, the culprit and owner of the foot being none other than Wooly.

'Come on will ya, sleepy head. You've been out of it for ages!' said Wooly as he kicked the bed again, only harder this time.

Jonathan sat up and rubbed his eyes to focus on his new lodgings. With a stretch of his thin arms, he slowly managed to feel more awake and had come to his senses a little.

With his consciousness now restored, he looked up at the cheeky faced Wooly. This morning, however, his expression was rather more happy and cocky. Jonathan could tell that Wooly wanted to say something of importance but decided not to coax it out of him.

'Get up and meet the rest of us,' urged Wooly.

Jonathan tilted his head and leaned sideways just as Wooly took a sidestep.

Jonathan saw the wooden table was in use by five other people, all sat round it. They were all of similar age, the youngest being close to thirteen and the eldest being around sixteen. They were in clothing that seemed to be many years passed its best but still managing to do the job. At first sight, they looked like bunch of ragamuffins and misfits.

Wooly lead Jonathan to the group in order to introduce them, pointing at each member as he did so.

'Far side is Twist, that's Tommy, that's Ginger, over there is Mary-Ann, and to ya left is my little sister Lizzie. Guys, this is Jonathan.'

The group all nodded as Jonathan gave a small, shy smile.

Wooly's sister, Lizzie, despite being one of the younger members of the group, struck him as being the most caring and astute. She was the first to notice that Jonathan was shy and fairly uncomfortable, as most people would be when confronted with a bunch of strangers, especially when they all seemed to know each other so well.

She kicked out a chair and asked him to sit down. Jonathan did so at once, and his small smile stretched a pinch wider.

'I bet you're hungry, aren't you?' she asked.

He nodded, and Lizzie stood up and made her way to the kitchen in the corner of the room. The kitchen was no more than a small stove with a few pots and pans scattered close by. '

Wooly sat in the chair adjacent to Jonathan and proceeded to talk and venture into more detail concerning his friends.

'Tommy is a mute, so don't take any offence when he don't chat to ya, and as I said before, Lizzie is my sister and Mary-Ann is her friend.'

'Why do they call you 'Twist'?' Jonathan asked as he looked to the other side of the table.

Twist opened his mouth, but before a single syllable had the chance to leave him, he was stopped dead in his tracks with laughter coming from Wooly.

'Oh please, Twist, you gotta let me answer this one.' Twist's eyes rolled with reluctant agreement.

Wooly began a story that he took much delight in conveying, as every time he told it, it never failed to stop him from giggling.

'Ya see how his nose is all crooked?' asked Wooly.

Jonathan nodded but did not make too much eye contact with Twist, in the fear that it may antagonise him.

Wooly continued. 'Well, 'bout six months ago now, Twist was in the middle of a dodge, can't remember exactly what it was - fink it was a wallet.'

Wooly paused and tilted his head up and to one side in an attempt to recall his memory. But failing, he continued, 'Anyway … the man caught him and went to grab him. Twist spun round, twisting his body like a little ballerina and ran -' Wooly could not finish the story because he was chuckling so much. This in-turn made Jonathan laugh, not solely through the amusing story but more so to participate and fit in to being polite, and hopefully would lessen the feeling of being an outsider.

'Get on with it if you must,' said Twist.

Wooly composed himself and held back his giggling, which had now turned into full-bellied laughter with a tear rolling down his face.

'Well, he turned to run away and BANG! ran straight into a lamppost. Bust his lip and broke his nose in two places. Looks like an ugly sod now, don't he? I've seen bare-knuckle boxers prettier than him.'

Jonathan was inclined to agree'', but he managed to stop himself at the last minute and just laughed politely instead.

Twist did not mind hearing this story, in which he played the rather unwilling protagonist, and even smiled at Wooly's laughter. Jonathan, with little knowledge of Twist's personality, remained cautious and did not presume anything. With his desire to join in, he still held back a little. ''

As time ticked by, it was clear to Jonathan that the whole group were friends and comfortable with each other. It was akin to a family. With Wooly obviously in charge, every member was happy and each had a say in all matters.

Lizzie returned to the table and lowered a bowl of hot chicken stock soup and a toasted muffin in front of Jonathan. His eyes lit up as the bread and apple from the day before had not satisfied his stomach.

'Oh gosh, thank you, Lizzie, thank you so much,' he said happily.

"Ere, don't he talk nice n proper?' said Ginger in a somewhat aggressive tone.

Lizzie sharply replied, 'Well I likes how he talks.'

Jonathan started sipping the hot soup to then follow with a bite of the muffin that he'd just dipped in to the broth.

As various stories came from Wooly, Jonathan learnt that, although this group of friends were very different to one another in certain ways, they had two things in common. They'd all had different upbringings but sadly similar conclusions.

The other unfavourable similarity consisted of each one having a troubling story to tell.

Jonathan listened with amazement, shock, and dread as each one spoke.

Tommy being a mute was the poor victim of a brutal assault a few years past, having his tongue cut out as a result. Ginger was a runaway and had been with Wooly for two years. His mother was a single parent and would bring a different man back every week, most of them beating or mistreating him in other ways, until one day he could not take any more. Mary-Ann's mother and aunty died from consumption, while her father was an unfortunate resident in a debtor's prison on the other side of London. Twist was an orphan and by some miracle had managed to escape the dreadful environment of the workhouse six years ago.

Jonathan was saddened and felt deflated from hearing these harrowing and cruel tales. If it wasn't for the soup, he would have felt most depressed.

After a few moments, his heart felt like it had dropped, with a deep, inner question he had and one only he could answer. Was he one of them? He did not feel like one of them, but he did take note of some resemblances of circumstances and desperation.

He quickly dismissed his inner question and focused on his food, which did seem to lighten his mood. He decided this soup tasted a better than any other simply because it was made by Lizzie, who he thought was very pretty.

It was abundantly clear that his new friends did not have much in terms of money, so he asked, 'Hope you don't mind me asking, Mr Wooly … sorry, I mean Wooly, but … how do you pay for this room?'

An unfortunate episode had happened to their landlord just one year ago, which happened to be very fortunate for Wooly and his clan.

"Bout a year ago, our landlord died, and funny fing is, we ain't heard nofing since. No one has asked for the rent and we ain't seen no bailiff, so 'ere's where we stay. God knows how, but I ain't askin' anyone,' explained Wooly.

'Yeah, and you better not say nofing either, you hear!' Ginger warned aggressively. Jonathan agreed to keep their secret.

'Anyone asks you, just say you're a mute, got it?' Ginger continued.

Lizzie stood up to clear away Jonathan's empty bowl and walked towards the kitchen saying, 'How can he *say* he's a mute? Twit.'

Most of the group, including Jonathan, laughed at Lizzie's quick response, but the reaction from Ginger was a huff and a look of warning. Ginger was the most wary of Wooly's friends, as he took the longest to trust strangers, be them man, woman, boy, or girl.

With Jonathan's age, size, and lack of muscular structure, it was obvious to even a simpleton that there would be no danger from him in terms of violence, but Ginger knew the risk of damage was still a possibility with the potential of loose lips.

After about half an hour, and when the chit-chat had wound down, Wooly told the group to 'go out to work' as he wanted to be alone with Jonathan. Twist, Ginger, Tommy, Lizzie, and Mary-Ann stood up, tucked their chairs in, and left the room.

Wooly reached underneath the table and produced a large brown glass bottle full of what looked like water. With a nod, he pushed it into Jonathan's open hand. Jonathan pulled off the crumbling cork, he brought the bottle to his lips, leaned his head back, and took a sizeable swig.

Within a moment of the clear liquid filling his mouth, it was spat out fast, in a long, wide spray followed by a gravelly cough.

Wooly laughed whilst wiping off his offering from his shirt and trousers.

'Oi, watch it, that cost four shillings," he said.

After a few seconds, when Jonathan felt the breath coming back to his lungs, he gasped 'What was that?' He had never tasted anything like it before.

The response was, 'Mothers Ruin'. The answer did not seem to help and he wanted Wooly to elaborate.

'What's that?'

Wooly took a swig and told him it was 'Gin' at the same time as he put his feet up on one of the empty chairs and leaned back to get more comfortable.

'The time at the moment is 9.47 exactly. How do I know that? Do ya see any clocks in 'ere?' Wooly said with a smug look on his face.

Jonathan looked around the brick and plaster walls and shook his head. Wooly pulled out a very fine-looking pocket watch, with bright gold face and hands, silver circling the edge and hung by a gold chain.

His first reaction upon seeing the pocket watch was confusion, then awe. Jonathan, having known Wooly for only twenty-four hours, was aware that he hardly knew anything about him. He did however know that Wooly was not the sort of person to own this impressive timepiece. With his appearance, this gold watch would have looked more out of place and unfitting than a bearded man wearing a corset.

He seemed extremely proud of himself as he explained that he could fence it for food and drink for three days, another coat, half ounce of tobacco, and still have a few farthings left over.

'Gosh, where did you get it from?' asked Jonathan.

'Dodged it this mornin', didn't I, early, when you lot was fast asleep,' he replied.

Jonathan had never even heard the term 'dodge' before, but it rapidly became obvious that he meant 'stole'.

His dropped jaw turned to a frown.

'You ... you stole it? From who?' he asked with a slight stutter of disbelief.

'Fink ya mean from whom,' Wooly replied with a smugness.

He could not fully answer Jonathan's question with much depth or detail as it was just another man in the street. Another addition to the long list of his victims.

Jonathan did not understand, not only with how and why, but what was more unnerving was the normality and pride that was present in Wooly at such an act. Jonathan's face and mannerisms made it clear that he thought it was wrong and he should give it back and say sorry, a task that should be simple and easy to do.

'Give it back? Say sorry? Gor, you are just a kid, ain't ya, green and stupid! Like that chicken soup earlier.' He guffawed. 'Well guess what? Dodged that two days ago, just like you did with that bread roll!' Wooly said with a meaningful tone.

Jonathan thought the two counts of theft were completely different, as he explained that when he stole the bread, it was because he was desperate and starving.

Wooly stood up fast and yelled, 'Well what do ya fink this is?' He went to explain that this was what they all did, softening the crime by stretching the truth and telling him that a quarter the population of Whitechapel were doing the same. A quarter of the population being somewhat a stretch of the imagination to say the least, but it probably wasn't hugely far from the truth. But, for Jonathan, a gold watch was not the same as food. His young and innocent mind and lack of knowledge of these parts could not distinguish between the two.

According to Wooly's rant, it was one and of the same. It was all about money. It was all interconnected where the next penny, farthing, shilling, or pound came from. Food was money, money was food, and a watch was money, so therefore food.

Not only did Jonathan now understand, but after hearing about Wooly's streetwise tricks, he was rather dazzled, especially with the fact that not everyone could do it, or do it well.

'If it was easy, then everyone would do it,' Wooly enjoyed saying, more than once in order to make the message crystal clear in Jonathan's mind. He was getting a crash-course in the ways, means, and lies of the world, at least from Wooly's perspective.

He went on, talking of humanity's lies, deceptions, and side hustles, especially in London, whether it was market traders short-changing their customers when they could get away with it, the crooked police cracking open the skull of a man down a dark alley just because they could, a prostitute ripping off a client, a man keeping a girl sweet for a week in order to bed her only to then leave, a beggar faking an illness for sympathy, and even the politicians spouting their lies in the Houses of Parliament.

Jonathan sat still, being a willing and keen student, taking in all the information that was being thrust upon him, nodding at every other sentence. The lecture only partly made sense, as he did not know what a 'prostitute' was or a 'politician' and had never heard of 'The Houses of Parliament'. He had more questions than answers, however the gist of Wooly's meaning managed to get through to him.

All this was very sad, but it was Wooly's world and he'd seen it every day for as long as he had been in Whitechapel. It was scary and depressing for Jonathan to hear that the world was not what he thought. Experiencing his father, he knew of some of the cruelty that man was capable of, but Wooly's words still hit him like a hammer blow to the senses.

Wooly was not evil, just a product of his surroundings and beliefs. Once, long ago, before moving to London, he was probably not unlike Jonathan. Full of innocence, as any child should be, but over time, his naivety and innocence faded away in order to just survive. At first for Wooly, the perils of Whitechapel became pearls of wisdom with his fear edging away and knowledge of the streets growing. It was rather sorrowful, but it was not through choice. In Wooly's mind, you could either be like him or be' dead.

However, Wooly did have a heart and was always upbeat. He could see the sad look on Jonathan's face and continued with the good that was around in the world too. There was much fun to have and he knew Jonathan would grow to love the tricks that would be taught to him. Jonathan's head was low, as if he had a great weight balancing on the back of his neck.

Wooly gently placed his hand on Jonathan's cheek. 'Come on, chin up, kid, all will be well. Ya got us now, and we'll look after ya. Ain't all bad, I promise,' he said, followed by a big smile.

Jonathan smiled and took every word to heart, the positive, as well as the negative.

'Come on, let's go and you'll see for yaself,' Wooly said in a soft and happy tone. With that, they left the room, Wooly taking a long coat with them. Being a warm day, Jonathan was very sceptical and looked questioningly at Wooly.

'Lesson one, kid' Wooly said with a cheerful wink.

Chapter 9

The two new friends, or teacher and apprentice as Wooly saw it, found themselves on the cobbled roads of central Whitechapel, not more than a mile's walk from Wooly's crumbling loft room. It was good for Jonathan to set sight upon his current surroundings and probable new home, without exhaustion and the pang of starvation. He could finally take in everything properly. He watched the hundreds of people going about their days. He could smell the scents of the street, with its mixture of alluring foods and goods.

Berries, baked bread, cooked meat, and strong coffee, with loose tea from China, perfumes from Paris and Italy, spices of yellow ginger root from lands far and wide; powders of coal dust, flour, vanilla, and lavender; pipe smoke and floral scents from fresh, colourful flowers.

If this was all he could smell, it would have been nothing but a delight for his nostrils. However, the old street, along with its inhabitants, also carried a strong displeasing odour. In parts of the area lay raw sewage, horse manure, and piles of uncollected rubbish baking in the sun. Not to mention the odorous slaughtering and processing of animals, including fish guts and rotting chickens' feet, that many people engaged in. With some of the street and side alleys being quite narrow, the smells would only be amplified as they drifted through the air and hovered in the atmosphere.

Wooly was by his side, with his hand in his coat pockets as he walked with his usual confident swagger. Wednesday was not market day, but the streets were still busy and a hive of activity. Many traders were still selling their wares, from buckets to bananas, candles to carrots, and soups to sausages, along with all the shop keepers offering their stock, services, and specialised skills to customers.

Wooly was to give Jonathan his first lesson on the tricks of his trade. How long would it take for Jonathan to pick it up and master them? Wooly had no idea, as everyone was inconsistent and contrasting, with divergent levels of morality and ethics being higher or lower depending on the individual. He had taught the whole of his group in past few years how to dodge and avoid getting caught, something he was most proud of.

When he had taken in Mary-Ann, many moons ago, she'd found it somewhat difficult to grasp at first and took over six months of trying every day to perfect the trade, whilst Ginger and Twist picked it up within a little more than three weeks and had never had their collars felt by a policeman or been on the receiving end of a citizen's arrest; they never even got a whack from anyone. With Jonathan's age and polite demeanour, Wooly guessed it would take a while, but time was on his side, and not being tied to anything or anyone, they had all the time in the world. Wooly did have high hopes for him though, having seen how he had stolen the bread rolls the day before.

They both walked a couple hundred yards and found an empty black iron bench with curved ornate arms to sit down on and watch the world go by, while looking out for any potential opportunity to lighten a heavy pocket of a passerby.

It was lunchtime and the street was full of shoppers, mainly consisting of maids and servants buying supplies for their household employers and masters. The maids stood out in their black dresses and white aprons and did not make worthy targets, for they had little money about their person.

Wooly explained, because they went out almost every day, they never held more than a few shillings at one time as it was not worth the risk. Also, the majority of the maids would shop in established places of business, where most of the purchases would be on account so there would be even less of a chance of them carrying money.

'Well, why can't *you* have an account in a shop? You don't need money then,' Jonathan asked innocently.

'You mad? Na ... no shopkeeper would give us an account. He won't trust us, 'tis only people of good stock and power that has fings booked down to pay at the end of the month,' Wooly replied, wishing it was that simple.

Just then, a very attractive housemaid walked past. 'Only fing she has that I'd be interested in is what's underneath her skirts,' said Wooly. Jonathan had a look of confusion whilst Wooly tutted and said, "Never mind, kid, guess ya a bit young for that."

Wooly wanted to test Jonathan by making him do his favourite dodge. The dodge in particular being "The Match Dodge", also known as 'The Peppermint Dodge'. Jonathan sat still and was happy to learn about it.

Wooly went on to explain that this dodge was all about what someone would do to avoid embarrassment. It was a very simple trick, but one that worked more times than it didn't.

The match or peppermint job consisted of a stooge, usually a little girl, the younger the better, walking round with a handful of either loose matches to sell or loose peppermints to eat. The little girl would deliberately bump into a passerby, one that looked like he or she was well-to-do, to then drop the peppermints all over the ground. The little girl would then feign heartbreak, cry out loud, and make a huge fuss. Nine times out of ten, the lady or gentleman who she'd bumped into would have a strong feeling of guilt and would give the crying girl a few coins in the hope to shut her up and to avoid a crowd gathering.

Upon receiving the coins, the girl would stop crying and the victim of this deception would walk off and think nothing of it. Five minutes later, the girl would do the same thing to another unwilling soul with a large heart and heavy wallet.

On a good day, the girl would do this over and over again, in different areas of the street without anyone cottoning on. Do it ten times, on average getting half a shilling a time, and the girl would have acquired five shillings. With the typical weekly wage for an adult shop keeper being between only fifteen and twenty shillings, when done right, this little venture would be very profitable and lucrative. All just by dropping a small handful of sweets or matches, even using the same handfuls at that. The mints or matches would rarely get damaged or wasted. The money being handed over was not solely for damages but more to cheer the little girl up, and fast.

'You have a go. Lizzie and Mary-Ann did it hundreds of times when they were eight,' said Wooly as he handed over a few sweets into Jonathan's palm.

Jonathan was impressed by the possibility of getting free cash through such a simple act. In a funny sort of way, he saw it as deception and not lying. He looked down to his open hand holding the sweets and was a little hesitant. Wooly pressured him into trying it, as he saw the perfect suitor walk past. A gentleman of about fifty years of age with a monocle and obvious wealth, walking straight and proud in his fine crisp suit, wearing a top hat and carrying a shiny black cane.

Wooly nudged Jonathan's arm as if to hurry him along.

'There ya go ... him, he's just right. Go ... go bump into him,' said Wooly.

'"But I'm not an eight year old girl. It won't work,' he replied in a slightly panicked tone.

Wooly explained that anyone could do this dodge, it was just easier with a sweet looking girl as any adult, at least one with a heart, would naturally do anything to stop a soft, sweet child from crying.

'Quick, before it's too late. Go will ya!' Wooly said with added pressure.

Jonathan stood up, clutching the rather dirty round peppermints in his hand, making a tight fist just in case he were to drop them prematurely. He was about ten paces behind the gentleman, eyes fixated on his back as he walked behind him and waiting for the right moment to run and bump into him apparently by mistake.

Wooly watched on as his little student walked faster, slowly getting closer and closer, catching up to the man. After about thirty seconds, Jonathan was within touching distance of his target.

Now was his chance. Jonathan was about to barge into the side of the gentleman when suddenly, without warning, the man swung his arm round behind him in order to scratch his back, hitting Jonathan in the face as he did so. He fell to the ground, landing on his backside, and forgot to drop the mints. His hand still clenched tight as his body became stiff and taut with shock.

The gentleman scratched his back, turned around, and upon seeing Jonathan on the ground, said in a very posh and calm voice, 'Oh I am sorry, dear fellow, I didn't see you there. The fault is all mine. I am a clumsy buffoon, aren't I?' He then simply walked off.

He stood up and looked back a few yards at Wooly, only to see him laughing his head off, falling sideways on the other side of the bench as he did so.

He wiped the dirt off his bum and walked back to the bench 'Spose you think that was funny?' asked Jonathan.

Wooly could not speak, he just nodded hard in between his giggles.

After a few moments, when Wooly had finally regained his senses and managed to stop his loud outburst, seeing Jonathan was not hurt, with only his pride being bruised and not his face, he knew all was well. He took back the peppermints and placed them back in his pocket.

'Can I at least have some sweets?' asked Jonathan, thinking he deserved at least one for his efforts, not forgetting he'd just had a slap on his face.

Wooly said no, but not as a punishment for failing the dodge. It was because the peppermints were at least two years old and dirty, as they had been purposely dropped on the ground a minimum of one hundred times.

'Even if I blew off the dirt, I still wouldn't eat 'em', said Wooly. 'Couple of dodges ago, they fell in some horse shit!'

Jonathan was happy not to have a sweet after hearing that. 'Told you I couldn't do it,' he said in a deflated tone.

Wooly reassured him and told him to cheer up as it was only his first attempt, and that the very same thing had happened to him on his first try years ago. This was a lie, but a lie not out of malice like most in this world, but to comfort Jonathan.

'Somefing a little simpler perhaps,' said Wooly as he thought of another dodge for him to do. He held a large wealth of knowledge, and a whole list of scams, tricks, cons, and dodges were present in his brain.

They both stayed on the bench, with Jonathan sat still as he happily looked around, doubting whether it was easy after all to dodge these streets and if he'd ever be as smart as Wooly.

'It ain't easy,' said Wooly. 'Just gotta be patient is all and look for the right geezer,' 'he continued.

He nodded in agreement. He went on to explain that although he found it fun and a huge thrill, even after doing it all these years, it was still a very dangerous lifestyle.

'Pick the wrong pocket, get caught by the peelers and bobbies, or even just upset the wrong man and you'll either get a good hiding or thrown behind bars, or worse, you'll end up growing daisies, know what I mean,' Wooly said with added seriousness, moving his fingertip from one side of his throat to the other.

Wooly had many a horrific tale to tell of adults and children meeting a fearful and bloodied end, but he knew that if he were to convey those scary tales, it would only frighten Jonathan. He wanted him to possess an element of fear, for he believed it would keep him on his toes, but not too much. A scared little mouse would not last long at all.

Wooly leaned back, crossed his legs, and, with his hands interlocked on the back of his head, he thought about something a little easier for his friend, his head turning left and right, up and down the street, watching and thinking. It did not take him long to find a worthy but easy opportunity for Jonathan.

'I've got it!' he said as he caught sight of an apple seller working across the road, almost exactly opposite from where they were. By the looks of the sweet girl behind the stall, it should be an easy pick. She couldn't have been much older than Jonathan himself.

He excitedly said to Jonathan to walk up to the apple seller and take just one apple and then come back. Jonathan looked at the seller and paused, for deep down in his heart, he knew it was wrong and it felt very unnatural to him to take part in such an act. The seller looking kind and soft made it all the worse. But he was in no position to turn back now.

Wooly said two things that made Jonathan a little less hesitant. One: it should be relatively easy and did not require some huge scam or ingenious tricks. With the second reason: (which at first sounded rather odd and random, but also felt strangely warming) Jonathan could then give the apple it to Lizzie when they got back home. Wooly knew his sister pretty well and had an inkling that she held a soft spot for Jonathan, and there was a chance the feeling would be reciprocated. With his looks and charm, he did have a habit and a great talent of persuading people to follow his words.

Jonathan stood up and made his way across the road and towards the apple seller. Wooly sat back and watched on with a large smile that slowly got wider with each step that Jonathan took.

Within just twenty steps, he reached the stall. He stood in front of the long wooden tabletop that was held up by three 'A' frame legs. The table was full of a huge variety of apples, from the light green Granny Smiths to the bright red Galas to the yellow Golden Delicious.

The apples that engulfed the table were displayed in a most ornate fashion, with the sole intention of attracting more customers, in direct competition with the other apple sellers. The attractive orchard fruits were sat on top of each other in four piles, almost in a pyramid or mountain shape, each one ten layers high with just one apple conquering the summit and balancing nicely.

Jonathan looked around in a casual manner and waited till the seller and other onlookers were facing away, even for a split second, just like he did when he snatched the bread rolls on his first arrival to Whitechapel.

After about two minutes, the coast was clear, and the narrow window of opportunity had come. He grabbed an apple, but before he could place it in his pocket and turn away, the whole pyramid collapsed. For he did not take the top apple, but one at random from the bottom of the stack. Within seconds, dozens upon dozens of apples fell, rolling left and right and all over the floor, causing a commotion with some of the apples rolling several feet in all directions.

Wooly watched and took a deep breath, slowly shock his head, and closed his eyes for a second in shear disbelief.

Jonathan stood still in shock, his mouth wide open. Not five seconds had past when a lady shopper at the stall looked at him and in a very loud, high-pitched voice, yelled, 'Oi! Thief! Thief!'

Wooly stood up and shouted, 'Run!'

Jonathan ran towards the bench, reaching it in seconds. Wooly grabbed his shoulder as they then ran off down the street together.

They both ran as fast as they could, having to swerve and weave through the crowds as they did, whilst looking back every now and then to see if they were being chased.

After about two hundred yards, they stopped at another part of the long street. Both gasping, with their lungs desperate for air and hearts fit to burst, Wooly looked back yet again to check that they were not being pursued. As luck would have it, they were in the clear. Either no one bothered to give chase or the two boys had managed to lose their pursuers in the mass of people. That was indeed one advantage they had: they blended in very well with every other child in similar stages of wealth or status. On this occasion, they were very lucky, for if a trader or shopper in the street did happen to see someone, not just stealing, but almost any crime, they would usually yell for assistance or would want to see justice against the perpetrator. Not forgetting the bobbies or 'bluetops' that, from time to time, would patrol. At least that was the case during the daytime.

They both sat down on the pavement and leant back against a brick wall down a drangway to a blacksmiths.

'I'm sorry, Wooly. I … I didn't know … I was scared,' Jonathan said sadly.

'Ya didn't fink, did ya? Fancy taking one from the bottom of the pile!' replied Wooly, but not with any anger to his voice. Wooly was not angry, nor was he really disappointed, as he appreciated that little Jonathan had tried, and it was his very first day. Instead of giving him a lecture, he simply smiled and said, 'You are a silly sod.'

'But I could have got us caught!' said Jonathan.

'Main fing is ya didn't. Relax, you're learning, kid,' replied Wooly. 'But no more o' that nonsense in future, eh? You gotta be able ta dodge on ya own sooner or later, and if ya get caught ... well, ya fate is on ya own 'ead.'

After a few minutes, the two friends turned to one another and laughed when thinking about all those apples rolling around like a waterfall scattering with the fruits.

Wooly stood up and said, 'Come on, kid, let's go home. Fink we've had enough for one day, don'tcha?'

Chapter 10

It was late afternoon when Wooly and Jonathan returned to the loft room.

Wooly kindly asked Jonathan to light the fire, to make it as warm and comfortable as it could be for when the rest of the group came back. Jonathan did not know when that would be. Their 'work' being somewhat random, with no set times or distances, it was difficult to judge where they would be, for Whitechapel had a hundred streets, side alleys, and courtyards. It was a vast playground of opportunity for those with criminal inclinations and tenancies.

Wooly, however, did have an inkling as to what time they would return, as Mary-Ann did not like to be out after dark. When the moon hovered over Whitechapel, it was at times a rather testing place for a grown man, let alone a child, or any being that held a nervous disposition. There were two sorts that were commonly present who were victims of crime. The ones that had suffered by the hands from another were hardened to it and accepted it. The others were ones that also suffered from similar acts but particularly nervous due to their experience and retained a first account of barbarism. Just as every blade of grass is different when examined closely, the residents of this area all appeared the same until one took a good look behind the eyes. The victims of muggings, assaults, rapes, and beatings took to street life in different ways. One act would stir a fright in some, while others saw it as nothing more than the norm and would even count themselves lucky that they could return to home alive.

When the group went out to work the streets, the majority of the time, they split up in order to cover more ground, and also because a lone child can hide or blend in more easily. But this was not the case concerning Lizzie and her dearest friend Mary. They both stayed together, not only for safety but more so because they worked exceptionally well with one another, for whichever dodge or trick they were doing usually needed a pair, be it for a diversion or a lookout.

Jonathan lit the fire in the centre of the side wall in the room. Having done it many times for his mother and father, he was skilled at building fires for his age . Wooly had little in term of household wares, but he did have an abundance of logs and paper for his beloved but very modest fireplace. When lady luck struck on certain days, he even had a few handfuls of coal that found its way from the docks into his tarnished copper scuttle.

With the fire lit, it's welcoming orange glow flickering behind the hand-made stone hearth, Wooly dragged his chair close and relaxed. He pulled out a white clay pipe from his coat pocket and reached for a burning twig to light his tobacco.

'Ya know, I should be annoyed at ya,' he said whilst puffing away.

'I said I was sorry," replied Jonathan as he sat in front of the fire with his legs crossed.

'Na not that. Roughly this time each day, we all come together and show our stuff, and I ain't got nofing to show, have I?'

Jonathan was soon to learn that 'stuff' was code for stolen loot. It was not a local colloquialism, nor was it long tradition of speech in these parts. It was merely elementary slang for Wooly and one that that the others gladly emulated, especially when in earshot of strangers. It would not have mattered what 'stuff' they had, as long as it was found or stolen in some shape or form. From a halfpenny all the way up to the priceless crown jewels themselves, it was all 'stuff' if they used their know-how to get it.

Wooly was not really annoyed at not being able to impress his friends with his ill-gotten gains, for he had nothing to prove, as he was the boss and the most successful in such criminal acts. Also, if Ginger or Twist were to voice a wise remark on the subject of his empty pockets, he could always blame it on Jonathan, saying that he was extra busy teaching and being the tour guide. Besides, he hadn't come back completely empty-handed, as he had two brilliant stories to tell about Jonathan's mishaps; his comedy of errors on his first day on the job. Wooly knew that it would certainly enthral and fill them with much amusement, lifting morale, and would be worth more than a few pence for sure.

An hour had passed, and one by one, Lizzie and Mary-Ann, Twist, Ginger, and Tommy all returned. All home, safe and sound, bar a new deep cut on Twist's elbow, all were now sheltered and secure.

This was always an interesting time for the group, when they all clubbed together to share stories and show off their stuff from the hard day's work, and it was sure to be an education for Jonathan.

Before the telling Wooly of the day's events and producing whatever was in her pocket, Lizzie first turned to Twist to treat his wound. The morals of Wooly and his sister were certainly lacking to say the least, however Wolly and Lizzie saw themselves with a duty of care for the rest. A burden which at times felt weighted, but a burden and responsibility they took on nonetheless, and at most parts were happy to do so.

Seeing as none of the group had any parents, or at least none of worth, Wooly and Lizzie saw themselves playing the part to the best of their ability. Between them, they could be a nurse, seamstress, cleaner, doctor, teacher, protector, caregiver, cook, and a gardener if they had the chance and all else that consists of being a decent parent.

Only Jonathan had a mother who excelled in all those jobs. But with Sarah many miles away, Jonathan was in much the same position as his new friends.

Lizzie sat down with Twist to inspect the bloody cut, much to his defiance and insistence that it was fine and 'just a scratch'.

'Just let her look at it,' Wooly snapped, and Twist finally relented and allowed Lizzie to play the part of nurse, a part she had played more than once in the past and had, over time, become somewhat proficient at.

Within just ten minutes, Lizzie worked her feminine and caring magic yet again. The wound was cleaned, checked, and wrapped in cloth, followed by the reassuring words, 'He'll live, but it will need a stitch or two.'

'A stitch – in my head?' Twist's eyes were wide open with terror.

'No, silly! There's a hole in the elbow of your coat.'

'The group sat round the table, all hungry and happy to know their stomachs would soon be filled. Mary-Ann and Lizzie were to start dinner, with the aid of the already lit fire and charcoal that had accumulated, which made it perfect timing for cooking.

Wooly turned his head and watched the two girls preparing the food. The anticipation on his face morphed to one of very slight discontent, with one eyebrow curving downwards in a questioning manner.

'Oh, soup … again. Brilliant. We had that yesterday … and the day before … and the day before,' he said slowly. Sensing her brother's meaning and sarcasm, the words were quickly parried away.

'I do the best with what we have,' Lizzie replied tartly. 'You want decent meat? Then tomorrow, go out and dodge us a pig and we would gladly make a meal fit for Queen Victoria herself. But until you manage it, you'll have what we make or go without.'

Sat at the head of the table, Wooly did a teasing impression of her, his shoulders moving up and down, mumbling her sentence word for word, his lower lip protruding. To then hit her lightly on the backside with a smile. An act which Lizzie returned in the exact same way, as brothers and sisters can do with one another full of charm and closeness.

The table was in full attendance as Lizzie and Mary-Ann served dinner. Mary- Ann placed a large black cooking pot with a ladle off to one side in the centre, whilst Lizzie walked round, giving everyone a small bowl. Wooly leaned forward and served the hot soup, giving each person a fair and equal portion, to then serve himself last.

'Hmm … soup … again,' he grumbled. 'I'm so glad we have it *all the time*,' he said with a sniff and sarcastic smile.

Lizzie sat down and quickly replied, 'Shut your cake hole, and before you ask, no we haven't got any cake.'

Dinner had come and gone within just a few moments, but this did not defect from the pleasurable feeling it left in its wake. Jonathan was the first to thank Lizzie and show his appreciation for her efforts, to which her pretty face lit up. There appeared to be some sort of connection with these two, like an invisible rope.. They could have talked about anything, even something boring or mundane, it did not matter. They were fulfilled just with talking away, and the subject of any genre would seem captivating. Every time either Jonathan or Lizzie spoke to each other, it was as if the rest of the world faded away.

'As the group were all together, chatting as the last drop of soup was licked out of the bowls, a cold darkness drew in as evening came. The loft room looked warm and cosy with the crackling from the open fire. It was a far cry from most homes, even ones in bleak areas, but the group had become accustomed to it and they still knew that some children had it worse. The thought of living on the streets outside was a threat that constantly hung over their heads like a black Gothic iron arch over a haunted cemetery gate. The thought of death was only a slight decree worse. Every winter, it would not be uncommon to see a wretched frozen corpse in the gutter or a doorway with a look of pain ever immortalized on its face.

The chit-chat had halted as Wooly announced it was time for his favourite part of the day. They all cleared away the table and, in turn, showed their

Chapter 10

day's achievements, accompanied with a tale of how exactly they had done it.

Instead of hurrying the pleasure by asking everyone to empty their pockets simultaneously, he would allow the moment to drag on, by going round each member one by one and allowing them to take it in turns. Wooly was not alone with his anticipation, for they all felt a sense of suspense with a slight feeling of trepidation as to whether what they concealed about themselves would be sufficient. It was akin to a crooked Christmas day, with the unknown knowledge of gifts, until the pile that always showed itself in the middle of the table looked back at the dozen eyes of the children.

From a dirty halfpenny to a gleaming solid gold bar, it was all feasible and achievable, although the items that held extreme riches were few and far between. The pocket watch that he had showed off to Jonathan days prior was the nicest piece the group had filched in over three weeks.

The time where the members could show off their gains was a pocket of happiness, for the majority of the time discontent was rife, not just within the confines of their home but moreso within the world as they knew to snatch a smile, even for moment in time where they could was not just of importance, but vital.

They were all well aware that losing one's spirit and essence in life could very easily spell death. Giving up when you do not get many seconds chances, you might as well pull the hangman's

117

trapdoor lever yourself and bid a fond farewell to all you know of this world.

'The whole group stood up and gathered themselves round the table. Some coat pockets were bulging and some looked almost empty, but Wooly had enough experience to know that this was not a clear indication of goods. A flat pocket containing a diamond would be far more useful than a pocket stuffed with apples.

Wooly had connections all over Whitechapel and could sell or swap anything, no matter the price or size, just as long as the trade took place well away from the sight of the authorities and the prying eyes of civilians yearning for a cash reward. Not always as easy as it sounds, for the long arm of the law at times stretched far.

The group, as if standing on ceremony, took it in turns to unload their pockets. Twist, from his left pocket, threw on the table for all to see a brown leather wallet. It landed open and was clear to all that it was void of notes. Wooly picked it up for a further examination and found three shillings, a farthing, and about twenty-six pence, made up of pennies and halfpennies.

'Nice … plus, we can get at least a ten shillings for the wallet itself. Anyfink else?' said Wooly.

Twist nodded, as he then pulled from his inner pockets three dark blue handkerchiefs, two of which were of particularly good taste and quality being made from French satin.

'Good lad,' said Wooly, then gave a nod to Ginger as if to say, 'You're next.'

Ginger, who leaned more towards shop thefts, pulled out four circular tins of cherry blossom shoe polish, two bars of soap, a small box of matches, and a handful of Bonbons mixed in blue and red sugar powder.

Only two lots down but the centre of the table was already looking rather pleasing to them all as the pile slowly grew larger.

The group took their gaze away from the loot and aimed it at Tommy, for he was next in line. He raised his hand up in a closed fist but then stuck out his index finger, pointing it upwards to indicate he only had the one item about his person.

Usually, a single item would come with a look of shame from the owner, but Tommy held a smug smile. Still holding his finger up, he put his other hand in his pocket and wriggled it around. The rest of the group looked on with confusion.

'Ya playing with your cock again, Tommy?' said Wooly to break the anticipated silence.

The group laughed, with Tommy smiling even harder. Not one decibel could leave his muted mouth, but with his head bobbing up and down from Wooly's remark, it was clear he was laughing inside.

After a few more seconds of wiggling around inside his pocket, his finger hooked onto the single item. He slowly pulled his hand out and showed the others a pearl necklace hanging down from his finger. It hung down at least ten inches and looked as good as new, each and every pearl looking immaculate and as smooth as silk, with its shiny pinky-white milk texture. Not one scratch, dent or graze seemed present among them. He gently placed the necklace in the middle of the table to add to the rest of goods. Wooly nodded his head with much approval, followed by a wink at Tommy to show how pleased he was.

'Nice one. Just for that, you can have tomorrow off,' he said.

Tommy gave a nod as a reply.

Lizzie and Mary-Ann were last but certainly not least. As they worked in a pair, the routine was to always show their efforts together. They produced from their pockets a small bag of flour, two packets of raisins, a shilling, four half pennies, a rolled up newspaper, a red leather bound book titled *'Mary Shelley's Frankenstein'*, a long black ladies purse, an apple, and two bars of Frys Chocolate with strawberry paste filling.

Jonathan's eyes were as wide as they could be as he looked on at the impressive mound of goods. Wooly and the rest also looked upon their collected endeavours with smiles as it was all quite an undertaking to acquire, and this particular horde was more successful than on most days.

Every item that lay before their eyes was of worth in some way. The food and money holding the obvious importance, but everything else that could not have been eaten or used as money would soon become money. The combination of the wallet and purse, the book, necklace, boot polish, and handkerchiefs had a collected value of around two hundred shillings, or ten pounds, if bought new. After Wooly had fenced them through the streets, they would probably, all being well, get around fifty shillings. Not bad at all for one day's work, and they were all well aware of that.

Wooly and his sister gathered up the loot and place it round the room accordingly, some if it going in a large wooden chest with a rounded lid, not unlike a pirate's chest, while the food was divided up amongst the friends. Wooly broke one of the chocolate bars into three pieces and gave it to the younger members.

The whole group gathered their chairs and sat round the crackling fire, snacking on chocolate, apples, and raisins, with gin to help wash it down. Laughter and merriment filled the air with tales of how each of them had acquired there 'stuff', with the apple being passed round, each taking a bite apart from Wooly. When the apple got to him, he simply threw it to Jonathan.

'Have a bite, kid, you like apples, don'tcha?' said Wooly with his ever-present smile on his face and continued, 'Fink our new friend has a story to share about apples … don'tcha?'

Jonathan tentatively looked left and right at the group and was hesitant as he did not want to appear the fool or be made fun of.

With the friendly feeling he felt from the entire room, he was happy to tell them his story about what had happened earlier. What followed was cheering and giggles in a most joyous fashion towards him, with added reassurance that they all made mistakes, and it was clear that the giggles and jibes were *with* him and not *at* him.

Lizzie leaned over and told Jonathan not to worry and it was a good thing in a way, for it took a certain type of cold-hearted, inhumane person to take to crime with ease and be proficient from the first minute.

Jonathan took solace that it was a compliment of sorts. He felt accepted by the rest and was now part of the group as the chatter and gin flowed into the night.

As the night drew in even darker, the orange glow from the fire and the smell of pipe smoke made the atmosphere somewhat comfortable, and Jonathan felt relaxed for the first time in a while. The gin seemed to help as his second and third sip did not seem to have the same reaction than his first.

Chapter 11

Six weeks had passed when Jonathan woke up in his narrow, rigidity, wooden bed in Wooly's loft room. He thought he had overslept, as when his eyes first opened, he did not hear the regular clitter-clatter from the rest as he usually did. He looked around the room and saw it was empty. He sat up to reach for his glass of water that lay on the floor when Wooly entered, slamming the door behind him.

It was evident that Wooly was not in the best of moods and much out of character. A rare thing indeed. Wooly was always a happy-go-lucky, cheeky lad, but not on this day, it seemed.

'Good morning, Wooly,' greeted Jonathan in a welcoming tone to cheer him up, even just a little.

Wooly sat down on the bed next to Jonathan and said nothing, with a look of palpable discontent.

'What's up?' asked Jonathan nervously.

Wooly was not angry, nor was he threatening, but he certainly was showing that something was at the forefront of his mind.

A silence resonated in the air between them for a few moments. 'Please tell me, Wooly, I don't like this,' asked Jonathan.

Wooly explained the reason for his apparent moodiness. He was not happy with Jonathan, and he had started to lose patience. Not with his personality, character, humour, or mannerisms. It was the fact that Jonathan had not yet completed one illicit scheme. Not one dodge, trick, scam, or theft had been accomplished to any beneficial fulfilment. All of his efforts showed less than a single halfpenny coin. A grain of sugar would have been more of a contribution than what Jonathan had returned from the streets.

Wooly was well aware that everyone took different lengths of time to learn the trade, but there were limits to his tolerance, even more so in desperate days when time was not on 'their side.

'It's been well over a month and ya ain't earned us nofing, not even a bloody apple core to chew on,' said Wooly. 'Ya gotta pay 'ya way 'ere. I ain't keeping no orphan or whatever you are for free. Ya know 'ow many people out there ain't got nofing? I ain't taking *them* on, am I? And I won't, neither. I ain't no mug.'

Jonathan felt guilty and sorry. It was a rather peculiar feeling, to feel guilt at not having committed a crime.

He had not intended to take advantage of Wooly, nor had he taken his hospitality for granted. He tried to do what he was told, almost every day attempting to pick a pocket from a stranger or pilfer stock from a shop, but every time, he would lose his nerve. What if he was caught? Even just the thought of being found out sent a cold shiver right down to his core. He had offered in the past to 'play mum', to cook and clean the room whenever he was asked in an attempt to offer something to the well-being of the group. But it was never enough as Wooly wanted something tangible from him, for a clean room did little for the survival of the rest. If you couldn't eat it or sell it, then a good deed meant nothing to Wooly. A rather hard line was taken by him, perhaps too hard, but one that had been forged through necessity and the difference between life and death.

His fear of being caught in the act was a very sensible emotion, as being caught was a solid possibility. Every day, one child or adult was either beaten or arrested for doing some criminal act. The bobbies walked their beats, and a good percentage of Whitechapel's workers and residents were streetwise and keen to catch a thief or anybody with ill-intent and disregard for the law, especially when it would cost them personally and financially.

Jonathan explained to Wooly that only a couple of weeks ago he had witnessed a little girl, trying to steal some meagre food being caught and grabbed roughly, taken away to god knows where.

'If a sweet-faced girl half my size was roughed up, what do you think would happen to me?' he explained.

Wooly did understand the risks and fears, for that was all he knew, but he would still not relent and told Jonathan that he must go out and 'do the trade'.

Jonathan was in a dilemma. He had to contribute just like the rest, but to say it was not natural to him would have been a titanic under-statement. His predicament was a vicious circle faced with a double-edged sword for he had to do as Wooly said and yet couldn't.

Wooly kept it simple. 'Ya either in or ya out. Get somefing today or ya sleep in the gutter tonight. And if ya fink Lizzie will keep ya, then fink again. I wouldn't allow her. Up to you, kid,' warned Wooly.

Jonathan's head dropped as reality set in, hitting him full force in one short statement.

'Look, it ain't gotta be much, one fing and that'll be a start. Come on, let's go,' said Wooly.

Jonathan nodded, and they both stood up to leave. It didn't take long for him to get up, for there was no brushing of teeth and no changing of bedclothes. He had lived and slept in the same clothes each night, which slowly began to fray as the days rolled on.

The two boys were in the centre of Whitechapel, sat down watching and waiting, as they did almost every day. Jonathan looked even more anxious than usual, for he knew there was added pressure for him to perform.

'It's easy when ya get the hang of it' said Wooly. Jonathan nodded with a nervous smile.

Wooly reached into his pocket and produced a small selection of coins. He picked out the lowest denominator, in this case being a penny, and poured the remaining coins back into his pocket.

'Watch this. I'm gonna turn this penny into somefing more,' he said.

He looked around for a potential victim. Not just anybody, as this particular pick-pocket dodge had to include a wealthy-looking lady or gentleman.

After a few minutes of waiting, Wooly saw his intended target. A gentleman, judging by the look of his attire, which consisted of black starched trousers, a clean white shirt under a crisp blue waistcoat, and a long black coat with deep-looking pockets.

Wooly watched as the man stopped outside a small bookshop. A particularly expensive shop, with several small, square windows in the front intercut with narrow wooden straights, with tables of books sitting either side of the door.

The victim took his time browsing, reading the odd page here and there. It was apparent that this man was and oblivious to his surroundings, entrenched in whatever text he was reading.

Wooly walked up to the gentleman and dropped his penny on the ground. It fell to the left of the man, landing within just a couple of inches of his shiny black shoe. Wooly stood to the man's right, and looking very innocent and friendly, he tapped him on the arm.

'Excuse me, sir, I believe you dropped your money,' said Wooly in a sweet tone and then pointed to the coin.

The man looked down and turned slightly to grasp it. As he did so, Wooly reached into the right pocket of the man's black coat and pulled out some coins. The man straightened up and placed the penny in his left pocket, without even noticing Wooly's actions.

'Oh, thank you, young fellow, most decent of you, I must say,' said the gentleman.

'No problem, mister,' replied Wooly as he then turned round and walked away, returning to Jonathan.

Wooly reappeared next to Jonathan looking rather pleased with himself, and said, 'There ya are, I lost a penny and gained ...'

He counted the stolen coins that lay in his palm, flicking through them slowly. 'Three pennies and two shillings.'

He smiled, but his joy was not fully reciprocated from Jonathan. Wooly could tell from the look on his face that he was still hesitant with too much conscience in his soul.

'Follow me, kid. Let me show ya somefing just to prove that it ain't just us fooling the public,' said Wooly.

They both walked a few hundred yards round the corner and arrived at a residential street. It was long, with rows of dozens of tall cream and white houses flanking both sides, each house looking the same as the next and having two flat stone steps leading up to each front door.

Wooly and Jonathan stood at the entrance of the road, leaning against some black iron railings that encircled a small patch of grass, with a single mountain ash tree growing there.

'Why are we here?' asked Jonathan.

'Just wait, you'll see,' replied Wooly.

They both watched as a short, skinny man sat down on one of the steps of the house. The man appeared to be a beggar in his torn and filthy clothes, as if the fabric was rotting away all over him, He had the look of weakness and desperation upon his face.

Almost as if he was about to drop down dead at any moment, the beggar held a rock-hard crusty piece of bread that looked several days passed its best. It resembled more of a jagged green stone than dough.

They both watched on as the beggar started eating his foul bread. On the second or third bite, he started choking. Whilst he was choking, upon seeing the choking beggar through his widow from the other side of the street, a resident rushed out his house towards him. The resident made sure the poor man did not choke to death and gave him some pennies, following with the kind order to buy a bottle of beer from the pub to help wash his throat out. The caring resident walked back to his house across the road with a happy feeling of his good deed. The beggar then walked off with half the bread roll in one hand and a few pennies in the other.

'See, kid? That was a dodge. That beggar will do the same fing again and again and again on every forth house. He'll do it twenty times and get a pound, maybe two in total, if the do-gooders feel extra kind'.

Jonathan was saddened and found it hard to believe there were so many crooks and liars around, but with what he had just witnessed, it was hard to believe anything else. It wasn't necessarily a case of right or wrong. The beggar probably was a real beggar with nothing to his name, and this dodge was just a way to get money. However, it still mislead people, and kind, decent people at that. Was it worse than a lesser-minded beggar simply asking passersby for help and money? Jonathan didn't know.

They both walked back to the main street and sat in their favourite spot. Jonathan sat in silence whilst he thought about the latest lesson from Wooly.

'I'm just not sure about this,' said Jonathan.

Wooly stood up with a wilful huff. 'Look, ya ain't getting it, are ya! Ya wanna be in the workhouse? Or dead? Well?'

After just a few more brief moments of deep thinking, Jonathan told himself he would do as was expected of him. He agreed to Wooly that he would not only attempt a dodge but would see it through to the end.

They both sat back and watched, waiting for an appropriate pocket to pick. It wasn't long before the opportunity presented itself. Another wealthy gentleman dressed in fine black clothing walked past and caught the attention of Wooly and Jonathan.

The gentleman walked just a few yards past and stopped outside a tobacconist shop. The window display showed an array of different coloured packets, bottles, and tins of the loose leaf. The variety of different blends and tastes of tobacco was vast. On one side of the window stood a glass display case containing two dozen types of clay pipe. The gentleman seemed to take much interest in these pipes, as he bent down a little to have a closer look through the fogged up glass panels.

Jonathan stood up and made his way towards the finely dressed man, moving closer and closer, his blood pressure rising with every step. Wooly watched on as Jonathan reached the man. Jonathan turned his nervous eyes head to face Wooly with a look of acute indecisiveness. Wooly tilted his head encouragingly.

Whilst standing beside the man, Jonathan slowly slid his hand into the pocket of the black coat. The gentleman did not seem to feel a thing as Jonathan's small hand slowly began to pull out a white cotton handkerchief. He smoothly pulled, inch by inch, as the handkerchief slowly revealed itself, half in the pocket and half out. The handkerchief being bright white stood out very noticeably against the black backdrop from the man's clothing. Halfway out and Jonathan's nerves and conscience got the better of him as he loosened his light grip of the handkerchief. The corner dropped down, with half of it hanging out the man's pocket.

A split second later, a voice rang out through the air, 'Oi! Stop! Thief!'

A vicious-looking bystander lunged towards Jonathan, both arms stretching outwards, with large dirty hands that looked like clawed talons from an eagle opening as wide as they could to grab him hard.

Jonathan looked across for Wooly, but his heart sank as he was nowhere to be seen.

Panic and dread filled his soul as the bystander held him. Jonathan twisted and wriggled his body and kicked the vicious man in the shin, forcing him to loosen his hold, and Jonathan managed to escape the man's grasp. He started to run away, with no time to think of which direction. He ran like the wind from the tobacconist shop. Whilst running down the street, he turned his head to look behind him and saw that he was being chased by the same man that had grabbed him.

Jonathan was certainly dodging now, but not in Wooly's meaning. He dodged and wove through the crowds, running for his freedom. His heart beat fast, and a second look back told him that the pursuer was not giving up. His expression paralleled an angry bull, fixated on Jonathan as he kept charging after him.

Jonathan ran down the main street and turned down a long, narrow side alley. He stopped for a seconds' respite and leaned against the brick wall, gasping harder than ever before. He looked round and saw the man still running towards him. With one big intake of breath, he started run again, racing all the way down the alley to then dash off to the right, down a side street. He did not turn his head, for his main goal was to do nothing more than focus on escape with as much speed as his little legs could take.

After about three minutes of desperate running, which felt like thirty with the lactic acid burning through his muscles, Jonathan had to stop. He found himself in a secluded square courtyard, no bigger than twenty yards, and surrounded by tall brick buildings. Every side of the square had an alley between the buildings. He sat down on the patio-style stone floor by the entrance of one of the alleys and rested to give his body a chance to recover. But his mind could not fully rest, as he still kept a look out for the man. Looking franticly in all directions, it appeared the coast was clear and he had managed to outrun and outmatch his chaser. He looked down and enjoyed a moment's peace.

Suddenly, he felt a large hand reach round from the alley behind him to grab tight onto his arm. Jonathan was pulled up roughly and forcefully and spun round to face the owner. It was the same man. Both his arms were held so tight, he could feel the squeeze down to his bones. He wriggled and contorted his torso as much as he could to escape but failed to do so. He was forced to look directly at the man holding him. Jonathan's heart raced and his eyes began to blur with tears. The man had a face as ghastly and evil as any. A violent and dirty-looking man who possessed yellow teeth, rough black stubble, and a short but thick scar over his eyebrow, with a look on his face as if he'd been possessed by the devil himself.

The anger from him was clear and very real, almost psychotic.

The man clutching Jonathan was certainly unknown to him. In the last six weeks in Whitechapel he had not come across him once. The man, however, was known by a select few and went by the name of Jack Hawkins. He also answered to 'Scarface'.

Most people probably would not have enjoyed being called such. But a man of this kind would relish in the idea of having that type of nickname, for he would happily brag like-minded men, in the darker underworld of London Town, about the violence he dished out. He took it as a complimentary pseudonym and believed it showed the world he was dangerous and tough. To this man, it was a badge of honour, which was ironic as he had no decency or honour whatsoever.

'Please … please … I didn't even take anything … I'm not a thief … please, mister,' Jonathan pleaded.

'I know your fucking kind, you little rat!' replied Scarface.

He continued pleading for Scarface to release him, shouting 'sorry' a half dozen times.

He didn't really have anything to be sorry for. Nothing deeply criminal, at any rate. An attempted pickpocket, which he'd abandoned anyway, and a kick to a shin was the extent of his criminal record.

But Scarface did not care for Jonathan's sorrowful cries of mercy.

It would be somewhat reasonable for the average and sane citizen to want lawful justice, but Scarface was not the breed to restrict himself with the limits of others, especially the law.

He certainly wouldn't be taking the boy to the nearest beat bobbie or the police station down Bow Street, and wouldn't bother return him back to the tobacconist's to find the victim of the attempted theft. Scarface not only thought he should deliver his own brand of justice, but more disturbingly enjoyed it far too much.

He clenched his fist tight and punched Jonathan on his jaw, forcing his head to swing back with a twist to his neck. Jonathan cried out again and again as a second punch was preceded by a third. His tears flowed down his face as he begged the man to stop.

Scarface laughed at the pain he inflicted on young Jonathan. A forth punch struck him on the mouth, knocking two teeth out and making the boy bleed from the inside of his cheek as the flesh split and gums opened.

'I ain't fucking finished with you yet! You kicked me in the shin! See what you get!' Scarface growled.

He was more angry that Jonathan had kicked him!

As Jonathan was forced to face Scarface over and over, with his hair being pulled back, so this maniac could land yet another punch. For Jonathan, it was as if pure evil was manifesting itself before his very eyes, even worse than his father.

He was in so much pain and so scared, he could not plead any more. His fear and anguish made it almost impossible to voice, 'Please stop, I'm sorry'. All he could do was take the suffering, his weak body giving up and going limp, as he began to feel dizzy.

Jonathan was just about to pass out when he heard footsteps coming from one of the side alleys that entered the courtyard. The footsteps slowly became louder as they got closer to him and his atrocious abuser.

The footsteps came from a very fine-looking gentleman indeed. Not that Jonathan could see with much clarity with the whites of his eyes now coloured red with blood.

The gentleman was dressed in smart black shoes, black trousers, white shirt, and a dark brown long coat, with a top hat cresting his head and a walking cane in his hand.

'What on earth is the meaning of this? Unhand that boy at once!' demanded the gentleman.

Scarface did not do as asked and bellowed, 'Mind your own, old timer. You don't know what this rat did!'

'Old timer? I stand before you forty and four. What did he do to warrant such cruel actions?' he asked.

'Nabbing a gen'leman's 'ankerchief, he was! Kicked me in the shin!' Scarface explained.

It was strikingly clear to the gentleman, as it would be to most, that this cruel beating was not justice but an unnecessary savage lesson and one which could easily be Jonathan's last, with death not far away if just one more blow were to hits it's mark.

'I said, unhand that boy! You shall do it now and I will not ask a third time!' he said in a more demanding tone.

'Piss off!' replied Scarface.

The gentleman looked Scarface in the eye and gave him a stern look.

Scarface took the look as a threat and released his grip of Jonathan, making him drop to the ground faster and harder than a cannonball.

Scarface turned to the gentleman, facing him square on, and took an aggressive stance.

'You want some, do ya!'

The gentleman polity asked him to leave, to which Scarface responded with the crazed smile of a madman and the slow shake of his head.

'No one tells me what to do!' said Scarface as he slowly circled the gentleman.

The gentleman kept calm and did not budge but kept his eyes on Scarface, with a second plea for him to leave.

Just then, Scarface pulled a knife from his waistband and growled, 'Or what? What you gonna do?"

The gentleman took a deep breath, for he knew the stakes had just been raised. 'I warn you, sir. Leave.'

Scarface was spoiling for a fight and began to threaten him, swinging the knife left and right.

Jonathan regained his senses a little and watched as the stranger and Scarface went face to face. The gentleman took a few steps back and gave his final warning.

'Think I'll make you bleed, old man, I'm gonna stick you like a pig!' threatened Scarface.

'You are thick as you are cruel,' he replied.

With that remark, Scarface launched towards him, blade first, stabbing through the air and approaching his target.

The gentleman took a sidestep, and with a twist from the top of his cane, he pulled out a thin blade, two feet in length.

Scarface continued attempting to stab him, but he was hastily stopped in his tracks when the gentleman flicked his sword in a smooth wave upward with perfect aim.

The razor-sharp end hit the jaw of Scarface with one short swipe. The blade moved upwards, ripping through his cheek and continuing to his brow, slicing through the pupil and taking out the eye as it did so.

Scarface dropped his knife and held his face with both hands, screaming in agony. Hot blood seeped through his fingers and poured down his hands.

Jonathan sat still, not quite believing what he just witnessed. The gentleman calmly wiped his blade and smoothly sheathed it back in the cane.

'I won't fucking forget this, you bastard!' yelled Scarface, with screams of pain in between every word.

'Jolly good, that was the intention. Now leave … odious man, unless you would like me to make a splendid reflection on the back of your head,' he replied.

Scarface turned and ran away down one of the alleyways.

Jonathan was gob-smacked and fascinated by the gentleman's sophisticated and high-class weapon, for he had never seen anything like it before. Upon closer inspection, the blade was a thing of unique beauty. It stood at three feet, with an outer covering of different types of wooden veneers. Oak and teak covered the handle that would reveal the blade when turned and drawn out, and embedded on the hilt lay a small silver St Christopher's medallion.

The gentleman could see the boy was fascinated with his cane. He raised it slightly.

'This is called a sword stick, never leave home without it, especially when one is venturing in these parts,' he said.

Jonathan looked up and for the first time managed to properly focus on his saviour's face. He felt safe straight away and smiled as the gentleman possessed a very kind face and had the demeanour of being incredibly strong and yet incredibly soft at the same time. There was something about him that gave off a feeling of pure kindness, even after witnessing a violent and bloody act.

Jonathan did not want the kind gentleman to leave. He was about to talk but before he could utter one word, he fell back and passed out. The gentleman picked him up softly in both arms and walked away, carrying him gently.

Chapter 12

Three days later, the sun rose with its golden rays piercing the cold, dense morning mist. This day, the warm sun showed itself in particular wonderful form, as if Apollo himself was personally responsible.

Jonathan woke up with a feeling he hadn't experienced for a very long time. Immense comfort. He sat up and found himself in a large white bed. It was bigger and softer than anything he'd slept in ever before. Every sheet and blanket appeared perfectly clean, fresh, and not even holding a single crease, even after a night's use. He was rather confused as he had no idea to what his current location was and simply couldn't recall how he had got there. However, he was so comfortable, it did not seem to matter to him at all.

As he looked around the large bedroom, he was in awe at all that presented itself. Directly in front of him stood a large black marble fireplace with lines of gold running vertically, hand-carved granite lion heads on each top corner.

He edged himself off the bed and landed on a thick, dark blue soft rug that stretched over most of the floor. He looked down whilst touching his chest and saw he was in a pair of crisp and snug pyjamas. His confusion grew for he had no recollection of putting them on. He walked to the window, which was several steps away, and pulled the thick, heavy, emerald green curtains open. Looking outside, he saw a green garden which was more like a small lawn, with short black iron railings surrounding it.

A moment later, three gentle knocking sounds tapped from the other side of the bedroom door. Jonathan rushed back to the bed and jumped in, and with a quiet, shy voice, he allowed the unknown man or woman to come in.

wide white wooden door opened, though which a man stepped.

Jonathan looked on, his mind first telling him he had never seen this stranger before. With a friendly smile, the man stepped closer to the bed, and it came to Jonathan that he had seen him before. He smiled as the memory came back to him, as he realised it was the gentleman who had saved him from Scarface and possible death.

The man sat down at the foot of the bed.

'Good morning, young sir, I trust you slept well. You have been asleep for three days,' the man said in a soft yet deep voice.

'Oh ...yes ... I did sleep good, thank you. I'm sorry for sleeping so long, sir'

'There is nothing to be sorry for. Now, what is your name? he asked.

'Jonathan, sir. Jonathan White.'

The man leaned back a little and gave a happy laugh.

'Well, well, By Jove, what a splendid coincidence, for I also answer to Jonathan. My name is John Huffham. I am a locksmith and fencing master,' he said, a warmth spreading through him. The young boy looked so demure and innocent.

'I do hope I did not jump to an error of judgement in bringing you to my house. You were in an awful state when our paths first crossed'.

Jonathan shook his head frantically as if to say that he was in fact overjoyed by the act.

'How about a little breakfast? One would imagine you are famished.'

Jonathan's frantic head quickly turned into frantic nodding at the idea of food.

Mr Huffham stood up and made his way the side of the fireplace. He pulled on a long thick cord that hung from the ceiling.

Not two minutes later, a girl of about twenty years of age and wearing a black working dress with a white apron entered the room.

'Yes, sir?' she said with a short bow.

Mr Huffham introduced Jonathan to his maid.

'Jonathan, this is Sally, a wonderful girl, without whom I would be utterly lost, and it is she who you can thank for your healing.'

Sally and Jonathan smiled and nodded to each other, with a polite and very meaningful 'Thank you' from him.

Mr Huffham placed his hand on Sally's shoulder and said, 'Some breakfast, if you please, for our young guest. Two boiled eggs with thick cut toast, and a few rashers of bacon, I think.'

He paused and looked at Jonathan and continued with, 'Would that suffice?'

Jonathan could not remove the smile that stretched across his face and nodded, his eyes bright and shining, so bright in fact you could almost see his soul glowing. Sally acknowledged the enthusiastic agreement and bowed again to then take her leave.

'You stay and rest a little longer, and Sally will return soon with your food. There is much to discuss ... all in good time, though. When you have finished and are ready, you may come downstairs and find me in the parlour,' said Mr Huffham.

'Oh, thank you, sir, a thousand times, thank you,' replied Jonathan, tears on his cheeks.

Mr Huffham left the room and closed the door behind him. Jonathan sat up in bed, happily waiting for his breakfast, his fingers brushing against the soft eiderdown that covered him. He had never felt such a soft texture.

To pass the time, he was fully content with doing nothing at all, not even to think with any degree of effort or consciousness. Just to soak up the palpable safety and comfort was more than enough.

This very simple act and being so tranquil would have been rather strange to some people of wealth, for these surroundings would be the norm to them. But this was not the case for Mr Huffham.

He was a prosperous and affluent man, but also a humble man, for he held great value in monetary but also in emotional terms in all he possessed. He was thankful and appreciated everything in his personal life and did not allow wealth to overwhelm his decency. It was only through hard work, a kind heart, and a keen brain that brought him this status.

Jonathan couldn't stop gawping at the size of his bed, and how incredibly comfortable it was. Like lying on a cloud. In the past, even sleeping would have held some sort of stress or uneasiness for him. In his hard, cold bed at home, he would hear the sound of his mother crying in response to her husband's yelling tantrums or feel the pang of hunger to the point of psychical pain. .

After a short time, Sally knocked on the door.

'Come in,' said Jonathan, like he was the Lord of the Manor.

Sally entered and laid a silver tray across his lap with everything Mr Huffham had ordered, as well as a silver coffee pot with the aroma of caffeine steaming from the spout and a fine bone china cup.

He did not even have to crack and cut the top of the eggs off, as it was already done for him. He looked down as the eggs were nesting in two delicate cups and saw the runny yoke, bright yellow encircled by white. The toast almost as thick as his wrist, with butter melting through and a side plate painted with a blue and white willow pattern holding three slices of freshly cooked bacon. His little head weaved all around at the fine and varied spread that lay before him.

'Oh … thank you, Miss Sally.'

'You are most welcome, Jonathan,' she replied in her gentle and pleasing voice.

'Why … why is your master being so kind to me?'

'All shall be revealed soon, I'm sure. I do not have the answer, I'm afraid, but rest assured, my master is a gentleman and his judgements tend to be correct. You will not find a finer man, not even if you searched for a hundred years.'

With those comforting and reassuring words, she bowed and left the room to allow Jonathan to enjoy his breakfast in peace.

He sat back and devoured the breakfast. His primal instinct was to gobble it all up within just a couple of minutes, almost without coming up for air. However, this was the most delicious food he had ever tasted, so he took each mouthful slowly, in order to savour every bite, his taste buds tingling with pleasure.

The somewhat crafty side of him also realised that the longer he took eating, the longer he could stay in bed. Not that he particularity wanted to keep Mr Huffham waiting, but the master of the house had come across as rather laid back with his mannerisms, and he did say there was no rush, a suggestion which Jonathan gladly exploited and indulged in taking literately.

Nonetheless, being polite was deep in his moral fibre, and he did not want to push the relaxed manner and kindness of Mr Huffham.

After all the food had gone, he jumped out of bed and left the room. He found himself in a long hallway and made his way to the end, looking around this grand house for the staircase to then try and find the parlour room. Within a minute of searching, after taking just one wrong turn, he found the staircase, long and wide, with a slight curve to its wooden structure. Whilst still in his pyjamas, he slowly took a few steps down the stairs. He was about halfway down when he could hear raised voices of two men, coming from what looked like the parlour.

One of the voices he recognised as belonging to Mr Huffham, but the other was unknown to his ears. Jonathan tiptoed down and edged his way to the entrance of the room, not entering, but stood still to one side..

The raised voices were not loud with malice, nor was it an argument, but with the occasional word he did hear, along with the volume, it was certainly a disagreement of sorts. Jonathan moved his head as close as he could without being seen so he could listen.

The parlour was the grandest room in the whole house. It was a large rectangular room, walls painted maroon, with a vast white floor-to-ceiling bookcase on one wall, holding at least five hundred hardbacks, all bound with coloured leather. With the text in many genres and tastes, but mainly involving history from all eras, from *The Birth of Caveman* thousands of years ago, to *The 1776 Wars of the Americas*. In the corner of the room stood a drinks cabinet, with tinted glass doors showing the contents of two dozen bottles of spirits.

In the other corner were positioned two fine pieces of furniture, one being a tall grandfather clock made from teak, the other being a delicately carved chess set. Each warrior piece was out, standing still, ready for battle and waiting for the next two challengers to play. What stood to the side of the ornate chess set and grandfather clock was a grand marble fireplace, mirroring the one upstairs. Opposite the bookcase on the other side was a Steinway & Sons piano, the ivory keys gleaming bright white. All this finery stood upon a carpet with pale blue edges showing the design of the fleur-de-lee.

In the middle, but slightly off centre, there was a velvet emerald-green chaise- longue, which the other man was sat upon. The conversation that was taking place was one of disagreement and concern, questioning why Mr Huffham had taken in Jonathan.

His uncle was a tall, thin man of years beyond sixty-five. He was of a stricter generation and had little time for street urchins, especially with at least half of them being some sort of vagabond or criminal. Petty crime or worse, it mattered not to his uncle. The discontent and disbelief was plain to see and hear, as he constantly questioned his nephew and asked him to explain his random act of kindness to a complete stranger.

His uncle was not a bad man, but he did have little tolerance regarding certain issues. He was a product of his years and wary of the unknown and of Jonathan's apparent calibre.

He was right to be dubious and concerned, as the actions of his nephew were quite out of character.

Getting familiar with, let alone taking in, a random street thief, criminal, lost soul, beggar, or prostitute held an unnecessary risk. In general, the wealthy had no reason to help lesser people. In a rare case, if some felt sudden guilt for their wealth, there were charities for that impulse. 'Arms for the Poor' and 'Feed the Desperate' being two of them, as well as tossing a coin to a beggar or giving a donation to a collection tin at church.

Mr Huffham was no fool. His heart, however large it was, not larger than his brain, and he was well aware of risks of welcoming strangers from certain areas.

Mr Huffham stood in front of the fire and listened to the lecture coming from his uncle's mouth.

'Have you lost senses? You bring this ... this vagrant into your home? Where did the notion of righteousness stem from, John? Why can't you give a donation to the poor like I do?'

'You do that?' John replied.

His uncle coughed and stuttered. 'Well ... well, of course I do, dear boy.'

Mr Huffham looked at his uncle with one eyebrow lifted, with the knowledge that he was not entirely telling the truth.

'Well, all right, I don't,' he confessed. 'But that is not the point.'

Mr Huffham went on to explain the circumstances that had brought himself and Jonathan together.

His uncle praised him for his act of doing the right thing and teaching Scarface a lesson he would never forget. The praise, however, stopped there as he did not and could not agree with the second act of kindness in bringing Jonathan home. His stubbornness would not relent as he refused to understand.

Mr Huffham went on to tell his uncle what he had planned, if all being well and agreeable.

'If the boy chooses, I intend to bring him down to the shop, where he shall work for me,' said Mr Huffham.

'The boy is probably a thief! They're all the same!' he replied.

'I believe it not so, sir. I saw it in his eyes that he is no hardened criminal. He has a kind face.'

'Poppycock! The ones with the kind faces are the worse for deceit! John, my boy, you're absent knowledge of this lad, your beliefs do not reflect fact. I wager five pounds that he's upstairs now pinching the silver!'

'If so, the fault would be mine, and I would confess to making a misjudgement of his character,' he replied.

'I pray that you are right and I stand in error. Good day, John.'

His uncle turned around, placed his hat on his head, and made his way out of the room, catching a glimpse of Jonathan peering round the door frame. The man looked down at him with a stern look of warning and yet also a look of hope.

Jonathan looked back and remained silent with a fearful look on his face.

The man left the house, so Jonathan was free to enter the parlour. Mr Huffham sat down and smoked his pipe as Jonathan stood still, his feet together and his arms behind his back.

'Come forward, Jonathan. Did you hear our conversation just then?' Mr Huffham asked.

'Oh ... yes, sir,' he replied with a slight hesitant tone in his voice.

'Tell me, do you think my uncle is right?'

He did not know how to answer. He did think his uncle was wrong in his judgement of him, but he was too afraid to voice his opinion out loud. Only one wrong word could have him thrown back to the street or in the workhouse before his feet could touch the ground.

'It's okay, dear boy. You may speak freely. Your honest opinion would fall on friendly ears and you will not receive punishment of any kind. I promise.'

Warily, Jonathan said, 'No ... no, sir ... he was wrong. I'm not a thief and I would not steal from you. I promise,' he said shyly.

With another puff on his pipe, Mr Huffham chatted to Jonathan and wanted to learn all about him. About his parents, upbringing, and how he had managed to get involved with the likes of Scarface.

Jonathan told him all about the last six weeks and was honest about it.

However, he did not tell Mr Huffham about his father. A lie did not technically pass his lips, he just skilfully avoided the topic. Mr Huffham was very curious about his mother. Jonathan simply said he had run away and came to London for work, a story that was close enough to the truth, he thought.

'Do you know where you are?' Mr Huffham asked.

'Whitechapel?'.

Mr Huffham told him that his present location was Westminster, just six miles from Whitechapel, but the differences were so vast in all aspects it could have been a different world.

'Before you came to London and fell on harsh times, let's call it, I trust you had some sort of education ... schooling of sorts?'

'Ahh ... some sir,' he replied.

'Splendid ... Timeo danaos et dona ferentes.' An awkward silence sat between them for a moment. 'Latin, Jonathan,' he continued.

Jonathan gulped and shook his head with a look of shame.

'You weren't taught Latin? By Jove, what do they teach children nowadays?'

He had no children of his own, so he was a little ignorant as to what knowledge the average child held. When he was a youngster, he'd had a keen interest in and a moderate understanding of Latin and Greek and had readily consumed the words of playwright Shakespeare, the poet Tennyson, and Wordsworth. A collection of classics that still held a proud and vital position on his bookshelf's today.

He did not want to be too hard on Jonathan but did want him to have at least the capability of learning, with some level of the basics.

'Can you read and write?' he asked.

Jonathan nodded, and Mr Huffham handed over a fountain pen that he had just dipped in an ink pot and paper, asking him to write down his name, today's date, and numbers one to ten. A simple task but one that could tell a lot, seeing as so many children around Jonathan's age could not accomplish it.

In relatively good handwriting, he wrote:.

Jonathan White
Saturday 27th October, 1880
1.2.3.4.5.6.7.8.9.10

Mr Huffham looked at his writing and smiled. He screwed up the paper and tossed it into the burning fire.

'Excellent, well done, for if a man can't write properly, then he can't read properly, and if a man can't read *or* write properly, then he can't learn properly.'

He continued an interesting proposal for Jonathan. 'Would you like to work for me at my place of business, for a standard wage? You could live in this house.' He paused to let Jonathan think a moment. 'Only if you wish to, of course. If not, I can get a cab to take you anywhere in London you want to go and you'll never have to see me again.'

Jonathan smiled

'Yes … yes … oh please, yes. Really, could I?'

Mr Huffham laughed and smiled, which made Jonathan laugh as if it was contagious. He stood up and faced the young boy. Mr Huffham was about to give him a big hug, but before he managed one step forward onto the carpet, his arms wide open, Jonathan ran into him and hugged him tight. The boy's soul beamed with joy and fondness as a single tear slipped down his little face with happiness.

Chapter 13

The following day, Jonathan woke up from a second night of wondrous sleep, which, for the first time in a very long time, contained soft dreams as opposed to hard nightmares. He looked across the room and saw new clothes draped over a chair in the corner.

Dark shoes with proper laces, brown corded trousers, a vest and shirt, both white in colour, and a black jacket. He later learnt that Sally had been shopping, just for this attire, due to an order from Mr Huffham.

He made his way downstairs and greeted his new master. Mr Huffham was delighted and very satisfied with his appearance.

'Splendid … thank you, Sally,' he said, his voice raising a couple of octaves towards the end so that Sally could hear him from another part of the house.

In her usual maid's outfit of black and white, Sally presented herself in the kitchen doorway, which was positioned at the rear of the dwelling. She looked at Jonathan from heel to collar and smiled.

'Ah ... you look as fine as any young man I've ever known. In fact, I'd say better,' she said.

'Thank you, Miss Sally,' he replied.

As the three of them were stood in the hallway, Sally turned to Mr Huffham and told him she had acquired the new clothes on account and that they came from 'Willow Threads' shop.

Mr Huffham looked rather gormless for he had never heard of that shop. Sally, knowing him very well indeed, was not in least surprised that the shop was new to his mind. It was, however, not new to his ears and eyes, as that particular shop had been mentioned in many a previous conversation with him. Sally wanted to tease him a little by saying how it was the nicest and most popular shop of its kind and that he should have been aware of it.

Mr Huffham still looked perplexed. 'My God girl, I am not one of the fine ladies who natter down at the Tudor Tea Rooms. I have no knowledge, wisdom, or experience in such matters.'

'You and I went there three weeks ago, sir,' she said with a cheeky look on her face.

'If that is so, my mind has expunged it,' he replied.

'Expunged it, sir?'

'Yes, Sally, expunged it ... expelled, eradicated, evacuated, terminated it!' he said.

Sally knew that the clothing shop in question was not one of her master's favourites, in fact, it was an establishment he detested. She stood there, giggling.

'I'm glad you like what I bought,' she said with a smile.

'Yes yes, jolly good, I'm sure they're the finest from Paris,' Mr Huffham replied in a joking and dismissive way. 'Come on, Jonathan, to work we go,' he continued.

Mr Huffham and Jonathan walked over the black and white chequered floor of the hall and made their way out the front door. Upon closing the door, Mr Huffham gave a friendly kiss in the air towards Sally and flicked her a shilling. It rotated through the air in a smooth motion and landed dead centre in her open palm. She smiled and wished them both a good day at work.

Mr Huffham lived in Greencroft Palace Road, so within just a few minutes they both found themselves on Westminster Bridge, crossing the River Thames, a bleak and filthy stretch of water that had flowed there for thousands of years. If dredged properly it would, with most certainty, reveal a whole host of worldly treasures, as well as many a rotting, poor soul. Jonathan looked down at the muddy riverbank and saw two people, one standing in the water up to his shins and the other on hands and knees in the wet sludge. He asked Mr Huffham who they were and what they were doing.

He learnt that these people were scavengers and called themselves 'Mudlarks.' They would search and forage for anything of value that they could sell on for food or rent. A desperate people indeed, who had their lives dictated to them by poverty. It was arguably one of the dirtiest and most vile jobs around. Their hands would often get cut to pieces from broken glass, with the constant threat of infection from corpses hanging over them. Excrement and waste would also be ever-present from the raw sewage. The one advantage of this dreadful trade was that the hours were scattered nicely, as they could only do their foraging when the tide was out. The short lesson ended with a strict warning to avoid the male mudlarks if ever possible, for a desperate type like that would think nothing of slitting a throat for even a few pence.

Westminster Bridge itself was a tremendous feat of engineering and was well maintained and cleaned regularly. Walking next to Mr Huffham, holding his hand, and jumping over the large flat stone slabs that passed beneath his feet, he was so fixated on looking down, he failed to see one of the many wonders of London.

Mr Huffham lightly pulled on Jonathan's hand and asked him to look up. The sight of Big Ben stood tall in all its splendour, pointing towards the heavens like a giant needle.

Jonathan looked up in amazement, his head tilted far back.

'Gosh,' he said in utter bewilderment.

Mr Huffham laughed. 'Gosh indeed. A splendid sight, is it not?'

Jonathan did not speak, instead agreeing with him with his head nodding and mouth open, still in awe.

'Largest clock in the land, I believe. I was your age when it was erected. Eighteen forty-four, if memory serves.'

Jonathan could have easily stayed for several minutes and would have done if it was up to him. But with a pull from his master, Jonathan nodded and gladly carried on their walk.

'Come on, my boy, or we'll be late. Tardiness is not a pursuit I often indulge in.'

After ten minutes of travelling, covering about half a mile on foot, they reached the main street of Westminster. It was similar to Whitechapel in the sense that both sides of the street lay shop upon shop, with the rows going on far into the distance. There, however, the similarity abruptly ended.

It was clear within the first sight that this was a charming place.Clean and portraying a safe feeling, the majority of morning shoppers being either ladies or gentlemen or house servants. For every beggar here, there would have been twenty in Whitechapel held. Crime was still present, but the levels were rather low in comparison. The bobbies on the beat were sporadically positioned accordingly and reassuringly.

Rather unjust perhaps, but unfortunately money was not unbiased and does have a voice when being directed by the rich, and controlled by men of power. The local politicians and council understandably having resources in areas where they themselves live, worked and shopped. As opposed to funds going to lesser areas which were in greater need. The rich had the feast when the poor had the scraps. With the wealthy paying more into the system, it was a situation that could not be changed. Such was life, just or unjust depending on ones viewpoint.

It was a quaint and curious sight, as they both walked along the pavement, passing tall, ornate, black iron lampposts with their distinctive square tops. They passed shops of all tastes to accommodate an array of customer demands, wants, and needs.

One shop was called 'Jones' Butchers', with clean pale blue and white tiled walls with a full pig hanging in the window. 'Hobsons Boot Menders' had a black wooden sign hanging forward in the shape of a long boot. 'Smith and Son's' soap and candle shop wafted the smell of bees wax and perfume down the street. 'Westminster Weavers' was for linen. The window display of 'Frys Treats Sweetshop' had a constant audience with high demand from children. 'Simpsons Chemist' sold tea and groceries amongst the medicine. 'Copycatz' printers and stationers also sold wares and trinkets included. 'Tops Toys' was a toyshop filled with colour and joy, selling anything from dolls to small wooden castles, which certainly caught the wondering eye of Jonathan, though he dared not say through fear of slowing down his master on this particular morning. Not forgetting Mr Huffham's favourite shop; 'Brown's Books', with an eclectic selection that outnumbered any rival bookshop ten to one.

The shops were nicely broken up and entwined with Blacksmiths, tearooms, coffee houses, and public houses. The latter and most often frequented was titled 'The Jewelled Crown', where Mr Huffham was known well. If the pub walls could talk, they would tell many a tale, a large percentage of which involved him.

After walking just a couple hundred yards and striding along the rows of shops large and small, they arrived at Mr Huffham's shop.

They stopped outside as Mr Huffham showed Jonathan the shopfront. The large sign that adorned the window proudly said in gold calligraphy script:

Huffham's Locksmiths Of London.
Finest Bolts, Locks, Keys, And Safes Made
To The Highest Powder Proof Quality.

The front also held a wooden signboard sticking outward, carved in the shape of a large padlock, which hung off an iron bracket, similar to a tavern sign, which would swing in the breeze with a distinctive screeching sound as it flapped to and fro in the wind.

'Wow,' Jonathan whispered.

'Thank you, Jonathan. This is the family business. It is mine as it was my father's before me. I have followed in his footsteps through business, as I hope I do in spirit, for he was a truly wonderful man. If I stand but a fraction of him, then I stand content and proud.'

Mr Huffham and his new apprentice entered the grand shop. Jonathan looked around all the curious items. His first thought when hearing that his master was a locksmith was that it was a simple trade with limited duties. As he looked around, he realised he could not have been more mistaken.

Each wall was of full display of locks, bolts, and padlocks, all with different designs and styles. From small, simple padlocks for securing small, simple treasures to giant, Gothic style iron padlocks, some the size of a tankard of ale. One of these padlocks was responsible for keeping away undesirable hands from the vaults of the Bank of England itself. There were at least one hundred distinct locks of one sort or another hanging like pieces of art on the walls. Down the centre of the room stood treasure chests fit for Black Beard himself, safes big and small, cash boxes, and lock boxes of iron and steel, adorned with golden brass.

What impressed him further was that Mr Huffham and his staff made it all by hand and on the premises itself.

Mr Huffham coughed loudly, and a second later, two people showed themselves from the back room, which was more of a workshop. One was a young man of about twenty, named Stanley Copperton; likeable, cheeky, hard-working, though with the tendency to put his foot in it more times than not. His clumsiness and wit tested his boss' patience, but it all came from a decent place in his heart. He stood before his boss in what he wore almost every day. White trousers, a white shirt, a red neckerchief when Mr Huffham would allow, and a green striped waistcoat. Everybody called him 'Koots', even Mr Huffham, except when he was being told off.

The other employee of Mr Huffham was a woman of similar age to Koots, who was called Jessica Jackson. A pretty girl with long brown hair and a joyous smile to match. A happy soul who thought herself lucky to be in the position she was. She stood beside her friend and colleague in a long purple dress with a white vest beneath and holding a smile that seemed almost constant.

Both were clean looking, as per their employer's rules. They were smart and glowed from inside out, as well as outside in. The pair had worked in the locksmith's shop for almost five years , and both wanted to stay as long as possible, earning an average wage and appreciating Mr Huffham and his, at times, unusual ways.

On the rare occasion, they'd be a little fearful of him, but only in a healthy sense, like one would a strict headmaster. They were very fond of their boss and were well aware that he was firm, but also extremely fair. A man such as he could be your best friend or your worst enemy. He demanded respect and received it, but he also gave it.

Koots and Jessica did not need reminding that their situation was more noteworthy than the majority of others, as they knew through previous experience. They liked their state of affairs and almost saw work as a second home. The work was spread evenly and appropriately, with Koots largely being in the workshop and Jessica being in the shop, though they did have to cross paths many times within the working day, with a helping hand here and there in either room.

Mr Huffham introduced Koots and Jessica to Jonathan. The staff were very friendly and polite and made the new apprentice feel comfortable within moments.

They all shook hands and greeted one another in a pleasant manner.

Jonathan could not help noticing that Jessica was in unfortunate possession of a limp and nursing a nasty ankle injury. He was so at ease with his new acquaintances that he didn't mind asking.

'Hope you don't me asking, miss, but how did you hurt your ankle?'

'Please, call me Jessica' she replied, but was stopped mid-sentence by Koots saying, 'She fell off Mr Huffham's wallet'

'Stanley!' he said firmly, with a stern expression.

'Yes, sir, sorry, sir,' he replied to then scamper back into the workshop.

Jessica giggled but held back the true extent of her outburst, as she was not more than two feet away from Mr Huffham. She explained to

Jonathan that it was nothing, her ankle felt better than the previous day, and it was just a slip at work. She returned to her duties and stood behind the long counter to await the next customer.

Mr Huffham walked into the workshop. 'Anything to report, Koots?'

'No, sir, except Mrs Richards is meant to be coming in at 10am.'

Mr Huffham's face dropped like a heavyweight. Mrs Richards was a loyal customer but was also a pain in the highest form. All her demands, be it key cutting or a new set of bolts for her house, had to be changed over and over again, her tastes changing as often as her petticoats.

'Ah, damn the crows, dreadful woman she is. 'Tis a miracle in the saddest sense that she found a man that could put up with her,' said Mr Huffham.

'And she ain't even naughty in bed, I'd wager,' said Koots.

'That's enough, she is still a lady … in a sense.'

'It's one minute to ten now, sir.'

Mr Huffham took out his pocket watch and saw for himself that it was indeed 9.59am.

He turned to leave the workshop, to then walk round the corner and take solace and hide in his office.

He was halfway on his journey, which was only a few yards, with the workshop and office being practically next door to each other, when he heard the small brass bell that sat above the door ring sharply, with a friendly ding-a-ling.

Tall, skinny, and dressed in a long pink dress, carrying a stern, strict look on her face, she walked like an army officer, as if she was leading a brass band. A large but very false smile adorned Mr Huffham's face.

Koots peaked round and tried to be friendly by saying, 'Ah, Mrs Richards. Can I get you a coffee?'

'No thank you. I tried it once and didn't like it!' she abruptly replied.

Koots placed his hand in his top pocket and produced a cigarette and offered it to her.

'A smoke, then?'

'Again, I tried it once and didn't like it!'

Koots returned the cigarette to his pocket and said quietly, 'Strange.'

'Not at all, my daughter is just the same.'

Koots turned around and said, 'Your only child, I presume?'.

Jessica and Mr Huffham laughed. However, Mrs Richards did not follow. Instead, she stood still and looked at the boss with a beady stare. He coughed to stop his laughter.

'Ah, Mrs Richards, how nice it is to see you again. You are looking radiant as always.

'Mr Huffham, I am not here to discuss flippant pleasantries. Will you please send your boy round to replace my safe! It's been over a week now!' she demanded.

'Mrs Richards, we have gone through all this before. We have come and gone from your residence three times in as many days. We have checked everything, including with your family and staff.'

'My family know nothing about this. I am in charge, thank you very much!' she snapped.

'I bet you are,' whispered Mr Huffham quietly to himself.

'I demand you come to my house again … in one hour!' she said.

Mr Huffham told her that it was not possible to fully submit to her demand. Her mean, strict, gaunt face turned to an expression of deep displeasure. She turned around and made her way towards the door, with a stiff, upright march.

'If you were my husband, I'd poison your tea!'

'Madam … if you were my wife I'd drink it,' he replied.

Upon hearing that last remark, which did not help in softening her facial expression one bit, she left the shop and slammed the door behind her. Instead of the usual dainty ding-a-ling from the bell, it was more of harsh thud.

Jessica, who was still standing behind the till, laughed and said, 'Well, at least I don't have to serve her today.'

'Oh, she'll be back, fear not,' Mr Huffham warned.

Jonathan had been watching with much amusement, thinking that his master was not afraid of an animal like Scarface and yet he wanted to hide from Mrs Richards.

Mr Huffham asked Jessica to take three shillings out of the till and leave to pick up some pipe tobacco for him. She nodded her head and did so at once. He then led Jonathan into his office to talk further of his present and future duties concerning the business.

Chapter 14

1888. Eight years later.

Jonathan was now twenty years of age and grown into a fine young man indeed, with a handsome face and a brilliant mind. Not just any man, either. He proudly stood as the highest calibre of man … a gentleman. With thanks from Mr Huffham, who was still his boss, but also a friend, Jonathan had a truly wonderful time in his teenage years. His tutoring was rivalled that of the great institutions of Oxford, Cambridge, and the public school of Harrow. Those masters in their black capes with tasselled mortarboard caps, being the finest in the world, would have been envious and enthralled at Jonathan's education and progress.

He remembered back to his first lesson at Mr Huffham's house and the very first sentence that has come from his master's mouth.

'Your young sponge of a mind will only remain so for a few years. There will be approximately two thousand days of learning, and you will need every minute of it. Tempus fugit.'

Jonathan now knew 'tempus fugit' to mean 'time flies' in Latin, two words that seemed to leave Mr Huffham's lips every day.

From the age of twelve to the present day, he was well versed in the works of many a great scholar, playwright, poet, and wordsmith. He studied piano and became a fine chess player. His mind and heart was filled with copious amounts of wit and wisdom. His marvellous teacher, boss, landlord, and friend, being well trained in various skills and being a man of the world, also taught him to be of strong body and kept his reflexes sharp. He did this through the ancient art of fencing. He knew how to handle a blade and had the desire to keep standards high with a friendly nod to tradition and our brave warrior ancestors. Mr Huffham passed on his comprehension of the full set of the Epee, Foil, and Sabre. He could handle himself inside his mind, as well as outside on the street.

Jonathan was lucky, to say the least, to have a teacher in his lord and master who not only held this vast wealth of knowledge but could also teach well. Through his life, he had come across people who had expertise, but their knowledge often conflicted with teaching. Merely holding knowledge was not enough if one could not enlighten others.

It was not all smooth and plain sailing, however, and not possessing the gift of a brilliant brain from god, as if it was a gift from the heavens, he would many times find it a huge struggle and extremely arduous to fulfil his endeavours.

Discipline would come swiftly and fairly, and at times, feelings of despair would befall him. Not once did Mr Huffham have to strike him when the learnings seemed to fall on ignorant and lazy ears. Any punishment would largely consist of the words,

'I am most disappointed in you, my boy.'

With the fondness, respect, love, and desire to emulate, just that simple line was enough to get emotions running and would aid Jonathan's tenacity. Luckily the punishments and tears of shame and sorrow were very few and far between. The manner of the lessons, with the friendly atmosphere of the household and Sally for support, made almost all the learning days pleasant. At times, Jonathan hardly even realised he was learning whilst doing it. A simple and fun jolly around the kitchen table with two bread sticks would unknowingly help teach him the parry, block, riposte, thrust, and lunge of sword skill, as well as tapping the different jars and china ware that lay on the kitchen table with the edge of a butter knife to create a unique and bespoke tune to help build a musical ear, much to the annoyance of Sally, of course, which bemused and enlivened Jonathan much in his early adolescence. But nine times out of ten she would smile and brush it off and see it as a harmless yet educational instruction for the boy.

Mr Huffham offered him almost everything a young man could ever wish for.

Furthermore, it all came from a place love. Jonathan was quite at home in his master's house and saw it was a place of sanctuary and comfort, as well as duty and hard work; nevertheless, it was all happiness with a plethora of contentment.

Today was Jonathan's twentieth birthday. He found himself in the locksmith shop, his most frequent haunt. Even though the day was somewhat different with his age turning, he did not mind in the least to be working. Not only did he have academic skills from Mr Huffham, he also had, by this time, all the skills a locksmith and safe maker needed. Every job and task that was necessary he did with distinction and merit.

The apprentice from years past had become an able workman. From a simple key-cutting job or handling money through the exquisite shiny chrome and marble cash register, to making a strongbox by hand, strong enough to withstand gunpowder and bullet.

The tools in the workshop at the rear of the store housed everything he needed,. the padlock mechanism being the most petite and delicate, almost resembling a clockmaker's tool set. I had taken Jonathan over a year to master this creation. Koots was present, by his side and by now also a firm friend. The two certainly went through many an adventure, largely consisting of wine and women, and the overuse of both, the lion's share of stories only fit for memory and not the boss' ears.

At ten o'clock, Mr Huffham entered the shop and greeted Jessica, Koots, and Jonathan with his delightful, 'Good morning!'

In response, he heard back in three different voices from his staff, 'Good morning, sir.'

It was a typical start to the day, with one exception. In Mr Huffham's hand he held a long object wrapped in brown paper and tied with string.

'Come forward, my boy,' he said to Jonathan.

Jonathan stepped closer with anticipation. A smile came from Mr Huffham, followed by a warming wish of a happy birthday, accompanied by a firm yet friendly handshake.

'Thank you, sir.'

Whilst their hands were still interlocked, Mr Huffham gently twisted Jonathan's wrist to expose his palm, face up, inside which he placed the wrapped object as a birthday present: a long brown parcel tied up with string. Jonathan smiled and began to pull at the string bow. Jessica and Koots both came to satisfy their curiosity. He tore away at the paper to reveal the gift.

What befell his eyes made them widen with astonishment. The gift was a seventeenth century rapier sword, as fine and elegant as one could ever imagine, its long and slender blade slowly widening to a silver base, with a golden curve arching from hilt to pommel to act as a handguard.

'Well fuck a duck,' said Koots in awe.

That sentence would usually prompt a strong word from Mr Huffham, but not on this occasion, who responded with a laugh. 'Yes, Koots, fuck a duck, indeed.'

Mr Huffham was equally impressed by such an antique and had been in two minds wether to give it as a gift at all. His heart, however, had got the better of him and was glad to give it to Jonathan.

Jonathan hugged his friend and master and could not remove the smile that came to his face so suddenly.

Mr Huffham raised his chin and asked, 'What can you tell me about this gift?'

Jonathan opened his mouth to answer but was interrupted by Koots.

'It's a sword.'

'Yes, thank you, Stanley. Where would we be without your invaluable input? Now please be quiet, you nitwit.'

Jonathan laughed and answered, 'It's a rapier, sir, Spanish style, and it became commonly used in around 1630, give or take a few years.'

'Splendid, well done. Enjoy it, for it is yours now.'

This was quite probably the most valuable and precious gift Jonathan had ever received, and it would take pride of place, hung up nicely in his study. It was something he would treasure for ever as it didn't just carry beauty but also the heartfelt fondness from the benefactor.

The working day carried on as usual, customers coming and going, the sound of the bell ringing every time the door opened or closed. Jessica was behind the counter and cleaning the store when she managed to get a spare minute. Koots and Jonathan were in the workshop, and Mr Huffham was in his office, dealing with paperwork and sorting the endless, tedious accounts, a job he did not cherish at all, but he was the only one who could do them.

Mid-afternoon came, and Mr Huffham asked Jonathan to work late to help with a single task. The task in hand had to be done at night, for that was the only time the client was available. The job involved collecting a payment from a certain establishment in Whitechapel, for a previous lock-box commission. The task was somewhat important and urgent. The money should have been paid three weeks ago, and the payment in question stood at eight pounds. Just this one late bill was the cause of the accounts not balancing for this particular period, a problem which had to be rectified as soon as possible. Jonathan accepted the job.

The client was a pair of brothel madams who ran their place of business together, only opening at 10pm and closing at 3am. The place in question was called Scarlet Cherries, coming from one madam named Scarlet and the other, Cherry.

'It is a house of ill-repute, but a client is a client,' said Mr Huffham.

'Consider it done, sir. Tomorrow, the money will be on your desk,' replied Jonathan.

'Can I come?' asked Koots, in an excited voice.

175

'In your own time, you may spend your wages how you please But tonight I need you here, in the workshop,' replied Mr Huffham with a regrettable tone.

'The shop will be closed, so Jessica could go,' Koots jokingly suggested.

It was no surprise that Jessica declined the offer. Whitechapel was not a place she would choose to go, and a brothel was not her idea of fun, especially after a hard day's work.

Chapter 15

It was ten thirty at night in Whitechapel. The night was bitterly cold and wet, the rain falling hard. The galloping sound of a horse drawn, two-seater cart pulled up on the cobbled roads, accompanies by the splash of puddles in the gutter.

It was only a thirty-minute ride, but Jonathan had not been to these parts since his first days in London, many years ago at the age of twelve. There had simply been no need for him to tread these streets since. Jobs connected with Mr Huffham's locksmiths seldom came to Whitechapel. Scarlet Cherries seemed to be the exception, and this job was most irregular.

Whitechapel in the day was harsh enough, but it passed itself off as average, and being on par with some other unfortunate boroughs. Be that as it may, at night, it became a different world. Just fifty paces away from the main street, lay an underworld hiding in plain sight, most of the residents, including the police, well aware of the activities during the hours of the night. Down back alleys and side streets stood a whole host of alternate places of pleasure and entertainment. Vice and crime in the seedy underbelly were not lacking in popularity, with the majority of the questionable businesses being a den of debauchery of one kind or another.

Taverns, brothels, gentlemen's clubs, and opium dens were used every night, not to mention the highly infamous Hellfire Club, where gamblers, deviants, and connected crooks with friends in high places and plenty of cash on the hip would frequent. The Hellfire Club was a place where crime and perversion would shock most of the people around. It was, at times, so infamous, some saw it as an urban myth and could not believe some of the stories that would spread, with talk of murder, torture, gang rape, bestiality, and bizarre cult-like rituals.

With the directions given to him, Jonathan made his way down the main street, walking with a quick stride to lessen his time in the rain, the wet pavements making more of a spittle sound as the droplets poured off the iron lamp-posts helping to break up the darkness with their yellowy-white glow.

He was off the main road and down a narrow street, with black brick archways looming over him. The gaslight seemed to become less frequent the further he walked, as he ventured into the heart and soul of the side streets. The blue-white moonlight bouncing off the dark bricks became his main source of light. After ten minutes of delving deep through the veins of inner Whitechapel, he finally found 'Scarlet Cherries'.

This was no ordinary whorehouse. It was a brothel that was more the size of a hotel. It was large and often proved that it needed two house madams, something that was quite rare in this trade and business of the flesh.

Two great wooden doors made up the entrance, with posters nailed up either side of ink-drawn prostitutes, with descriptions underneath of their so-called talents. It was a sexual profile that was not unlike a wanted poster, that adorned the billboards in the street or outside the coppers station.

Jonathan knocked on the door and awaited the response. Whilst he did so, he glanced around and read the posters that hung before him, merely to pass the time. The drawings were sensual and seductive, and the text beheld much allure.

Lilly Smithers: A wild, airy, thoughtless girl, about twenty years old. Honest, well-meaning disposition and no one's enemy but her own. Fair complexion, good teeth, and genteel with her loose attire. Deep penetration with any hole.

Nelly Anderson: This pretty bit of luscious stuff is not above nineteen.

A round-faced wench, she is remarkably full-breasted for her age. Her temper is affable and complaisant, however, a couple of shillings will have its due influence.

Jane Sexton: A submissive maid with legs lean and long. Her mouth wide open for all. Well-turned limbs, plump and round. Upon the bed she lays as she were slain, till his breath breathed life into her again.

Betty Ellis: A lecherous hussy with golden locks, who has some very odd tricks, which, however pleasing to those depraved appetites, will cost a pretty penny, but worth an elegant debauchee. Soft skin and one of the best at giving pleasure.

The door was opened by Madam Cherry herself. She stood petite and slim, in a pink and black tight corset, with a large bosom deep cleavage. She looked Jonathan up and down and smiled, as she could sense a heavy wallet that she thought would be easily depleted.

'Hello, handsome. Come on in, get out of the cold'.

Jonathan entered and saw a large open parlour room, with at least a dozen women spread about, attempting to charm and appeal to the punters.

He stood on the thick red carpet and looked on at the enterprise that lay all around. Madam Cherry took his hand and walked him down the three wide steps that preceded him. The décor and furnishings were of the highest quality, but he knew it was a beautiful home in an ugly world. He looked around him and noticed a bar to his left, with a long staircase beside it. It was clear the rooms of trade were upstairs, from the to and fro of prostitutes either taking or returning with their clients. It was a conveyor belt of flesh, a cottage industry of titanic proportions.

With a hand from the Madam on his shoulders, he sat down on one of the four French-style, long, ornate couches, covered in purple velvet which was at centre of the lobby.

He told Cherry who he was and that the reasoning for his presence was indeed of business matters, with the debt having to be settled.

'Ah, not a problem my lovely, you relax and I'll fix you a drink. Give me ten minutes and I'll have your money. Have one of our girls, on the house of course,' said Cherry.

'You are most kind, but the drink and payment will be all, thank you,' he replied.

With a click of her red silk-gloved fingers, a house worker girl arrived with a tray of drinks and offered one to Jonathan.

He sat comfortably with his glass of gin and lime and awaited payment. Whilst doing so, he observed three side cubicle rooms, with just a curtain as a door to each one. He stood up and walked closer to the curtains, behind which he heard strange and intriguing noises. He stood by the first curtain, listening to the ravishing sound of carnal lust from both male and female. The rapid sounds of moans from a woman, accompanied by the deep growls from a customer, and more than one by the sound of it, grew ever more, making his curiosity increase with every second that passed. He slowly pulled open the curtain, just a few inches, and peaked through at what was taking place.

He watched as a fully naked prostitute appeared to be tied down, bent over on a horse-like bench structure, with her wrists and ankles tied to each wooden leg. A large naked man with a full and swollen erection pounded her hard back and forth from behind, pulling on her hips and slapping her arse. As the bangs became more vigorous, he thrusted like a bull as it forced her breasts to bounce in unison, as they hung down to the rough rhythm. At the same time, another naked man was to her front, pulling on her hair and holding her head level to his waist as he fucked her open mouth again and again. The moans were complemented by her gags, as she simultaneously took the two stiff, flesh shafts inside her pussy and mouth. Behind each man stood a few more punters, waiting in line to take turns on her, each one standing by to fill her up and use her as a cum holder.

Jonathan was in shock, for he had never seen anything like that before. It was not a pleasant shock, and yet it was not a bad one either. He returned the curtain to its original position, for he had seen enough of that particular cubicle. He could not help but think what was behind the middle curtain. He wanted to explore what was beyond and if it was just as bad a shock as the first. Just like with his actions prior, he peaked through the next curtain. It was another prostitute, naked from the waist down, with her top half exposed but held on by an open-buttoned, white-laced vest. She was standing up and leaning against the back wall, her sight momentarily taken from her with the use of a blindfold. Her body was in an 'X' position, her legs wide apart and her arms matching. She had five paying customers surrounding her body, moving all around as she stood still with anticipation. They all touched and caressed her, running their hands along her skin concurrently as if worshipping a goddess. Ten hands were exploring every part, from a grope of her breasts to a tickle to her inner thighs, to fingertips running along her neck.

Jonathan observed that each and every man in this specific cubicle wore nothing but a colourful face mask, each mask portraying a cruel picture, one in particular of the devil himself, with horns settled sticking out of the forehead. Each mask was different, but they did all hold one similar characteristic. Every nose on each mask stuck out long and rigid and took the shape of a cock. It was a bizarre mixture of dark age plague masks and a masquerade ball face attire, each with the protruding nose like Pinocchio himself. At first it was the stuff of surreal nightmares, but soon the masks began to serve their purpose. He watched as one man knelt down and positioned himself between the prostitute's open legs. The masked man tilted his head back, so the tip of the long nose was rubbing against her wet, dripping slit. He slowly rose up, inching his way off the floor as the fake cock slid inside her, only to be removed again to start the motion over and over, going in and out, just with the balancing movement from his head. Jonathan's eyes widened with bafflement and perplexity. With a deep breath, he pulled the curtain closed.

The noise from the third and final curtain was one that was very contrasting to the other two, as it contained a man screaming with pain and pleasure.

With yet another piece of his curiosity needing to be quenched, he looked through the third curtain and saw a man stripped naked and tied to an upright wooden board. He was facing it with his stomach flat against the grain, so his back and rear was on full show. A prostitute stood beside and held a short cat-'o'-nine tails in her hands and would whip the man over and over. Her blows would not weaken as the commands and orders bellowed from the man. Again and again, he asked for more. The thrashes were so harsh that every one of them would leave a bloodied mark on his torn flesh. His back and posterior resembled a chequered picture of red blood in fine lines zigzagging their way far across. Jonathan could not help but flinch every time the lash of the whip struck the raw flesh. The paying man would scream and cry and yet beg for more, as if testing himself as to how much he could take, testing his own threshold and tolerance through flogging.

Even though it was certainly a sight for sore eyes, there was one thing that flabbergasted

Jonathan's eyes more than anything else he had seen in the last ten minutes. He looked to the side of the cubicle and saw a judge's red cloak, with its white fur collar circling the top rim, hung up on the hook that lay on the rear wall with a white judge's wig hanging over the top. He laughed at the sight and quickly closed the curtain. He would not have waged that a man such a judge, or any man with authority, power, and high education, would and could be the reciprocate of such base desires. It is one thing to harbour illicit salaciousness, but to have them fulfilled was quite scandalous. After a moment of thought, he corrected himself and thought that even men of worth and standing taller than the many were still flesh and blood with needs of release. It was also clear to him that these working girls were there upon their own choosing and were not prisoners or hostages. It would be true that many of them, given easier ways to make money, would grab at the chance. But this fine, warm, and comfortable place held more serenity than other bawdy brothels, let alone the cold rough streets. A well-kept bed or fur rug for a 'hump', no matter in what hole, would be more appealing than a stone wall.

Madam Cherry approached him and handed over her debt in full. Jonathan counted the notes and placed them in his inner coat pocket.

'Thank you, ma'am, the account is settled.'

'You have our sincere apologies. sir, and you have our word that we will not be late next time.'

'Not at all, it's been an education, one could say, and one I shall not forget for several days. Good evening, miss,' he replied.

Jonathan placed his hat on his head and made his way out of the building. The pull of temptation to stay was present within him, but he did not weaken and left through the way he came. His strongest desire at that moment was of sleep and home. The pull of those two thoughts were greater than the pull of lust.

He made his way back to the partly welcoming glow of the gaslight from the quiet main street. He looked up and down for a cab void of passengers and available to return him home. Whilst turning his head, he noticed some movement out of the corner of his eye. He turned further and saw someone he had not seen for a very long time.

Chapter 16

The movement was a young lady of about twenty years of age, with long hair and wearing a long dress that was heavily frayed at the hem from the scuffles of the ground. She stood, pulling the door closed of an ironmonger's shop. Jonathan was no more than five yards away when the silhouette of this lady revealed itself more clearly. The side profile of her was very familiar to his memory. He walked up to her just as she was locking the door. He stood still and removed his top hat.

'Milady,' he said in a gentle tone.

She turned to the voice with an indifferent expression on her face, thinking it would most probably be a man wanting to perturb her in some way.

Her indifference turned to joy with sudden recollection. 'Jonathan! Is that really you?'

She was almost certain it was, but she looked closer for a few seconds before opening her arms to give a fond embrace.

'Lizzie? Yes, it is I,' he replied, as he received her with much enthusiasm. They both smiled and folded in each other arms with a warming touch.

Almost in unison, they said, 'You look much the same, and yet …'

The pair laughed.

'It is so good to see you,' Jonathan said, and Lizzie agreed.

'Has it been … eight years?' she asked.

'Yes,' he replied thoughtfully.

'I cannot believe my eyes,' said Lizzie.

'Nor I. Would you care to join me for a drink?' he asked.

His previous desire, when he left the brothel, for home and sleep, was very powerful, but it was expeditiously taken away when given opportunity to share a drink with Lizzie.

'Yes … yes of course' she said with elation.

Jonathan removed his coat and placed it over her slender shoulders for warmth and an extra layer from the rain. His large coat wrapped around her shoulders and torso with ease and encased up like a cosy cocoon. They walked the pavement with anticipation and glee. The cold, bitter dark, with the rain, did not feel like what it did before. The only item on their minds was to sit down and catch up on everything and anything.

Within one minute of walking, they were passed by two empty cabs, throwing up a wave of gutter rain over Jonathan's legs. Luckily, there was an abundance of public houses on the main street, so after just a short moment, they found themselves in The Red Lion. This was picked for no other reason than it was the closest and most convenient to dodge the rain. They were desperate to talk further, and Lizzie was worried for Jonathan's soaked state.

The Red Lion was a comfortable enough pub, a spit and sawdust type, holding a typical London boozer feel.

They were ten to a penny but offered an small, empty, round table for intimate conversation, right next to a large open fire, which was all they sought. The time passed with haste as the parlance flowed with merriment and laughter. A light bitter was enjoyed by Jonathan, whilst Lizzie relished her double gin and orange. They learnt all about each other's lives over the last eight years, the trials and the tribulations, the successes, as well as some sadness.

Jonathan was pleased to learn that Lizzie was no longer with her pickpocket friends and that particular skill had been substituted for honest, albeit humble, work in the ironmonger's shop. Lizzie was equally happy to learn of Jonathan's fortunate encounter with Mr Huffham and his job and home, which sounded to her like it was from another world.

Their emotions of joy and delectation came together with ecstasy when they discovered that each one was unattached and not half of someone else or promised to another.

When asking of what became of Wooly, Twist, and the rest, the reply was some of regret and some of cheerfulness. She could not be sure of Twist, Tommy, and Ginger's fate, as only a few years prior, they had simply gone their separate ways, losing touch and having no knowledge of each other's whereabouts. However, she did know the exact whereabouts of Wooly and Mary-Ann. His heart sank upon hearing the news that Wooly was dead and his location was six feet under in Whitechapel cemetery.

Six years ago, back in 1882, Wooly had 'gone too far' as Lizzie put it. His dodges became evermore risky and dangerous as time went on. Jonathan listened carefully and heard that Wooly had endeavoured a house breaking and was shot in the attempt by the owner. A sad end to a sad tale.

He reached over the table and held her hand for a moment for comfort and support.

'I am most sorry for your loss. He had his faults, but the thought of him being no more saddens me. I thought of Wooly as being a survivor who would live forever,' he said.

'Thank you, Jonathan, you are as sweet as you ever were. It's all right. It's not fresh news to me as it is to you. I knew something like that would happen to him. He became wilder and more reckless as time went on. There can only be one end if you insist on dancing with the devil,' she replied.

'That is most true.'

Jonathan ordered a tot of whiskey to help the sad news soak in a little easier.

The feeling was lifted when he heard that Lizzie was as close as ever to her old friend Mary-Ann, seeing her regularly and only being a few hundred yards away from one another, with the two keeping company at least once a week. Lizzie explained that Mary-Ann was a lady of the night. She had tried many times in the past to steer her away from that distinct line of work, but the attempts always failed with temptations of easy money, gin, and the everlasting hope that maybe one day she would keep a punter forever and call him husband.

It was not as sickening and desperate as Jonathan first thought, for Mary-Ann, as well as many other working girls, were happy enough selling their bodies.

Being a prostitute was a status that had varied levels of hardship. The lowest being a dock-whore who would do anything to anyone for just a few pence. Then there were the street workers who, most of the time, chose their clients as well as their hours and were their own bosses. They would enjoy, to a certain extent, being in the pubs and taverns applying their trade, with food and drink not being in short supply. The next level were the ladies who lived in the brothels and, if lucky, were given a certain level of respect, especially if they found themselves in a whorehouse that was a cut above the rest, like Scarlet Cherries. Not to mention having a roof over their heads and a bed every night, as long as the rent was paid, which was a percentage of what they earned on any given night.

From the dock-whores to the brothels, there was always the threat of danger hanging over and ready to strike with malice, with evil doings happening frequently and almost consistently. Such was the norm, and having wits sharpened in conjunction with a blade for protection was commonplace.

Jonathan and Lizzie spoke for hours about Mary-Ann and the unfortunate demise of Wooly. But the bulk of their conversation was largely about each other, each of them more interested in the other and not themselves. The feeling was divine and heart-warming, the pair agreeing that the last eight years seemed to suddenly fly by fast and that their first encounter when they were children only felt like yesterday. The connection to one another back then was still present as if it never left, softly lingering in their eyes.

The landlord of the pub rang the bell and shouted for the last few patrons to leave, just as the fire was dying down, as the flames struggled to keep their hold on the dark charcoal from the last log.

Jonathan slid his hand across the tabletop, weaving in between the glasses that had accumulated, and reached to hold Lizzie's hand. She accepted the gentle and yet protective, strong grip with ease and a smile. He could not believe the time, but the face with two hands that hung on the wall above the bar was a face that did not lie.

The feeling of twenty minutes was the fact of two hours as time passed.

'I must apologise, Lizzie, I only meant to take your attention for a short moment. I have kept you long enough for tonight,' he said.

'Don't you dare apologise. this simple drink has been the best evening I've had for a long time,' she said and continued with a sorrowful tone, 'Is it just tonight that our paths will cross?'.

'Good lord, no ... well, that is if you'd allow, I'd love to see you again, as soon as possible, if it pleases.'

A smile beamed across her face and her head nodded fast. 'Yes, yes it does please me, and I hope it pleases you,' she said. The pair arranged to meet up again the very next day.

Jonathan walked her home, which was the flat above her workplace at the ironmonger's shop. They stood outside the front door and ignored the rain that still fell from the heavens.

'Tomorrow it is. I shall see you very soon,' said Jonathan.

Lizzie agreed and said 'Yes' again, with a smile that she could not seem to shake off.

He slowly pulled her towards him and kissed her gently. As their lips touched through the night rain, a moment of pure happiness manifested itself in both their beings, right down to their cores.

'Good night, Jonathan. I shall be thinking about tomorrow.'

'Good night, Lizzie, I shall be replicating the same thought as you.'

She entered her home and waved a goodbye to Jonathan.

He waved and stepped backwards to bid a fond farewell, until the morrow.

Chapter 17

The following day, Jonathan woke up with a certain spring in his step. Being a happy man, content with his life, this was not rare. Nevertheless, this morning, his steps held a little more bounce than normal. He had only been up a few minutes as he got dressed and made his way downstairs to Mr Huffham's dining table to indulge in breakfast. Within a single sip of his tea, he was already looking forward to his lunch break. Not for the release of work, nor was it to enjoy a midday meal. The sole reason was his rendezvous with Lizzie.

Sally entered the room holding a full silver-plated toast rack and a white china butter dish.

'Good morning, Jonathan, I hope you slept well. You didn't get in till one o'clock last night. I was getting worried.'

Jonathan sat back and glanced at the morning's paper.

'Good morning, Sally. Didn't the boss tell you? I was working, picking up a payment for the shop,' he replied.

'Well, yes, he did, but I was still worried.'

He explained that his late return home was because he'd had a drink with an old acquaintance.

'I'm not surprised in the least, you do seem to be rather popular with women.'. 'It was not what you think,' he said whilst smiling and tapping the side of his nose in a friendly way.

'Yeah, yeah … you and that Koots always seem to wander off and be lead away, or rather *mis*lead, when it comes to women.'

'Not at all … that is slander, I'll have you know. Not me … Koots is a bad influence,' he said with a cheerful wink and continued with, Besides, this is different.'

'Mmm, if you say so, Jonathan. It's only been one meeting.'

He did not answer, but his face said it all.

Jonathan and Sally had a marvellous relationship, a mixture of duty and affection. It was not commonplace in most houses, but it worked here. Given the nature of when they'd first met, with Sally being close to her master and Jonathan only being a child at first, the relationship had morphed into friendship and familiarity. Sally knew where the line was to be drawn concerning her words and actions. Jonathan was above her in status, and she served him happily and with pride, but the two were close and stood as more than just master and servant.

Sometimes, she would refer to Jonathan as 'Sir', but that, at times, became rather confusing when Jonathan and Mr Huffham were in the same room, as they would both turn their heads. Despite the mixture of class, positioning, and friendship between the three of them, their system worked and everyone was happy. Mr Huffham would not have it any other way and would refuse to live where discontent was present.

It was rather unorthodox, perhaps, but it succeeded to the fullest.

The masters' needs were of the highest priority, but even so, Mr Huffham still really cared for Sally and would often take time to consider her thoughts and well-being. If he was an unkind man, he could easily replace Sally in an instant, but he had no cause to partake in such a dismissal. Furthermore, he would be rather sad if Sally were to ever leave his household. Luckily, no thought of that or even anything akin to that was on the horizon.

Sally, being happy, fond of, and devoted to where she lived, thought herself incredibly felicitous and lucky to be in service, to have a room in the house but also having their company such as it was. Whenever Mr Huffham asked if he could help her in any way, she would laugh and smile and say, 'No.' She felt it was not right for a master to help a servant, but she did revel in those words when they came and enjoyed hearing the offers of help.

'Where's the boss? He's usually up at this time' asked Jonathan.

'He's at the shop He had to go in earlier than normal today,' she replied.

Jonathan understood as he recollected that there was a certain matter of urgency, a job of most importance to do in the workshop. He hastily stood up and left the house to make his way to the locksmith shop.

After his routine fifteen-minute walk, he arrived at work and shared a friendly greeting with the staff and Mr Huffham. He hung his coat and hat on the brass hook that hung by the door and walked to the back of the shop to work with Koots, who was in the middle of working on the delicate inner mechanism of a small padlock that had been returned the previous day for repair.

'Koots, Jonathan, if you please?' asked Mr Huffham.

The pair stepped out of the workshop. 'Yes, sir?' they both said in unison.

'Ah, chaps ... what is on for today?'

'Apart from this padlock repair, nothing, sir,' Koots answered.

'Splendid. Are you sure there is nothing else on the agenda?'

'Yes, sir,' he replied.

'Very well, carry on,' said Mr Huffham.

Koots and Jonathan turned around to return to the workshop. Koots took one step, only to then turn back to face Mr Huffham.

'Actually, it's an agendum,' said Koots with his usual cheeky grin.

'What?'

'If there's only one item, it's an agendum, not an agenda.'

'Yes, thank you, Koots. Where would we be without your contribution?'

'Always here to help. Are there any other English lessons I can help you with?'

'Stanley!'

'Yes, sir, sorry, sir. I'll be getting back to my work now.'

'That would be most wise,' said Mr Huffham with his stern look, which set sight on Koots almost once a day due to his mouth opening before his brain engaged.

When Koots' back was turned as he left the shop floor, Mr Huffham smiled. Koots was a cheeky fool, but Mr Huffham saw knew this and knew he had a heart of gold, as well as being a hard worker and highly skilled in all jobs that came and left the workshop. Also, being well versed in Latin, he knew that, technically, Koots was right. Therefore, he would not punish him for that remark, and actually, his happiness increased with his quick wit, even though it was misplaced from time to time.

A simple snap of 'Stanley' and a certain look was enough most of the time to remind Koots of his place. Mr Huffham, through his charisma, voice, and air of authority, had the amazing ability to say 'Stanley' and actually mean 'Sod off' at the same time as putting a fright down Koots' spine.

The morning's work seemed to drag by as Jonathan could not stop himself looking at the clock every ten minutes. With each and every glance, he hoped an hour had passed. Alas, that was not the case. The work consisted of many a customer to attend to. The tedious boredom did not change even as the bell that hung from the door rang frequently, matching the frequent 'ding' from the till every time notes and coins entered it. But the hands on the clock still seemed to rotate, as if it was in slow motion.

Being very fond of Lizzie, he was wondering and hoping that she too was wishing away the time and that her heart was beating as fast as his own. He was almost certain she did reflect his feelings. Nonetheless, he did not take anything for granted and dared not presume her intentions, no matter how much he wanted to. Jonathan was modest, unaware that he was quite a catch, turning many a head, his status, kindness, home-life, health, and appearance being somewhat a little higher than the norm.

However, he also knew that love, when not returned, stood for nothing. Unfortunately, through hearing of Mr Huffham's past, he knew that a being could possess the world, but in order for true love to flourish, the one thing you need is the other's heart.

Twelve o'clock came at last. He could finally have his lunch hour to meet with Lizzie. Jonathan had insisted he would travel to Whitechapel to save her the cab fare. Lizzie had then insisted she would travel all the way to him to save him any bother. They'd finally agreed the meeting place would be a large park that was conveniently situated equidistantly between Westminster and Whitechapel.

At one minute past midday, Jonathan managed to find a free cab to take him to the park. After giving the driver the instructions, he heard the comforting words, 'Right oh, gov,' and the cab trotted off with the driver holding Jonathan's promise of a gold sovereign if he did not dawdle.

Within ten minutes, he arrived at the park, which was possibly the most beautiful setting for many a mile. He took the two steps from the cab and flicked the driver the promised gold sovereign and followed with, 'Thank you, my good man.'

'You're welcome, any time,' he replied as he smiled and took the gold coin to his mouth for a bite of the edge.

The entrance of the park consisted of a long line of wide, flat stone steps that lead down to the grass. The grass was cut immaculately and to the highest of standards, resembling a vast lush green carpet.

He made his way down, looking left and right for Lizzie. Within but a moment, he saw her standing by a waist-high redbrick wall and looking right at him, with a smile accompanying her stare. As the bright sun shined high, it caught her face and made it look more beautiful than ever. He walked up and greeted her with a light kiss on her cheek.

'I pray I have not kept you waiting too long, Lizzie. I came as fast as I could.'

'Not at all, for I have only been here a minute. I too came as fast as I could,' she replied.

Jonathan held out his elbow and offered it to Lizzie as a comforting and gentlemanly touch of affection. She placed her hand in the crease of his arm as the two took a slow wander through the park.

The setting was as picturesque as could be. The three-acre park was awash with love and beauty, as if Aphrodite and Venus themselves had a blank canvas to stain it with a plethora of watercolours and oils with colourful pigment.

They walked side by side, favouring the sights and smells of their rainbow-like surroundings. All around them lay immense beds of bright flowers saturated in varied complexion. As the minutes ticked by, they passed vivid pink roses, pale blue irises, crisp white lilies, deep purple orchids, dark centre poppies, lime green tulips, and tall yellow sunflowers that glowed in the sun. The rain that had fallen the night previously gave even more life and strength to the well-being of all the flora.

The epicentre of the park held a circular bandstand, with a dome roof that was supported by six dark blue iron posts. Wanting to stay in the sun, they voted to rest on the grass and lay beside each other to continue their dialogue. They had shared much already, but with the mutual feeling they had for each other, the conversation flowed as each of them just wanted to learn more and more about the other.

As the park steadily became busier as the midday hour approached, Lizzie noticed that her attire was not quite of the same standard as her contemporary's. The majority of the other users of the park were ladies and gentlemen, walking side by side, enjoying each other's company, and dressed smartly. Even the dog walkers were dressed in their finest, even the grounds staff wearing crisp striped waistcoats and bowler hats.

Not much could get Lizzie down, for her soul was a contented kind. But upon seeing all the fine ladies walk close by, she felt a little deflated, if only for a moment. She sat up and looked down at her somewhat worn clothing and carried a slight look of sadness, with two melancholic thoughts going through her mind. The first thought was of selfishness, that she could not afford to look as beautiful as all the rest. The second was totally on the contrary, with a thought of Jonathan and why he would bother with her when there were all the other much better choices around far more tailored to him than herself.

Jonathan sat up and noticed the slight change in her tone and general feeling. He could tell exactly what was going through her head, which made him even more attracted to her. Her humbleness and soft vulnerability was very endearing to him.

'Look at all those people walking round smart, dressed well, elegant, and tasteful,' he said.

Lizzie carried a smile that was slightly forced and said with a small break in her voice, 'Mmm, yes, they certainly are pretty, aren't they?'

Jonathan leaned over to Lizzie and whispered in her ear, 'Nowhere near as much as you, my dear. You are worth a million of their posh frocks.'

Her smile suddenly held more weight as it was injected with joy. 'Thank you, Jonathan. You make me feel better than anyone else does'.

'I only say the truth, and the truth is I'd rather have your company than any of these ladies, and forgive my forwardness, but I find you extremely attractive.'

Lizzie kept her smile and nudged his shoulder with hers and replied, 'I find you extremely handsome and would rather have your company than any other.'

Jonathan laid back on the grass with his hands interlocked behind his head. Lizzie laid beside him with her head over his stomach.

'Would it be peculiar if I said that, back when we first met, I, a child of twelve and you at thirteen, was attracted to you, even then?' he asked.

'I was just about to say the same thing,' she said with a laugh, and continued with "Tis not peculiar, and if it was, I wouldn't care.'

They laid together enjoying the warm sun, with the sounds of birds chirping, and the gentle splish-splash of fresh water flowing from a large and distant fountain made a gratifying background sound that was interspersed with their voices. They chatted freely and easily, as if they'd known each other all of their lives.

After what felt like only a few minutes, Jonathan and Lizzie decided to have a change of scene, for both their stomachs rumbled with hunger. He rose to his feet and offered is hand out to pull her up tenderly from the grass. He made the suggestion to remedy the hunger, if she'd allow him to take her to the nearest tearoom. She accepted with glee, as she was certainly ready for food. However, the strongest reason for her agreement was nothing more than to share more time with him. Be it a minute or an hour, an oyster on a street corner, or a five-course meal, it mattered not, for the loving feeling and gaiety would be present within her as long as they were together. She linked her arm in his as the pair left the magic of the park to find a rapturous and refreshing bite to eat and to extend their time with one other.

The area of their whereabouts was somewhat unfamiliar to both of them. They had no wherewithal as to where such a pleasant tearoom was situated. As they walked along the pavement looking for such a place, they continued to talk and enjoy each other's closeness. The search was not a trouble or burden of any kind. Instead of filling their stomachs with food, they were consciously and subconsciously filling their hearts with fulfilment of desire and a sense of belonging to one another.

Just round the corner from the park, they came across the local tearooms, an old but well-maintained establishment that had been serving hungry customers for almost one hundred years.

Jonathan looked up at the well-preserved black, square, swinging sign that said in white lettering:

Mrs P Williams' Tearooms
Est 1790

'If it pleases, we can try here. I hope it's nice,' said Lizzie.

'1790 ... she should have got the hang of it by now,' he replied with a smile.

Lizzie giggled as they entered the tearoom, Jonathan stepping forward in order to hold the door open for her.

The tearoom was very welcoming, carrying a smell of chocolate and cream, dough from freshly baked bread, and fruit that was piled high in the centre of the room. It was a popular place that was almost at full capacity during midday, with people, mostly of higher standing, enjoying the offers that lay before them.

Many of them worked in the local district and could afford it and would venture their daily.

The tea maids looked very similar to the female servants, chamber maids, and parlour maids of posh households, in their black and white uniforms, the only difference being that their top half would button up to the neck, which then supported a choker with the logo of the tearoom sown on. These girls were allowed to have a ribbon hanging down from a bun in the hair, providing of course it was clean and attractive and in the employer's choice of colour.

Jonathan and Lizzie found an intimate table for two and indulged in petite square sandwiches with the crusts cut off and a pot of tea to share, only to be followed by a cream cake with a custard mix and glazed in icing, which was on display amongst a large selection of other tempting delights, some of which she had never seen before, let alone placed in her mouth to adore and joyfully consume with exuberance.

With the last taste of the delicious food being devoured and satisfying her stomach, she leaned forward over the table to thank him for the glorious meal. Her stomach reflected her heart with content. Jonathan took out his wallet in order to pay when he was stopped for a moment by Lizzie.

'Please, allow me to pay. This has been one of the best days of my life. I would like to contribute in some way.'

'Not at all, young lady. I asked you to accompany me. I am not a gentleman of vast wealth, but I am a gentleman ... well, most of the time anyway. I am better placed in this world than our first meeting all those years ago.'

Lizzie smiled, laughed, and replied, 'Well that doesn't take much. We had sweet Fanny Adams back then.'

He nodded in agreement. Whilst doing so, he carried his nod to the tea maid, for her to walk over so he could settle the bill.

They left the tearooms with arms linked. He placed his hat on his head just as the fresh air hit their faces. Whilst straightening the rim, he noticed a tall green, iron post opposite them that held a large clock on the top, towering high enough that it would be clear to even a pedestrian fifty yards away.

'Blimey, that cannot be the time, surely!' he exclaimed as he took out his pocket watch with the hope that the street clock was erroneous and in need of repair.

He looked down at his watch and expressed a deep huff. 'It's a quarter past two.

'What time do you have to be back at work?' she asked.

'One o'clock. Once again, Father Time has played his tricks and flown by.'

Lizzie was concerned that Jonathan was angry, so was about to apologise. But before the first sound left her mouth, her concern was quelled by his smile and the words,

'It matters not. In fact, I believe it to be a good thing. I would not have changed anything for the world. But I must dash, I'm afraid. I can see you back to Whitechapel first though if you like?'

She would have wanted to accept but knew that would not be right or fair. Her having the afternoon off, with Jonathan having to work, her head overruled her heart and she declined. She turned her gaze from the clock face and aimed it at his. Whilst standing very close, she caught sight of a small smudge of cream on his lower lip. She stepped closer still and leaned into him, just as he pressed closer to her. They shared a long kiss that was firm and yet tender simultaneously. The rhythm of their lips connecting in chorus felt sweeter than the iced cakes they'd just eaten. Just as they were pulling away after such an amorous moment, the tip of her tongue purposefully gathered up the cream off his lip, with the creamy whiteness on full display, to then retract it slowly back into her own mouth, to then swallow with a playful and teasing look.

With another smile, followed by another kiss, Jonathan raised his hat off his head for a second, to then replace it back.

'I must take my leave. I shall see you again very soon.'

'You promise?' she asked with joyful antici-pation.

'I promise. A thousand strong cavalry charging could not stop my desire to see you.'

He paced away across the stone road and jumped into a cab. He voiced loudly with exertion, 'Westminster, my good man, if you please!'

As the cab trotted off with the horses' hoofs clattering hard, he leaned out and gave a final wave of his hat back to Lizzie, with his heart booming.

She walked off into the distance in a carefree, jovial spirit, with a million amazing thoughts flowing through her body and soul and a fixed smile that not even the devil himself could erase.

A while later, Jonathan's cab pulled up outside his place of work. He rushed through the door with a curious look on his face, wondering what sort of reception he would receive.

Mr Huffham was standing with his back facing the door, only to then turn around when he heard the door open. He held his pocket watch in the palm of his hand but close to his body as the golden chain kept it attached to his jacket pocket. Jonathan opened his mouth, but it was forced shut an instant later when he saw Mr Huffham's finger raise up, pointing towards the ceiling.

Mr Huffham's most stern voice flowed out from his mouth. 'Unless my eyes deceive me, according to my watch, is it two thirty-four in the afternoon. Now … is my assertion false or do I stand correct?'

'You are correct, sir.'

'Jolly good. Now, you will tell me why you are over an hour and a half late?'

'I am sorry, sir, I really am.'

As he was mid-explanation and apology, Koots walked by to get to the counter and said, 'Horse stopped for a piss?'

Mr Huffham tilted his glare to Koots.

'Stanley, it is better to just remain silent and be thought a fool than to open your mouth and remove all doubt.'

'Pardon, sir?'

'Shut up.'

'Yes, sir, sorry, sir.'

'Jonathan. Explain yourself.'

He walked closer to his master with his hat in his hands, with a genuine sorrowful and slightly fearful look on his face. He explained in full truth why he was late and that such a crime would never repeat itself, but continuing with this particular girl was somewhat special and held a place in his heart that no other previous maiden had accomplished. He apologised profusely, over and over again, as Mr Huffham stood in silence, listening on.

In usual circumstances, he would not accept that a lunch date with a lady was good enough reason for such lateness. However, when hearing that this was no mere casual girl to join a long list of others, just in order to bolster his ego, and that Jonathan really did seem extra happy with this one, accompanied with the knowledge that it was the first offence of its kind, he simply smiled and told him that love, if indeed it was that, was a decent enough reason. But he did follow with a strict warning that it would not become habit, and if unpunctuality and tardiness were to emerge again, punishment would occur.

Mr Huffham's heart was as big as any, and he ended the warning with a smile, and with a tilt of his head, he kindly asked Jonathan to return to the workshop and said that would be the end of the matter.

Jonathan nodded and carried a look of happy relief as he left the shop floor. Mr Huffham gestured for Koots to come forward.

'Yes, sir?'

'You will not interrupt when I am talking to Jonathan again in future, do you understand?'

'Yes, sir, it's just you were late the other day.'

'Stanley ... do not make a catalogue of my mistakes. I know them better than you. You are a great salesman, you could sell rice to the Chinese, sand to the Arabs and ice to the Eskimos, but you should be grateful for your talents. If not for them, I would be tempted to sling you out, you understand?'

Koots, with his usual clumsy, happy, and daft face, nodded his head in full understanding and agreement. But he had one question.

'What's an Eskimo, sir? And why would an Arab want to buy sand?'

Mr Huffham smiled, for he knew it was a genuine question for the quest of knowledge and not intended to test his patience.

'Never mind, Koots, just get back to work, if you please.'

Chapter 18

A few days later, darkness descended upon Whitechapel. It was early evening as the sun gave way to the moon and stars.

Lizzie and Mary-Ann were enjoying their weekly catch up, Mary-Ann being all ears to hear the excitement that her friend was conveying, listening all about the previous week's events and sharing the joy that Lizzie seemed to hold.

They were in one of the many pubs that Whitechapel had to offer.. Being in the centre of the district, it was most handy for Mary-Ann and other prostitutes. There was always an abundance of possible punters and offers of free gin that the ladies of the night would see as a well-earned bonus, as well as a means to an end, for they had little else to do. For they had little else to do. Whoring and drinking was the main activity, and the one that took up the vast majority of the passing hours, only to be broken up with sleep and rest.

Mary-Ann would be in this pub every night doing just that. But the nights she was with Lizzie, she saw as a night off, with no thoughts of either earning money or finding a husband. The only man she would take interest in this night was the one that her friend seemed to speak of so highly.

After a couple of hours and three large gins, Lizzie and Mary-Ann decided to bid farewell to the evening's pleasant and much-needed catch up. It was getting cold and the two of them wanted the comforts of their beds.

They left the pub and gave each other a tight and meaningful hug, with the intention and promise of meeting again very soon. They both wished each other a safe walk home, as Lizzie then walked across the road with Mary-Ann staying on the pavement. She waved goodbye to Lizzie to then set off on her short walk home.

As the distance between the two friends slowly became greater, Mary-Ann decided to take a short-cut. Her room was not far, but the night was so cold, all she had on her mind was home and sleep. If a ten-minute walk could be turned into a five minute walk, than that would be most pleasing on such a night as this, with its numbing and freezing bite in the air. The shortcut was in the form or a long, narrow side alley, with dark brickwork on all sides. It was laden with wooden pallets leaning against the walls and archways sporadically, empty barrels that stood in rows piled two high, and small cargo boxes scattered around. It was awkward to manoeuvre through, but it certainly had the potential to shorten her homeward journey. The alleyway in question went by the name Buck's Row.

She wrapped her shoal around her shoulders and walked fast to keep warm. She was halfway down Buck's Row when she heard a rustling sound not too far in front of her.

The outline of a dark figure slowly manifested itself before her and approached her through the shadows.

'How much?' a deep and husky voice rang out from the darkness.

Mary-Ann did not answer but kept walking and managed to see the face of the man. The figure stood there, still, like a phantom in the mist. She looked upon him as he stood all in black and positioned himself directly in front of her.

His tortured face moved closer, catching the gaslight. His features held a long, deep scar running from chin to brow and carried an eye patch, which became ever clearer as he inched closer towards her.

'Not now mister, I ain't working tonight.'

His rough and bitter face got even closer as he asked again, although this time, the words shot through the air with anger.

'Are you deaf? I said I ain't working,' she repeated, and continued, 'Go and find a dock whore, they'll do a cripple.'

The man proceeded to grab her by the arms and pushed her against the brick wall. 'I ain't no cripple, bitch!'

'You look like one with that face! Leave me alone!' she ordered, then spat in his face as she tried to wriggle out from his strong control.

He pulled her away from the wall, only to slam her back again.

He faced her head on, so close that their noses were touching.

With his vile, bad breath he said to her with venom, 'No-one's gonna want to fuck you after I'm done with you!'

He violently back-handed her across her cheek, to then wipe the spit from his face. He slid his hand up her dress, between her legs, moving up and up as far as it would go to feel her most intimate part. She struggled and tried to pull away his fingers, as they slithered along like loathsome, creepy tentacles. After fighting his violation for a few seconds, he did remove his hand, only to then grab her jaw to force her head to one side. He licked her face with his rough tongue. She was disgusted as she felt the wetness roll over her skin, only to be followed with his coarse and jagged stubble, which felt like sandpaper rubbing up and down. She wrestled and screamed and did everything in her power to stop the savagery.

Her attempt at escape was futile as her screams were instantly muffled with his hard grip covering her mouth. He raised his fist and punched her unyieldingly to try and weaken her fight. He pinned her even harder as he tore open her vest, the small white buttons flying off in the air before landing on the ground. The curve of her breasts and her sensitive nipples hit the cold air abruptly as he groped and seized them viciously, like a baker kneading dough, squeezing so hard it hurt. His fingers and hands compressed her bust tight and deep enough to leave an imprint in her flesh.

He pulled her like a ragdoll from the wall and bent her over an oaken barrel that stood waist high. Standing behind, he forced her legs apart with a kick from his boots. She cried and wriggled as he held her down. He hiked up her petticoat and threw it over her back to then pull at her pantalettes, yanking them hard over to one side, ripping them as he did.

Half-stripped, she was at her most vulnerable as could not move and her pale, naked, rounded backside was on full display. She yelled again as she could hear him unclasp his belt and unbutton his trousers that were inches away from her hole.

'No! Please, no!' she begged and cried.

'I'm gonna fill you up, bitch, and teach you a lesson you'll never forget!' he growled as he fumbled with his trousers to release his stiff, fleshy weapon.

Just as his shaft was in his grasp, as the tip was about to ram her hard, she heard a familiar voice.

'Mary-Ann!'

With those words, the attack stopped forthwith. Lizzie ran towards them, her face appearing from what felt like out of nowhere.

'Lizzie. .. help!' Mary-Ann cried.

'Leave her alone, you ugly pig!' she demanded.

The man's angry face contorted and held more anger than before, as he had been stopped in the nick of time. He grabbed Mary-Ann by the waist and pulled her hair and flung her to the cobbled ground. He ran off into the distance to disappear into the dark night. Lizzie rushed to the ground to help her friend.

Mary-Ann sat up with tears rolling down her marked face and holding her top together to help restore at least a little dignity.

'I'm all right,' she said in a broken voice and continued with, 'another two seconds and it would be different.'

Lizzie helped her to her feet and walked her back towards home, holding her close, with her arm wrapped around her tight and protectively.

'Come on, Mary, What have I told you about Buck's Row'

'I know, I know,' she replied.

'You would have got a lot worse than a that if I hadn't shown up, and if it wasn't for your screams, you would have been ravaged and possibly dead!'

'Didn't even get a shilling for it,' said Mary-Ann with dark humour in an attempt to lighten the mood.

Lizzie laughed awkwardly.

Buck Row was notorious and particularly dark and secluded, but so were a many other alleyways. It was dangerous, but it did not stand alone in side streets and back alleys where evil men lurked.

The majority of the street workers normally carried some sort of protection, usually in the form of a knife. It was no fashion accessory, nor was it an ornament, but a tool and one that showed itself invaluable on many times. Mary-Ann herself used to carry such a weapon but was put off doing so. A year before, she had been mugged and lost her purse for quite a few days. The perpetrator fought with her and managed to disarm her, which in turn gave him the weapon. In her mind, a madman was scary enough, but a madman with *your* knife was worse still. Since that incident, she had chosen to use her experience and her wits as a weapon. Ninety-nine times out of a hundred, it worked.

Chapter 19

wo days had passed, and Lizzie was working hard for her boss in the ironmonger's shop. She worked from seven-thirty in the morning till six-thirty at night, six days a week, only having one week per year holiday. She felt that her position in life was typically standard and ordinary, with some who she crossed paths with far lower with a harder life, and others being higher, with a more undemanding lifestyle. Her experience was somewhat limited, having been in Whitechapel almost her whole life. Her workday was long and arduous, not to mention that the work of ironmongery was not exactly light-handed. She was not aided, for there was only one other person in the shop. That being Mr Fenchurch, an old and cranky man that wasn't cruel or harsh and never mistreated her, but at the same time wasn't entirely the easiest man either.

She only had to be one minute late for Mr Fenchurch to dock her wages, a lesson that she'd learnt early on and would always do her best not to duplicate again. Her work was varied and consisted of serving customers, taking orders, sorting deliveries, sharpening blades, and cleaning tools when needed.

One of her simplest roles was also one of the hardest, a task and duty that should be easy, but thanks to her boss, that was not the case. Stocking taking, selling, and weighing nails of all sizes was a job that would be part of her daily work. Nuts and bolts, wooden screws, and nails was the shop's main trade, with tools coming secondary. The nails would come in a large box, not too dissimilar in size to a hat box, and would weigh around fifty pounds. That was around half a large sack of coal. The boxes of nails would be stored in order according to size, going from quarter inch tack, to long five-inch nails. In the centre of the shop stood a large wooden cabinet, with long black draws underneath, each one full of different sized nails. They would be sold by weight, with the weighing scales and large galvanised bucket sat on top of the cabinet. The normal routine would be to gather handfuls of nails and fill the bucket to whatever the amount the customer wanted. Mr Fenchurch insisted that it was not the done thing to simply fill the scales by hand, but to hold the tray of nails up and tip it into the bucket. The top of the cabinet was as tall as Lizzie's shoulders, making every transaction and movement of nails back-breaking. Picking up these boxes and trays overflowing with nails would make many a muscle ache.

Mr Fenchurch was so peculiar in his ways that if he ever saw Lizzie reaching up with handfuls of nails, as opposed to carrying the whole container to fill the bucket, she would receive a telling off, which would not only cause upset but would also carry embarrassment to herself as well as the customer.

There was an occasion many years ago when she did complain and question his methods.

The response was a warning with the words, 'There's twenty other girls that could replace you in an instant!'

Those words did not answer her question and carried little explanation as to why he was stuck in his old, strange ways. It did, however, tell her not ask or complain ever again. It was a harsh statement, but it was also unfortunately very accurate. Plus, with her living in the flat above, for a relatively cheap rent, she realised she had to toe the line. No matter how bleak and jarring things became, she knew that others had it worse. She was surrounded by unfortunate souls, for there was one every few feet in Whitechapel. They stood as a constant reminder to appreciate what she had and not dwell on what she did not have.

This day, however, blossomed a nicer, kinder emotion than normal. The feeling of Jonathan in her mind lifted her spirits whenever needed, and even when it was not. There was also a physical feeling of comfort with her on this day. Folded up neatly and small, in her apron pocket lay a short love letter that she had received that very morning. She had read it more than once, the words of affection in ink drifting from the parchment and directly into her heart. Every word, letter, and punctuation made her smile, feeling wanted and yearned for.

If Mr Fenchurch was in the middle of one of his arbitrary, erratic rants, she'd glide her fingertips over her pocket, just to feel the outline of the folded paper, to help her mind drift off.

The words circulating into her heart was of yet another chance to meet, with the invitation to share more time with each other. The arrangement was for Jonathan to travel to Whitechapel for the pair to enjoy a drink and conversation.

Lizzie had the idea of surprising Jonathan and for herself to go to Westminster and wait for him outside his house, or rather Mr Huffham's house. The aim being that they could both travel back together to Whitechapel.

When she'd finished work at 30 minutes past six, that was exactly what she did. With the final job being ticked off at the shop, and the 'Open' sign that hung in the door glass being flipped over to 'Closed', she rushed upstairs to change into her best dress, wash her face, and brush her long hair. She made herself as appealing as possible, with the little she had. Unfortunately, and rather regrettably, her wardrobe was lacking, with only a few options. Nevertheless, her long, pale brown dress would have to do, for it was the least marked and frayed. It was hardly the latest from Paris, but it hugged her body slenderly and showed the natural feminine curves of her body with purpose.

She hopped into a cab and made her way. Whilst the large, spoked wagon-style wheels rolled over the rough ground, she hoped that her actions would not be improper and the surprise would not be an ill-timed one. With the knowledge she held about Jonathan's ways and personality, she was almost certain it would be satisfactory and suitable. She knew not to intrude and would never invite herself into Mr Huffham's abode. Her intention was to wait outside in the hope that the sight of her would make Jonathan portray a beaming smile and that the surprise would be one of unexpected joy. Also, sharing a cab back would allow an additional thirty minutes together.

She seldom had the opportunity to be in a cab. The necessity was not usually required, but also the lack of funds prohibited her doing so. To be in one was a rare but pleasant activity that carried the feeling of being a proper lady. The thought of a worker actually serving *her* and treating her well with relative respect was uncommon. She celebrated as she travelled onward her journey, fizzing with feelings of happiness and excitement, albeit accompanied with the odd shaking nerve and butterflies circling in her stomach.

After around thirty minutes of being pulled along by the magnificent black stallion, guided by the trusted cab driver, she arrived in Westminster and only three minutes away from Mr Huffham's house. Over Westminster Bridge, past Big Ben, and two corners later, the cab pulled up at the short row of black railings that squared off his house. She paid the driver in full, only leaving herself a small amount of loose change. If her surprise landed on a welcoming face, it would all be worth it, she thought.

It was around seven o'clock as she stood waiting, looking up at the large front door. She was very tempted to approach and give a loud knock, but she dared not. The wait did not bother her, for she knew it would not take long for Jonathan to appear. It was simple time keeping. The journey was thirty minutes, give or take, and the original arrangement for the meeting was to be at 7.30pm.

'He must be leaving around now,' she said to herself.

A couple minutes drifted by. Five minutes past the hour, then ten minutes past, and still no sign of Jonathan. Then a dreadful feeling swept over her.

'What if we missed each other and passed one another on the road?' she asked herself.

Maybe her romantic gesture had backfired and he was already on his way to the meeting point in Whitechapel, only to be stood-up upon his arrival!

Her heart began to pound hard as she wondered what to do. She felt she could not bang on the door of the gentleman's house, nor could she afford a cab to return her to her own district. A sad and isolated walk back was to be her only option.

Just as her stomach was churning and turning like a cab wheel, the front door of Mr Huffham's house opened with a silhouette of a man, with the words echoing 'Good night, Sally, I shall see you later.'

The silhouette was Jonathan. Lizzie was certainly pleased as she stood awaiting his response. He closed the door and, within two steps from his porch, he saw her, looking up, arms behind her back and smiling.

'Lizzie! What on earth are you doing here? I was on my way to meet you,' he said with a gleeful but startled look.

She told him that she thought it would be a nice change. She wanted to give him a sight that was unexpected and that, if he were agreeable, it would be gratifying to ride back to Whitechapel together.

He was still in delighted shock and agreed to her suggestions effortlessly. As she was right there, he insisted she come inside to meet his lord and master, hero and friend, Mr Huffham. She'd heard all about him, and as she was only a few feet away, she agreed freely and painlessly to finally make his acquaintance. If it was important to Jonathan, it was important to her.

She was nervous and hesitant, but Jonathan eased her worries, assuring her all would be well and that she would more than enjoy his company. With her hand in his, he lead her back into the house.

'Gosh that was quick,' Sally said jokingly, as she stood in the hallway looking at Jonathan and Lizzie.

He introduced them, the pair taking a liking to each other instantly. After a minute of conversing, he lead her further into the house, from the cold black and white chequered floor, to the warm study, where Mr Huffham was at his desk. He sat there with his head and mind deeply entrenched in one of his history books, as he did on regular occasions. Lizzie looked at the varied interesting artefacts that surrounded her as if it were a museum, but one that also harboured a warm, homely feel with the furniture scattered around eloquently and comfortably. Swords from many a different era hung from the walls, and a glass case of ancient arrowheads sat to one side, a dinosaur skull taking centre stage.

She took a step closer to the desk, (even that was of interest), books and manuscripts piled high and flanked by a golden quill, round copper inkwell, and a large magnifying glass. A miniature sword was used as a letter opener, next to which was a small sandstone and marble bust, fresh off the boat from Greece, of the Spartan warrior, King Leonidas himself.

With a deliberate cough from Jonathan, Mr Huffham pulled himself away from the pages of his text and looked up. 'Sir ... this is Lizzie'

Mr Huffham's face promptly turned from concentration to one of joy and cheerfulness.

'Ah ... milady, so this is the wonderful Lizzie I've heard so much about. Jolly pleased to meet you,' he said as he stretched out his open hand.

She smiled at his amiable face and affectionate words as she shook his hand.

'Pleased to meet you, sir,' she said with a curtsy. 'I too have heard all about you.'

'My, my, not all I hope!' he replied with an exuberant look.

Lizzie's smile continued, for she felt that she was in the presence of nothing but charm and affability.

Mr Huffham stood up and asked the pair to follow him to the parlour room, and they happily did so. He walked towards his drinks cabinet and asked her if she would care for a tot of something, with the added warning that it may be a little too strong. She turned to Jonathan, who nodded to reassure her that she should accept if she so wished.

'Thank you, sir,' she said as she gingerly accepted the glass.

'Please, girl, have a seat and make yourself comfortable.'

She sat down with her drink, a liquid she had no knowledge of, but it did smell rather nice, and chatted to him. Her initial nerves became a distant memory within just a few moments, for she felt quite at ease, safe, and more than content.

Their classes were a million miles apart, with the two different standings in life scarcely crossing paths, let alone sharing a drink and happy chit-chat. But Lizzie and Mr Huffham did so almost as if she was his equal, with him not only accommodating her, but being jubilant to have her there.

He knew that Jonathan was very fond of her, so he, in-turn, followed suit and accepted her as a lady of importance, with no concern of lack of social standing or wealth. He trusted his teaching to Jonathan to be a rather decent judge of character, so he felt a certain closeness to Lizzie, and that was good enough for him. He did not need to be aware of her bank balance or if her parents were titled, or indeed if her etiquette was on form. He could tell within the first two minutes of talking that Jonathan's judgement and heart fell to a suitable girl and that him being happy was of the utmost priority.

Jonathan poured himself a drink and sat back by the fire, looking on with fulfilment as the two of the most important people in his life were getting on so well.

As he placed another log on the fire, he realised a full hour had passed, close confabulation practically toing and froing between them continuously and easily. He smiled and looked on at what could almost be father and daughter sat before him. The adoration on her face was paramount, and that gave him nothing but exhilaration. He was his own man and held his choices, be them good or bad to himself, but Mr Huffham giving his approval still meant the world.

The dinner bell rang in the distance.

'I'm afraid that is my calling, my dear. My table awaits. Would you care to stay for some late super?' asked Mr Huffham.

Knowing Lizzie would not feel easy saying 'No', Jonathan said, 'Very kind, but we must be off. I am taking this young lady out for the evening.'

'Of course, dear boy. You go out and have fun.'

Mr Huffham stood up, Lizzie doing the same a second later. She did not know whether to hold her hand out, curtsy, or nod. The awkwardness of unknowing action of appreciation was taken away when he opened his arms to share a hug.

She hugged him and thanked him for his time, with an apology for any intrusion.

"Twas no intrusion,' he replied. 'And if it were, then a pretty face can intrude on my books at any time. You are a welcome distraction. Any ... er ... friend = of Jonathan's is a friend of mine. You are a lovely girl and welcome here at any time, now the two of you be off and have fun.'

He lead the pair out the door to see them off, before handing over a one-pound bank note to Jonathan.

'Be *totally* irresponsible, won't you, both of you!' he said with a cheeky wink. Lizzie and Jonathan laughed as he took the money and waved goodnight, with the promise not to be too late back home. They hailed a cab and made their way to Whitechapel.

They arrived at the main street of Whitechapel at nine o'clock. Jonathan asked the driver to drop them off half a mile or so from the pub, so they could enjoy a short walk in the night air. They walked across the serene, cobbled road, to the rough, uneven pavement, savouring the coldness and the quiet, before the loud volume of the busy tavern later, and sharing each other's body heat as they walked side by side.

Five hundred yards ahead was The Red Lion, the watering hole that was the location for their first meeting as adults. It was frequented by all manner of customers, including prostitutes and their punters. A prostitute and friend of Mary-Ann and Lizzie was one of ladies there, this pub being one of her favourites. She called herself Daisy and was well versed in the ways of the street. This night, she was leaning against a wall that made up a dead-end alley that situated itself right beside the pub. A handy location to apply ones carnal trade, for well-experienced workers could ratchet up quite a tally of men and coin through sex or ripping off a drunkard.

Daisy was quite the pro, almost an entrepreneur of her trade, for she had many years of experience. Her favourite trick to weigh down her own purse would be to find a fine-looking gentleman, who appeared to have much wealth, as well as much fondness for the consumption of alcohol, to play her little sexual scam on. She would entice such a drunk, lonely man for his pleasure, always taking the money first, an easy feat when dealing with a drunkard who is so intoxicated he has no wherewithal as to even his own name, making standing still look like he was balancing on a log floating in water. In fact, the more inebriated and incapable the victim the better for her trick.

After taking payment, which would usually be more than the initial asking price, as the bladdered man would effortlessly empty his pockets and hand over all he had. She would pull him into her as she leaned against a wall. Then, with her dress and petticoat lifted, she would simply grab the man's piece and place it between her thighs, several inches away from her genitalia. The man would slide forward and back in a daze before cumming over her legs, not realising the difference at all.

Deceived Dick Daisy, her friends would call her whenever she told them that she pleased a man just with her trick of her thighs acting like a hole. She, to a certain point, liked her work, but if she could dodge some money without spreading her legs, parting her arse, or opening her mouth, she thought that was quite an achievement, and it would be seen as an accolade to the other street workers.

She also had the great advantage of her beauty and aesthetics, with her delicate blue eyes that looked so pure and sinless however the contrary lay behind them, with long flowing hair and lustful, erotic lips that puckered up thick and dense.

In the alley adjoining The Red Lion, she leaned against the wall, looking for a man of wealth, which unfortunately was not commonplace. An average of one in twenty did possess enough riches to grab her attention and make a possible client. After a couple of minutes, such a man walked past, wearing a top hat and black tails. He was no young stud, but his coin was as good as anybody's, if not even better.

She unhooked the top of her corset to catch his gaze and tempt his fascination.

'Evening, mister ... take your pleasure, sir,' she said as she lifted her dress to show no pantalettes and only stockings, so he could gawk at her intimate offerings.

The gentleman passerby stopped and looked her up and down.

'Oh, no thank you, miss, I have plenty of that at home,' he replied as he held up his wedding finger to show a golden band.

'Oh, go on, help a poor girl out, will ya? Shilling a suck?' she said to try and seduce him as she licked her pert upper lip and continued with, 'I can suck the Thames dry.' The man looked left and right and stepped closer to her as they took three paces in the dark alley. She sat him down on a wooden box to then unbutton his trousers. He handed over a shilling that glistened as it caught the gaslight from the street lamppost. She lowered herself to her knees and took his throbbing shaft in her mouth. He pulled her hair and held it tight in a makeshift ponytail to guide her head as it bobbed up and down fast and deep into his lap. The wet, slurping sound of saliva over flesh increased with slight gagging, as he pulsated and thrusted.

A final twitch came from his hips, accompanied with a satisfying grunt as he climaxed heavily, exploding with power in her mouth like the white froth of champaign spurting out of a shaken bottle. Smoothly lubricated with the aid of the combination of spit, pre-cum, and cum, which poured out and ran down her chin and dripped onto her showing cleavage, she raised her head and smiled as she took a deep breath of fresh air.

Just as he was buttoning himself up, Lizzie and Jonathan walked past the alleyway and caught sight of her.

'Daisy,' said Lizzie in a greeting tone.

'Ah, hello Lizzie love, just finishing up, will meet ya inside in a bit for a drink.' Lizzie, with a slightly awkward nod, agreed then continued walking just a few steps to enter the pub.

'Tip?' asked Daisy.

'Tip? cheeky cow, I paid what you asked.'

'Oh go on, mister, you must admit you liked it.'

The gentleman stood up and flicked her a penny.

'Wow ... a penny. I'll buy myself an oyster,' she said in a cutting tone.

'Will match the smell from between your legs,' he replied as he then walked off into the night to carry on with his journey.

She walked to the pavement and yelled to the back of him, 'Arrogant prick! And you're the size of a mouse. I feel for your wife!'

There was no response from him as he disappeared into the night. He became another punter that came and went and was just the latest member of her list.

Upon entering the pub, Lizzie saw Mary-Ann in the background sat on a sailor's lap. Mary-Ann looked up and saw her friend entering and gave a friendly nod. Lizzie and Jonathan found an intimate corner booth and sat down, still holding hands across the tabletop. It was clear Lizzie was well known in this watering hole, as the barmaid walked over.

'Evening, Lizzie, evening, handsome. What can I get ya?' she asked.

'An ale for me, a double gin and lime, and two cheese sandwiches please,' said Jonathan.

Just as the barmaid took the order and walked off, the empty space where she stood was filled instantly by Mary-Ann.

'Watcha, girl,' she said.

'Ah, Mary-Ann, have a seat.'

She looked over at Jonathan.

'Well, I was going to say who is this stranger, but I'm going to guess this is Jonathan?'

He stood up in politeness as she sat down and replied, 'Your guess would be right. How the devil are you? It's been a long time.' The three of them chatted away and felt comfort whilst sharing stories and reminiscing times past.

The barmaid returned with the drinks and sandwiches as Jonathan then paid and told her to keep the change, for he was nicely surprised at how low the price was.

Mary-Ann looked at the food as if she were a
child scrutinizing a toy shop window. Jonathan
beckoned over the barmaid and ordered food for
her.

'Ah, ain't you nice? He's a keeper, Lizzie,' she
said in a happy manner and continued with,
'Might take him for myself.' She gently shoulder-
barged her friend in a jocular fashion.

'Mind my asking, Mary, but how on earth did
you get your cut and bruising?' he questioned.

Mary-Ann answered in a very casual manner.
'Rough customer, let's say.'

'Really? A man did that to you?'

'Yeah, real bastard he was too. Luckily, your
Lizzie scared him off.'

Lizzie wanted to change the subject and asked
Mary-Ann how she was getting on with her sailor
chap.

'Ah, lost cause that one. He ain't got no money.
Smart guy, though. He can speak Mandarin.'

'Seems like he and I have something in
common,' replied Jonathan.

'Really? You can speak Mandarin?'

'No ... I had one for lunch today.'

Lizzie and Mary-Ann laughed and continued to
chat and giggle and enjoy each other's company.

After twenty minutes, Daisy walked in and
joined them and sat beside Jonathan. 'Evening,
girls ...and you, mister.'

Lizzie introduced her to Jonathan as the three
occupiers of the corner booth turned into four.

'Ah ... I need a strong drink,' said Daisy and continued with, 'Anything to wash my mouth out. I've taken three loads in the last half hour.'

Jonathan laughed and offered to buy her a drink. 'Double gin?'

'Triple, please.'

Mary-Ann leaned forward and said in a witty way, 'Thought I saw you earlier in the alley. Didn't recognise you at first with a face full of cock.'

The friendly banter encircled the group with laughter and jibes back and forth.

Much of the conversation that flowed from the mouths of Mary-Ann and Daisy mainly consisted of amusing sex stories of what they'd experienced over the last few days. The talk was varied and ranged from one extreme to another.

Mary-Ann laughed along with Daisy, but it was a little stilted. Deep down, she wanted out of the game, her heart and mind harbouring dreams of a husband and her own home one day and sharing her body with just one person and not hundreds. It had become almost a hobby of hers to indulge in her endless pursuit for such a man and being lead on with hope. Alas, so far, the hope stayed at just that, no matter how tenacious she was.

'I'll find my husband one day.'

'Claptrap, ya ain't gonna find a husband from a client, are ya? Men are strange folk with the attention span of children,' replied Daisy.

'Some of you ladies are an enigma too, you know,' said Jonathan.

Daisy leaned into him and said, 'Ah, I like that. Ain't ever been called that before, and I've been called everything under the sun. I likes how you talk. Lizzie, can I have him?'

Lizzie replied with a smile and just one word. 'No.'

The jubilant chat carried on with more drinks and time ticking.

For a moment, a troubling thought came to the forefront of Jonathan's mind. The rather unsettling thought that maybe once Lizzie had been a working girl. She knew some of the local prostitutes, and it wouldn't be totally in the realms of fantasy to assume that it could have been a possibility at one point in the past.

'Lizzie ... dear.'

'Yes, sweet?' she replied.

'Forgive my line of questioning, but I must ask ...were you ...well ... were you once ... um ... you know?'

With the atmosphere that embodied all present, she knew exactly what he meant. She decided to tease him a little and take pleasure in his edginess and coyness.

'Was I what, sweetheart?'

Jonathan tilted his head towards Mary-Ann and Daisy 'You know ...'

Lizzie laughed and could not torture him any longer.

'A lady of the night? A hole like these two unfortunates?' she said in a cheery way. He nodded. Wanting to tease him a little more, she said with a playful look, 'Would it matter if I was? Would your feelings suddenly drift away?'

'Well, no ... umm, yes ... no ... well, maybe ... probably not ... but still ...' he replied in a staggered way, making the sentence last several seconds longer that it needed.

She giggled in her mischievous way and said,

'Fear nothing, my dear. I just have friends in that trade, that are is all.'

He took a deep breath as the relief shot out of him.

Daisy looked over to him and said in a voice of tomfoolery, 'You look relieved. What's the matter? Don't like the thought of dozens of men filling her and covering her with creamy sex juice?'

He squinted at such a thought but also laughed, for Daisy was always one to talk freely with a talent of having any inhibition eradicated within a moment.

Momentarily, the smile from Mary-Ann's face turned to fright, as Scarface entered the pub.

'What is it?' asked Lizzie.

'It's him, the one from the other night,' she said in a scared tone.

Lizzie moved her hand over to her arm to try and comfort her a little. Scarface looked over and saw Mary-Ann sat at the table. He walked over towards her with a brash and cocky look on his twisted face. He approached the table and looked down at the four friends. Mary-Ann looked up, her heart beating hard, her bosom heaving up and down rapidly over the top of her bodice.

'Well, well, maybe I can buy you a drink? Or can you not sip it with that swollen lip?' he said while laughing in a horrible, bullying manner.

Daisy, who was always one full of confidence, at times her passion coming before her head, looked up and said, 'Get lost, or I'll give *you* a swollen lip!'

Scarface laughed again. 'Ah, the battered-faced whore has a friend, does she?'

Lizzie then stood up and faced him. Jonathan looked on with deep concentration, his reflexes and instincts on edge.

'You are deaf, aren't you? We said, get lost,' said Lizzie sternly.

With those words and an easy target in front of him, he grabbed her by the hair and pulled it back hard to force her head back, so hard, in fact, her body tripped off balance and was just being held up by his grasp.

The second he touched her hair, Jonathan stood up.

'I suggest you remove your hand. Do as the lady said and leave!'

Scarface let go of Lizzie, making her fall to the wooden floor.

'Who the fuck are you?' yelled Scarface.

'It matters not. Final warning. Leave now or else,' warned Jonathan.

Scarface paused as if time itself stood still, as he tilted his head and studied Jonathan's face.

After a few seconds of a stand-off, his brain filtering through a thousand images in his life, his face changed as he remembered that Jonathan was the same person he had grappled with eight years ago and the one who he held responsible for the huge scar on his face and the loss of his eye.

'You! he snarled.

'I do not know you, now leave!'

It was clear that Scarface seemed to remember Jonathan, but the resemblance was not reciprocated.

'It is because of you that I have this face!'

'No, it is not. You can blame your mother for that, and your father … if that is you know who he was,' replied Jonathan.

The three girls close by, along with a few other patrons that were in earshot, looked on and giggled as a small crowd gathered, forming a semi-circle.

Scarface became enraged, not only by the words, but more so because he felt belittled in front of others, and he certainly wasn't the type to just let it go. His evil face shrivelled up, with his stained teeth on full show, snarling like a lion.

Jonathan took a step closer and calmly said, 'You've been told many times to leave. What more do you need to hear?'

He could tell that words alone would not be enough to make him go. Out of the corner of his eye, he could see that Scarface was about to launch at attack in some way, the muscles tensing in his forearms and the veins protruding.

Scarface raised his arms and moved forward to grab him. Before his hands could grip Jonathan's shirt lapels, he instantly grabbed the beast's wrists

241

and stepped aside to pull them back behind him, using the man's power and momentum against him.

Scarface fell headfirst into the wall, cutting his forehead as it smashed against the plaster. Jonathan turned round at the same time as Scarface, who raised his fingers to his head and wiped off the blood that had started to seep and flow.

There was about five feet of empty space between them. Jonathan stood still and kept his sight forward. Scarface's demeanour resembled that of a wild bull. He yelled out a gritty scream, his black eyes and mouth opening wide, then ran towards Jonathan, who stood his ground as the threat lunged towards him. A second had passed when Scarface was two feet away, as he threw a punch and aimed the swing for Jonathan's face, who yanked his head back to avoid the contact, at the same time pushing away the man's large fist. An instant later, another swing came for his face, Jonathan managing to block it just in time.

He kept his calm, knowing that a relaxed body could react and move far quicker than a stiff, rigid, and angry one.

A third punch came as he side-stepped fast yet smoothly, almost like a dance or parrying away a sword blade, making the man's fist hit nothing but smoky air.

Scarface was clearly out-matched, even though he sustained a fuller muscular physique. He did not have the intelligence in foresight or spirit, but a strong arm that lacked speed and fluidity. He became evermore livid and aggressive, his own thug-like efforts coming to nothing by Jonathan out-witting him and out-manoeuvring him at every turn.

Another punch came for Jonathan's face, with a swing hard and powerful. He ducked, making Scarface's fist curl right over his head. Whilst ducking down, he punched him solid in his stomach, with a thud. He then followed with a single blow to the beast's face, which knocked him to the floor, forcing his eye patch to fly off into the air.

Jonathan stood over him and looked down to see if he had hod enough. After a few moments, he thought he had. He was not one for fighting and had no desire to inflict more pain and damage to Scarface, especially seeing that the intimidating threat was now gone. He would always fight for himself and his love but would only do so when absolutely necessary. Mr Huffham had taught him many skills regarding combat, but the most valuable and decent lesson was one of inner strength, the repeated words going through his head: 'Any savage can throw hard, but it's our wits that make us gentlemen.'

'Get up!' ordered Jonathan.

Scarface stood up and looked dishevelled with his spirit gone. Jonathan grabbed him tight by the scruff of his neck and marched him to the corner booth.

'I believe you owe these ladies an apology.'

Scarface twisted his body but could not escape the tight hold. 'Shove it up your arse!' he yelled.

Jonathan shook him forcefully, tightening his grip even harder, with a stern look in his eyes.

After a few seconds, Scarface relented and reluctantly apologised to Lizzie, Mary-Ann, and Daisy.

It was obvious that the admission of guilt and expression of regret was not wholly and truly meant, but it was satisfactory enough. Jonathan released his grip and pushed Scarface away, making him stumble back several feet.

The girl's faces all held the same smile, and they were about to thank and congratulate Jonathan as they were impressed to say the least. Jonathan smiled and felt relieved that the violent ordeal was over.

Just as he thought all was done, and as he was about to sit down, he heard the terrifying sound of glass being smashed and saw the girls' faces turn from smiles to dreaded shock. He turned around and saw Scarface walking at speed towards him with a broken bottle in his grasp. He looked down and saw the jagged edge of sharp glass pointing towards him in a fearsome and petrifying way.

As the broken bottle was raised up in order to be plunged into his neck, Jonathan moved quickly, stepping forward, and in a blink of an eye, he punched Scarface hard in the face. With a crackle sound ringing out and droplets of blood spurting from his cheek, the large man flew back six feet, falling like a dead weight to the pub floor.

Jonathan had hit him so hard, he'd made sure there would be no further brutal attack. He did not turn his back; instead, his eyes fixated on his fallen nemesis.

After ten seconds, Scarface came too but had nothing left to give. His fight had been dissipated in one huge blow. He slowly rose to his feet and bumbled out the door, with his tail between his legs and his barbaric ego in shreds.

Jonathan took a deep breath and returned to his table, with a pat on his back from an unknown onlooker and a round of applause from the crowd, which for them in relative safety looked at the last few minutes of events as captivating entertainment.

'I need a whiskey,' he said as he sat down beside Lizzie.

She wanted to be the first to buy him one, but she lacked the funds in order to do so. From what she lacked, she made up for ten-fold in attention and affection and was more than happy to hold is shaking hand and wipe off the claret-coloured gore from his knuckles.

Mary-Ann ordered a whiskey, demanding it come as soon as possible.

The barmaid approached the table and handed round four whiskeys and said, 'These are on the house. 'We've had trouble with Jack before, and I don't think we will again for a while. Thank you.'

Jonathan smiled but did not reply. He was content with Lizzie by his side and the aroma of strong grain and malted barley emanating from his short glass.

The barmaid continued with, 'We keep a fine establishment here and don't want the likes of him around. I like to have gentlemen to serve, and I always give utter respect to my patrons.'

Just as she finished talking, a voice came from the distance. 'Same again when you're ready, miss, please.'

'All right! I've only got one pair of bloody hands, wait a sodding minute!' she yelled back.

Jonathan laughed at her unintentional comedic timing as the barmaid walked off to carry on with her duties.

After a few moments and the dust and drama had settled, Daisy said, 'Wow, you were amazing just now. Bet you weren't even scared.'

'Of course I was scared. Only a brute with no soul wouldn't be scared,' he replied. The merriment and chat carried on with the four of them, as if nothing had happened. Lizzie looked at the clock and wanted to leave as it was getting late.

They finished their drinks and said goodnight to Mary-Ann and Daisy. A hug and a kiss on the cheek was had by all. They left the pub with the intention of Jonathan walking Lizzie home, to then hail a cab for himself to return to his home. They stood outside the pub, just as Jonathan was putting his coat and hat on.

'I'm so sorry,' she said.

'Sorry for what?'

'The company. I had hoped we would be alone, and I'm sorry for Daisy's candid words.'

'No need for that, Lizzie. Her vocabulary is wondrously vulgar and did not bother me one bit. But I am glad it does not frequent my ears too often.'

They walked side by side along the short distance to her flat, with Jonathan walking on the roadside of the pavement. Lizzie held on to his arm, and she felt her usual happy self because she was with him. Little did they know, they were being followed.

They arrived at her flat and held each other tight and kissed passionately in the dark air.

'Thank you for seeing me home safe, my dear,' she said.

'Not at all'

I'm very proud of you. You know that, don't you?' she said with a heartfelt smile.

He smiled in response.

'I'm already looking forward to seeing you again. You're all I think about these days,' she said excitedly.

'And I you. You're never getting rid of me,' he replied with a happy expression.

They kissed again, the feeling of electricity flowing through her body, from her head, right down to her soles, tingling her nerve endings with euphoria.

Lizzie entered her flat as Jonathan whistled for a cab. Within just a few seconds, the horse drawn hansom cab pulled up. He pulled himself up onto the low-slung bodywork that sat next to the two large wooden spoked wheels and sat on the seat, with the request to return him to Westminster.

Trotting along behind him was another cab, virtually identical to his, as they all were. Thirty minutes later, Jonathan's cab pulled up outside Mr Huffham's house, the pursuing cab pulling up a short distance behind.

He left the cab and entered his home, closing the door slowly so as not to awaken Sally or his master, after paying three shillings for the journey. Ten pence more than normal due to the hour being as late as what it was.

One dark eye next to an empty eye socket approached from the darkness of the stationary second cab and looked upon the address of the current location. An evil laugh roared out, and then the gravelly voice ordered the driver to return him to Whitechapel.

Chapter 20

The following fresh morning had arrived, Jonathan waking up somewhat later than normal. He bolted upright from the mattress, sensing that something was quite irregular. His eyes squinted, and he touched his temples, rubbing them slowly as he felt the inevitable aftereffects of a little too much drink from the night before, thinking to himself, *Maybe gin, whisky, and ale don't mix so well.*

After a few minutes of trying to wish away the inner thunder and booming resembling a loud storm that beat inside his skull, and failing to do so, he looked up and saw the clock, which showed he had overslept by almost a whole hour.

He threw his clothes on and rushed downstairs. Sally greeted him and offered him some breakfast, with the friendly recommendation that it be suitably light, seeing as the hour was late, with the added offer of a cold flannel to help with his evident headache.

It was a peculiar situation, the fault falling entirely at Jonathan, but at the same time, Sally did hold at least some responsibility in the general mechanism of the household. It was not her duty to wake up either of her masters, but being aware of the comings and goings and routine was one of her many and varied responsibilities. He did not cast blame on her for his oversleeping, but was confused as to her casual manner.

There was no time to talk about how and why he had not woken at the typical hour, as no usual and comforting routine of morning banter flowed between them. A smile and wave was all that could be shared between him and Sally. He briskly left the house and walked to work in record time, turning a twenty-minute walk into ten.

This urgent and hurried act was quite rare, for a gentleman seldom rushes. Mr Huffham, being a wise man, one to emulate and admire, was a fine example of this calmness and elegance, with style and dignity. Jonathan was torn between two dilemmas, both of which were only a dream to most other men, but a dilemma nonetheless. His class was above the majority, but he was respectful and looked up to Mr Huffham, for he owed almost everything to him. This respect made it all the harder when he ran into work with the thought that he had disappointed his boss.

Mr Huffham was very firm and strict. This was not an opinion, or a boast and nor was it a belief, but shear fact. However, due to his character, he was also very fair. Jonathan knew that his primary action was to knock on his office door and explain why he was so late. Being a young man of principle, which was another lesson in life that had been taught to him, he chose to face whatever Mr Huffham had to say.

'Morning … or is it afternoon?' said Koots as he greeted him.

'Yeah, yeah, I know,' Jonathan replied as he walked past to present himself at the office. He knocked hesitantly on the frosted glass panel on the door and opened it after hearing a raised voice from the other side.

'Morning, sir. I know I am late, and I carry my sincere apologies and regret. I'll work extra hours for free and do anything you command to make up for it.'

Being a person of intelligence and understanding, Mr Huffham did not yell, scream, rant, or lose his temper without sufficient cause. Such undignified actions were not befitting a man of his calibre, without firstly listening to reason.

He looked down and noticed the marking on Jonathan's knuckles. He knew him better than most and so far had not needed to worry about him acting out of sorts. He did however want to learn about how and why such markings had come about.

'Seeing as your knuckles are marked but your face is not, I gather the other chap came off worse?' he said.

'Yes, sir.'

'Need I say, you are aware that you represent me and this establishment when you are in public?'

'Yes, of course, sir. Last night, or on any night, I did not dishonour you.'

Jonathan told him about the incident previous night. Mr Huffham sat back and listened . When hearing the events that took place, his facial expression was indifferent and plain. However, when the explanation was over, he stood up from his wooden, curved swivel chair and smiled, his face beaming with emotions of pride.

'Wonderful … just wonderful,' he said in a joyous tone.

Jonathan was very pleasantly surprised, as those words that fell before him were not ones he had expected, quite on the contrary in fact.

One of Mr Huffham's fortes in life was to experience and rejoice in other stories of good battling evil, with the good being victorious. It did not matter if it was from something grand like the colossal battle of Waterloo in 1815, where Napoleon was defeated, or King Leonidas and the great three hundred holding back the million strong Persians, to a common bar room brawl, for the principle was the same. He never grew tired of knowing, reading, and hearing about whenever evil and wrongdoing were defeated in conflict. The idea of justice and morality being one of his many key ethics in life. He was content that Jonathan fought because he loved what was behind as opposed to hating what was in front.

He had every reason to believe Jonathan. He knew he was numerous things, and his imperfections were many, such is mankind, but a liar was not one of his traits.

Coupled with the understanding that Jonathan was, by his own account, rather scared and needed the whisky to help dissipate his fear, not to mention that is heart had apparently been taken over with little resistance by Lizzie.

He opened his office door and walked onto the shop floor, with Jonathan in tow.

'Even though this is the second time your presence has been late, in just a few days, your record of eight years still stands with distinction and merit, and one which is rather exemplary.'

'Thank you, sir. I will make up the hour.'

'Fair enough. I don't think I need to throw you out my house and place of business quite yet,' Mr Huffham joked and continued with, 'We'll hear no more about it.'

'Many thanks indeed.'

'Tell me … you love this, Lizzie don't you?'

'Yes … I think so, sir.'

'I have seen the smartest of people doing the stupidest things chasing love, but you, my boy, are not one of them, for I believe love has chased you just as much. Your devotion for Lizzie is granted by me, for she is a truly splendid girl, and I hope you have a love which shall last forever more.'

Jonathan smiled and hugged him tight. Mr Huffham placed his hands on his shoulders as they stood face to face.

'There is one thing, just one thing, that is truly important in this world, the secret of life, which is to love and to be loved.'

The atmosphere was radiant in its profundity when the wise words left his mouth.

Just then, the voice of Koots bellowed out, 'That's two things!'

Huffham replied, 'Stanley! My office at once!'

Jonathan laughed and went on with his work in the shop.

Koots walked from the workshop, onto the shop floor, and made his way to the head office.

'Yes, sir, sorry, sir,' he said, with his head drooping down like a child who knew he was about to be told off.

Twenty minutes later, Koots returned to join him in the workshop.

'So what did he say to you?' asked Jonathan.

'Ah., the usual. Think before I speak and all that.'

'You're lucky he holds you in such high regard. Don't push him too far.'

'I know, I don't mean to, just comes out is all.'

The two friends continued to work and enjoy each other's conversation, as they did almost every day.

They were working together on this particular day, accumulating their talents and both their efforts on a cash box for a very deluxe ladies dress shop that was only a stone's throw from their shop. Jonathan was working on the lock, whilst Koots was filing down some metalwork for the lid hinges. Koots carried on the conversation with a question.

'So … this Lizzie?'

"Yes?'

'So … have you porked her yet?'

'Koots, do you really think I'm going to answer that?'

Koots' head inched back in confusion.

'Why not? You usually do.'

His confusion was justified to some extent, as over the last few years, an average of twenty per cent of their chats had involved the candid topic of women and sex.

'Lizzie and the feelings I have for her are different to previous lusts.'

'Why? How is it so different? She got three heads and a wooden leg or something?'

'One day, if you're lucky enough, you'll understand,' said Jonathan, and after a cheeky smile that he could not shake off, he continued with, 'Yes, course I have, now let's get back to work.'

Koots laughed and said, 'Ah ha … see, I knew it, well done.'

'How did you know it?'

'Because if you hadn't have bedded her, you would have looked sulky, instead of smiling, and you would have tried to change the subject to pratt on about the weather or something.'

'True enough,' said Jonathan.

The two carried on talking, laughing, and working hard as the day moved on.

Chapter 21

The night came upon Whitechapel with a cold stillness in the air. A light dusting of snow began to fall with the flakes falling from the heavens like confetti. Lizzie and Jonathan were revelling in each other's company with an evening stroll. Lizzie loved the snow and would hold out the palm of her hand to see each snowflake gently flutter down and land on her pale skin.

Unfortunately, with the dampness on the cobbles and walls of brick and stone, it could not settle, but it made the air prettier than normal, nonetheless.

Meanwhile, just half a mile away, Mary-Ann was on the streets, woefully not doing the same as her friend Lizzie, and not side by side with a love, but touting for business. It had been a slow night. The men just wanting to drink in the pubs or were not feeling the urge at all for the company of a woman with it being so cold out.

She must have said, 'For your pleasure, sir?' at least two dozen times, with only one taker, that one only wanting hand relief at that, with the sum total of five-pence being her evening's profits.

Without being able to afford a gin, she decided to call it a night and chose to swap the coldness of the outside for her bed.

She stood at the entrance to Buck's Row, wanting to use the short-cut to get home as fast as possible. She paused for a moment, considering the harsh memory from a few days prior. As one back alley was more or less the same as any other, she quickly shrugged off her concerns and made her way through the infamous Row.

She walked down the narrow alley that presented some protection from the cold wind, its walls and archways making natural barriers. It was surprisingly quiet. The only sound that was present were her footsteps that tapped along and the odd drop of water that dripped off glowing gaslights.

These gaslights that reached out from the walls were scattered sporadically, with the odd yellowy glow flickering down. It was as if God himself was flicking a light switch on and off again as she took her paces forward.

She took a right by one of the curving arches, when suddenly she was grabbed and thrown into the dark and onto a wall. After half a second, she look around and saw nothing; it was like a ghost had just shot out of nowhere. She looked in front of her, facing the other wall, but saw only darkness. She reached forward into the pitch black and felt nothing but air.

Her fingertips stretched out another inch when she felt a stubbly face on rough skin. She gasped as the dark outline of Scarface slowly showed itself directly in front of her. She went to run, but his hand gripped her arm in a vice-like tight hold, forcing her back to the wall.

'Mary-Ann Nichols … I told you I'd be back,' he said in a cruel and gravelly voice. Her mouth opened wide to scream, but his hand smothered her a split second later. Her cries turned into a quiet but continuous hum as the sound hit nothing but his hand, which gripped so hard it made her jawbone ache, and brought the feeling of her teeth being squeezed from her gums.

Her eyes widened upon seeing a glistening silver knife in his other hand. He held it up high, hoovering above her in order to prolong her freight. It did the job, as her twitching and writhing became more desperate and a single tear seeped from her eye. An instant later, he slashed down at her neck with the edge of the blade running across her gullet and sinking into her flesh. The warm blood sprayed out as her muffled screams ceased.

She fell to the ground, landing hard on the stone. He knelt down beside her and looked upon her body. He smiled when he noticed she was still alive. He stabbed the side of her breast, plunging the knife in deep. Part of his blade was still showing when he then pushed further in, right up to the handle, only to then twist it as he felt the metal churn up her insides. He then moved his position and straddled her.

He pulled out his knife and licked the blade in a ravenous and psychotic motion, to then thrust it in hard with full force into her abdomen, using her bellybutton as the central target. She let out a final gasp as her body arched with the impact, before her head tilted back at an awkward angle as she let go of the fight for life.

Keeping the knife in her belly, he proceeded to force it upward like a butcher gutting a carcass. It was hard work, but with his sawing motion, the blade managed to cut from stomach to chest with his savage slicing.

From the waist up, her entire torso was covered with her thick blood, with white bone showing through. He raised his bloodstained knife to then launch it into her slender neck. He hacked away at her throat so hard it almost severed her head. He wiped his knife on her hair to then place it back in his waistband.

The gruesome attack was not over. His twisted mind had not yet had its fill, as he then placed his hands inside her to open her rip cage, pulling apart and snapping the occasional bone as he did. His touch felt the squash of her stomach and liver as his hands delved in. He rummaged around her vital organs to proceed to pull out her kidneys, placing them neatly beside her corpse. The entire heinous act took several minutes, but his fun had to conclude when from somewhere in the distance he heard a noise. He stood up and looked at his achievement, to then dash off back into the dark night, turning himself into a shadow once again to flee as fast as he could.

Her tortured and mutilated body lay totally still as the blood flowed from her. The amount of blood was so great, it spilled over the stone and formed red lines in between the square cobbles. What surrounded her corpse was a chequered ground of miniature streams, in a maze-like formation of blood, pieces of flesh combined with small shards of bone scattered left, right, and centre, the dark red making its way as it flowed into the natural contours of the stony floor.

For the moment, no help came, and if it had, it would have been too late anyhow, much too late, a lost cause. Her motionless body was alone, only the bitter night and the drips of water for company.

Half an hour later, whilst Lizzie and Jonathan were still enjoying their nighttime walk, they heard a high-pitched ringing in the distance. As they kept moving forward, they were swiftly overtaken by a police constable, running past with a whistle in his mouth. The whistle rang through the air at an almost deafening rate as he passed them. The whistle seemed to match another whistle, which came from ahead. It was if it was a reply or some sort of response, like birds chirping to each other, although these sounds carried more urgency than our feathered friends.

They followed the policeman to see what he was running towards. As they travelled closer to the source of the noise, they heard other whistles coming from East to West. They approached the pub and saw three other policemen running down Buck's Row. They passed the pub and made their way in the same direction.

When they were just fifty yards down the narrow alleyway, they saw a small group of people and a couple of policemen huddled round something. They could not tell what it was as the view they had was only of the back of the group that stood in front of them. They stepped closer and saw a pair of legs, dressed with black stockings and black heeled, laced boots. They got closer still and saw the mangled torso of a young lady in a dark blue dress.

Jonathan was keen for Lizzie to turn away, for such a sight would easily stay in the mind longer than one would choose. They were about to turn their gaze away from such the dreadful sight when Lizzie focused on the detail of the face. They both filtered themselves through the crowd and saw the whole nightmare. It was like a hammer blow to her senses when she realised it was her close friend, Mary-Ann.

Her face turned to dread as she yelled, 'Mary!' to then rush forward, only to be held back by one of the policemen.

Jonathan was by her side as they both grappled with two of the officers.

'Constable! I know this girl!' cried Lizzie.

'I do not care, madam. Now get back, will you!' He ordered, whilst manhandling her.

Jonathan stepped forward. 'Show some heart, will you! They were dear friends'.

The policeman grunted and, with much reluctance, twitched his head in order to allow them through the human barricade. The body was only a couple feet away when Lizzie fell to her knees, tears rolling down her face.

Jonathan knelt down beside her, his knees dropping into the pool of blood. He placed his arm round Lizzie's shoulders to offer any modicum of support. He did not say anything, for no words could help. She leaned into his chest as they both felt the shock.

The magnitude of the horrid revelation was palpable, not just due to the sight of a deceased loved one, but also how horrendous the scene was. It was as if a wild animal had feasted on its prey; a hyena or a piranha leaving an open, bloody, and torn carcass. It was such a spectacle, even one of the experienced officers of the law had to hold back his vomit, that naturally tried to regurgitate upward from the pits of his guts.

'All right, that's enough, now hop it!' commanded another constable.

Jonathan looked up and saw two constables reaching out in order to forcefully drag them away from the scene.

'Come on,' he said softly and calmly to Lizzie.

He helped her up to her feet before the police could do it. She stood up as her tears rolled down.

'No ... no!' she cried as she fell into his arms.

One of the constables, who seemed a little more short-tempered than the others, guided them back towards the crowd, which by this time had doubled in size. 'Come on, sweetheart,' said Jonathan tenderly.

They did not stay with the nosy onlookers. She leaned into his arms and clutched him tight and close, as if she would not even have the ability to walk without him. He held her as they both slowly walked away.

Chapter 22

The next day came, but did not feel like a new dawn, as Jonathan and Lizzie had been awake all night. They could not close their eyes, even for a moment's sleep. They both lay on his bed with heavy hearts. Lizzie's eyes were dry as she had been crying for many hours, and she had no more tears to shed. An aimless, hollow look cast from her face and did not seem to wane.

It was approaching seven in the morning when she slid off the bed to make her way to Whitechapel for her work. Most bosses, even the hardest ones, would allow at least a single day off for a worker experiencing such a great personal loss, but Mr Fenchurch was not set that way. In his mind, that was not enough reason for a staff member to take the day off, especially with the victim not being a family member and a prostitute at that.

Jonathan, realising the situation as it was, did not fight for her to stay, as he knew what the unfortunate answer would be. He did, however, offer to walk with her, part of the journey to the locksmith shop, so he could then pay for a cab to take Lizzie back to Whitechapel.

They both walked from Mr Huffham's house to Westminster centre so he could go to work and for Lizzie to do likewise.

'Are you absolutely certain I can't help? I can talk to your boss and explain. He needs to give you some time to grieve,' he said.

'Thank you so much, but it would do more harm than good,' came her response.

Lizzie needing her job as well as her flat, unfortunately there was nothing that could be done.

With some reluctance, Jonathan agreed that she must go to work. He felt that with his standing and influence he could persuade Mr Fenchurch to be more tolerant, whether it be a strong word, a favour to be owed, or even an offer to pay for a day's wage, but, if any negative repercussions were to emerge from his actions, they would only fall upon Lizzie, and that was a risk he would not take.

They shared a brief moment of loving cordiality as they kissed outside his workplace. Just as their lips parted, the moment of solace was shattered when a paperboy, standing no taller than four feet and dressed in grey from head to knee, with long black socks and a grey flat cap, marched down the centre of the road. Doing nothing more than his job and not knowing his words would add sorrow to an already sorrowful heart, he yelled his business. 'Extra! Extra! Read all about it! Prostitute slain! Extra! Buck's Row murder, another woman butchered!'

An innocent voice that belonged to a young, innocent soul, but the words bellowed out for all to hear, carrying heartfelt foreboding, trepidation, and sadness for some.

They heard the paperboy yell his latest news, as each word felt like a stab to the stomach. Luckily, only a minute had passed when Jonathan managed to hail a cab. He kissed her a goodbye, both of them swearing they'd be together again later that evening. She journeyed off into the distance as he waved then entered his shop.

Meanwhile, in Whitechapel police station, Mr Dallyard, who carried the high position of Police Chief and held his occupation with much pride, made it his priority to catch the culprit of the latest killings. However, Mr Dallyard was not all he appeared to be. He also had a temper that was much on the short side. He was a large man, with shoulders as broad as an ox, and carried a large brown and grey moustache that would twitch and flare whenever he lost his temper. Trying to find the killer was not an easy task. At least half his staff didn't consider the taking of life serious enough when concerning prostitutes. His staff followed their orders, but with minimal effort regarding such crimes, with some even laying the blame on the victims for allowing themselves to be in harm's way in the first place.

'Comes with the trade, don't it?"

'What did she expect?'

'Was probably asking for it.'

'That's what a whore gets.'

These were the words and feelings that floated round the station ceaselessly, morning, noon, and night.

Mr Dallyard sat at his desk in his very own office, bickering and quibbling with one of his sergeants. The smell of fresh teak wax filled the room, as every piece of wooden furniture was habitually polished and cleaned.

'We will find this villain if it's the last thing I do!' he yelled as he found it hard to encourage his sergeants and officers to reflect his urgency, and continued with, 'What have you got for me so far?'

'Nothing, sir, it's only been one night, and tis just a whore,' replied the sergeant. 'There have been many a killing in these parts! This Mary Ann case is just the latest!'

The sergeants and officers knew Mr Dallyard very well and were well aware that all he cared about was the number of convictions he could achieve, not always convicting with hard evidence. All he cared about was position, and was never satisfied with his current status, always looking for more. All that took place in his head was promotion and all the delights it carried, money and greed being the primary objective. Even being able to call himself 'Chief' did not quell his appetite for the pursuit of power and wealth.

He did however do his job to some extent, and, possessing more tenacity than most officers in the station and district, some justice was achieved. His intentions were maybe less genuine than what he would pretend to hold, but such was the way of some bobbies whilst policing in Whitechapel.

With the exception of The Bow Street Runners' in the mid-eighteenth century, the police force was relatively in its infancy, as Mr Dallyard's great cousin, Sir Robert Peel, had founded the force only fifty years prior. Sir Peel had honourable intentions with his creation and his staff and would pay a healthy wage of one pound a week to not tempt bribery of any kind. His police officers would be untouchable, or so he thought. Mr Dallyard still found great family pride that his officer's nicknames of 'Bobbies' were after his late cousin, but the temptation of coin often became a more attractive weight than a clear conscience. The police had a backlog of crime files and would more often than not play by their owns rules when they could. A pay-off, a back-hander, a nod, and a wink would sometimes be enough to turn the odd blind eye, or to beat someone within an inch of their life if they felt were deserving enough.

The uniform was a dark blue tunic with gleaming round buttons and dark trousers, with hat and cape, and the equipment had not greatly changed since the creation of the Metropolitan police, but attitudes with some regrettably had. The original noble goals were carried by some, with crime in various aspects lowering as time went on. But the bad apples were not few and far between, as the tree and vines spread distant as some districts were sounder than others.

Mr Dallyard's pursuit of the killer was not with the aim of making the streets a safer place to be, nor was it to help the ladies of the night, or any other unfortunate soul that would cross paths with the Grim Reaper. It was to impress his superiors and better himself.

It wasn't so much bent coppers, but more, the thin blue line was a little elasticated at times with its flexibility in the difference between justice and street justice. However, whether it be reasons right and wholesome, or wrong and conniving, Mr Dallyard wanted the killer found as soon as possible.

'I want results, damn it! There are too many killings here, and this last dead woman is the thin end of the wedge!'

'Give it time, sir. We'll catch him,' replied the sergeant.

'I don't have time, you moron. If my boss isn't happy, than I'm not either. Shit rolls downhill, do I make myself clear!'

'Yes, sir.'

Just then, his office door was banged twice. 'What?' he snapped.

A young and nervous constable entered the office, holding a piece of folded paper in his thin, shaking hand.

'We … we have another one, sir,' he gingerly said as he handed over the paper over to his chief.

He snatched the paper and open it up to read aloud the note to his sergeant, who was second in command. Mr Dallyard's eyes dilated with shock as cast his gaze on the writing.

Dear boss, your police officers have not caught me yet. I shall keep on ripping whores till I get bucked.

I want to get to work right away. The last job was a grand one.

It took me a long time to do. My knives are nice and sharp.

You will soon hear of my funny little games. Yours truly,

Jack The Ripper.

Mr Dallyard read the dreaded words that warned and taunted him, for this was not the first letter of its kind. This only enraged him further, for he felt that the killer was having much amusement in his writings.

'Do these words stem from the same hand as the others? Have you compared the handwriting?' he asked.

The sergeant looked upon the writing, and at first glance it did appear to be from the same hand. By this stage, they had four letters in as many weeks, so he had become familiar with not only the handwriting, but with also with how the sender wrote and formed words.

'I will not kow-tow to this … this man … this Jack, with his taunts! He is making a mockery! A notion that will not succeed while I am in charge!' He angrily expressed as his moustache twitched.

The young constable looked his boss in the eye and said, 'Tis just a whore, sir. Wanton violence is part of their way of life, especially round 'ere.'

'I realise that, but don't you see that this murder will startle the streets? It was more brutal than the previous ones.'

'The culprit could be any man when dealing with vice, the list is endless sir,' the sergeant replied.

'Make your enquires to every surgeon and butcher within a ten-mile radius. I feel that the killer has some sort of extra skill with knives,' Mr Dallyard ordered.

'Don't mean to question your brilliance, sir, but that isn't necessarily the case. The poor girl was torn to pieces, and almost any man with time on his hands could do the same.'

'I have had my fill of arguing with you today, Sergeant! Do as I say!'

The sergeant nodded and left the office, along with the young constable. Mr Dallyard leaned back in his chair, contemplating his next move. His tunnel vision and stubbornness often got the better of him when his temper was not as it should have been, especially for a man with such responsibility.

He turned round in his smooth, wooden swivel chair and faced the back wall to his office. The wall did not show plain plaster or an oil painted portrait of Sir Peel or Queen Victoria. Taped to the wall was a large map of Whitechapel. Black and white blocks and lines spread over to cover every square foot of roads, streets, side streets, alleys, back alleys, houses, factories, shops, yards, and green spaces. The map was almost the same size as the wall, with only a couple of inches in between the paper and the floor.

He studied the map and compared charts, surveying them carefully over and over again to try to learn how the killer could apply his disgusting work so freely. If any possible escape routes were obvious, he hoped that something, anything, would leap out from paper to brain.

In previous cases, if the victim list was greater than four, the police would always look for the central position of the collective crimes for a clue to the location of the perpetrator. With this case, there appeared to be no rhyme or reason, no pattern or system to the killings, and at first glance they looked random. Yet he knew there must be some framework and method involved somehow, for nothing is truly random. He was an avid believer in the chaos theory with the apparent predictably of random events.

Most of his staff thought it was nothing more than a quack hypothesis, a pseudo-science that only failed mathematicians and alienists indulged themselves in.

The largest burden and complication was the amount of killing that took place. Only a mathematician could accurately answer how many possibilities there could be. Does ten killings mean ten separate killers? Or were there two killers with five killings each? Or one killer being responsible for all ten?

Even though the manner of brutality with Mary-Ann was different, vastly contrasting other slaughters, Mr Dallyard was not naive enough to jump to the conclusion that it must be separate to the rest.

He went over the hard facts he had at hand, as he had done many times.

This so-called 'Jack the Ripper' was a madman, was literate, had a dislike for prostitutes or women in general, held at least a basic awareness of knives and anatomy, knew the area, and was organised. Those were six known facts, but in reality, it just heightened the gospel truth with added certainty that the task at hand was grinding and strenuous. Those combined facts covered at least a quarter of the male population, which in turn would mean the culprit was around one in five thousand, and that was just for the local area.

Mr Dallyard was desperate for a conviction, for he had pressure thrusted upon his shoulders from his superiors, which were powerful and held little time for a chief who couldn't deliver what they ordered. Also, with high profile and the attention the case had accumulated in the newspapers, there was always the possibility of some maniac wanting to re-enact such dreadful deeds with copycat killings for their five minutes of fame.

After almost an hour of tranquil quiet, with just himself and his thoughts, he heard three knocks at his office door.

'Come.'

The door squeaked open, and in came the sergeant.

'Yes, what is it?' Mr Dallyard asked.

'Sorry to bother you, sir, but there is a man at the front desk who insists on seeing you.'

'Oh ... not now, Sergeant. I do not have the time. Send him away or deal with it yourself.'

He looked at his sergeant with a stern and bitter look as his moustache twitched yet again.

The sergeant continued with, 'But he says he has information regarding the Ripper case, sir.'

His expression changed in a heartbeat, with a sudden look of interest covering his face. He gestured with his fingers, accompanied with a nod to allow him in. The sergeant left the office, leaving the door open as he did.

Whilst waiting for the sergeant to return with the man at the front desk, he looked down at some paperwork spread across his desk. The silence in the air was evident and distinct as he was so entrenched in the details of the manuscripts, only the gentle sound of the quiet ticking clock was heard.

After two minutes, the silence was stopped in its tracks when he heard a rough voice say, 'I witnessed the murder. I know who Jack the Ripper is, and what's more, I know where he lives.'

He looked up, as Scarface stood directly in front of him, with a devilish and smarmy smile on his face.

For that moment, nothing else mattered, and all his attention suddenly focused on this new source of information, so much so that even the sound of the tick-tock seemed to silence itself as if time had stopped. Mr Dallyard's tunnel vision became evermore narrow with every millisecond that passed.

Chapter 23

Later that evening, Jonathan and Mr Huffham were at home, sitting down in the parlour room enjoying the tranquil feeling of allowing their dinner to go down and settle, with the aid of a scotch and brandy and a thin cigar and pipe. Once again, Jonathan's latest and most favourable subject was of Lizzie. His conversation consisted of the time, location, and activities he had planned for their next rendezvous, which was to take place in just a couple of hours. Mr Huffham sat back and held a more than willing ear, with the added advice or opinion when asked.

The flames from the large open fire cracked and spurted as they weaved upwards in a smooth and natural motion. Sally entered with four freshly cut logs for extra fuel. She knelt down by the stone hearth and placed the logs deep into the fire to help the cosy home feel that little bit more sultry and snug.

'Sit down, girl, and rest for a minute. I shall make you a cup of tea,' said Mr Huffham.

'Do you know where the tea caddy is in the kitchen?' asked Jonathan with a smile. 'I'm sure one could find it,' he replied.

Sally giggled and thanked Mr Huffham for the kind suggestion, with the pledge that she would take up the generous offer when her next job had been completed.

Her loyalty and faithfulness to her obligation and duty was tangible. Her undertakings were many but were also civil and amenable to a certain extent, with her breaks being up to her as to when she would take them.

Every single one of her friends who were in service for other households had a far stricter timetable to keep to, with breaks and rest periods being short and few, hence, one of the many reasons she was so happy to be where she was.

Everyone in Mr Huffham's house, including himself, adored the status quo, and all knew they had duties and would not want to swap for another role. It was a well-oiled machine that smoothly ebbed and flowed like a penny farthing rolling downhill.

She would feel great loss and much unhappiness without her boss, as the case would stand the same if the vice-versa came to him or Jonathan.

'Your next job can wait. I am still lord and master in my own home, and you will sit down and get warm,' said Mr Huffham in a nice and friendly way and continued with, 'Jonathan, go into the kitchen and make Sally a cup of tea please.'

Jonathan placed his half full crystal cut glass down, along with his short cigar, balancing it on the edge of the ashtray, and made his way to the kitchen, with a silent laugh flowing from his mouth at the correct prediction in his head at his boss' words.

Mr Huffham offered Sally a seat close to the fire and told her to relax. She took the offer with glee and made herself comfortable.

She looked across at his latest book that sat on a small side table beside his chair, and judging by where the bookmark was placed, it appeared he was about two thirds through.

'What book are you reading now, sir?' she asked inquisitively.

'Napoleon Bonaparte's War Diaries. Man was a tyrant, of course, but also a genius,' he replied and continued with, 'Of course, he should have been called Napoleon Blownapart when you think about it,' he said with a large grin.

She giggled and agreed then very nervously asked to borrow the book when he had finished with it. He noticed her anxiety and squashed it at once with his kind voice, saying, 'Of course, of course you can, my dear. You may take it when you like, for I'm on my second read of it.'

'Thank you, sir.'

Her question would not have come from her lips on her first arrival to his household many years ago. In most large houses, no staff member would dare ask such a thing, especially early on in a professional relationship, besides, back then she had been illiterate, her reading skills barely surpassing the sounds of the alphabet.

It was just another of life's problems that he had remedied through the affection he held for her. Reading was one of the very first things he'd taught her. It took up much of his time and it was something the vast majority of masters would not do.

One intention and hopeful result of his teachings were that one day in the future she would play the part of nanny and nurse his children. Alas, so far, that was not to be needed, with some regret.

His heart filled with joy that Sally asked to borrow the book. He would always say 'Yes' to a request of that sort and had said before that his impressive book collection was always available to her whenever she pleased.

'Sir?'

'Yes, Sally?'

'As we're sat down, I have a question that I've been curious about now for a couple of years, but I fear it may result in a tempered reply,' she said with a scattered hesitation to her tone.

'Ask away and fear naught,' he reassuringly replied.

Sally sat upright and prepared herself for her rather personal question to land on his ears. 'Well ... I hope I do not offend by asking ... I'm just curious. How is it that a man such as you has not taken a wife? I can think of a dozen women who would gladly be by your side.'

He did not reply straight away. Instead, he scratched his cheek and stood up to pour himself another brandy. She quickly stood up to pour it for him but was guided back to her seat with the order to stay in her comfortable position.

'There was one lady once, but it was not meant to be. The good Lord decided to take her somewhat early, an act I disagreed with, you could say, as at the time I would fall to my knees to argue with him and offer to swap places. Rather foolish, of course, for it was too late,' he said with a downcast manner.

'No, sir, it was not foolish at all. Did you love her?' she asked courteously.

Mr Huffham's eyes began to show a shiny glaze and did not answer. No verbal answer was needed, for his face said it all. He sniffed and veered off the current line of questioning.

'I have you. Almost everything I need is in yourself'.

She smiled deeply.

After a minute, he changed the feeling in the atmosphere with a slightly raised voice and a command for Jonathan to hurry up from the kitchen.

'The kettle is boiling as we speak, give it a minute,' Jonathan replied from the distance, to then mutter quietly to amuse himself, 'You've lived in this house over twenty years and still don't know where the tea is kept!'

Just then, a somewhat loud noise of horses hooves resonated from outside. It was not the common sound of a cab, but dozens of them in a beating rhythm.

BANG! BANG! BANG! went the front door, instead of the gentle ring from the bellpull. Just two seconds later, the hurried bangs came again in trilogy and carried even more franticness then before. The result was so that the wooden door vibrated and shuttered with the impact, almost hard enough to shake any woodworm from its hole.

Sally stood up and made her way to answer the impertinent banging. She was but a few feet away when the door was suddenly and violently smashed open, forcing the door to swing rapidly as far as it would go. Large splitters flew from parts of the door frame in all directions. She gasped and stopped dead in her tracks with the frightful shock.

A group of around ten uniformed constables, in their bell-shaped helmets and short capes, barged in and scattered themselves in the hallways, with two running upstairs and another two running straight through to the back kitchen. Mr Huffham stood at the opening of the hall to see what was the cause of all the pandemonium.

'What on earth is the meaning of this?' he demanded.

Sally stepped quickly towards him, but he held her arm to gently push her backwards into the parlour behind him.

He looked to his right, down the hall, and saw the two constables grappling with Jonathan, throwing him around, only to then grab at him again. The sounds of smashing and crashing emanated through the house, as china plates and cups were demolished with the inhospitable skirmish that was taking place in the kitchen.

Mr Huffham stepped forward, only to be held tight by the elbow by one of the policemen, who was making an attempt to push him against the stair bannisters. Mr Huffham squeezed the officer's hand, gripping it and cupping it deep, like a bird of prey holding its victim in its talons. The grip was so hard, it was enough to make the officer loosen his grip instantly, for after another second his fingers would have been broken.

The sounds from the struggling and violence from the kitchen did not seem to wane, as it continued for what felt like minutes. Mr Huffham demanded to know what was going on, in the hope at least one of the constables could answer. The police sergeant parted his men and walked though as he approached from the outside.

'All right, all right, that's enough of that!' he said.

Mr Huffham noticed the three stripes of his uniform's upper arm. 'I gather you are in charge of these men?'

'Yes, I have the authority here!'

Mr Huffham laughed to himself and replied, 'You hold no authority here, for that is my position. But you *are* in charge of these men.'

The sergeant was vexed and his face curled up with irritation.

Mr Huffham continued with, 'What the hell is going on here? Why have you charged into my household in such a manner?'

'I will ask the questions if you don't mind, sir,' replied the sergeant.

Just then, the two constables from the back kitchen showed themselves, with Jonathan being held in the middle, his arms held behind him and his wrists cuffed.

The sergeant looked Jonathan up and down. His face changed from the irritation he felt from Mr Huffham's words to satisfaction.

'Five foot eight, around twenty years of age, hair, face, and build ... They all match. Perfect.'

Jonathan looked highly confused and panicked. 'What is going on? Why have you arrested me?' he yelled.

The sergeant took two steps towards him, closing in, with only an inch separating their faces.

'You're coming with us, Jonathan ... or is it Jack?'

'What are you talking about?'

'You'll see. Now take him away!'

Mr Huffham stepped forward, which caused a few of the stationary constables to raise their truncheons in a prepared and ready stance.

'You will answer him!' he ordered.

The sergeant turned to address Mr Huffham and said, 'You want to be arrested too, do you? And the maid for housing a murderer?'

'Sergeant, whatever you think he has done, I can assure you, you have made a grave error.'

'Any more lip and we'll take all of you!'

With great reluctance, he looked over at Sally and did not say anything else to the officers.

The sergeant whistled for the two policemen to return from upstairs so he and his men could leave the house.

When the two officers who held Jonathan passed Mr Huffham, he looked him straight in the eyes and said in a trusting and calm way, 'Do not worry, all will be resolved in due course, I'm sure. A mistake which shall be rectified.'

Jonathan gave a half smile as he was then pulled away roughly.

All the constables and the sergeant left the house, leaving the damaged front door wide open.

Mr Huffham stood still in his hallway and hugged Sally as she ran towards him. They both looked out into the dark night and watched in upset as their dear friend was thrown into the back of one of the police carriages. The narrow, barred door was slammed shut and locked behind him.

They stared out into the cold darkness, totally powerless as the two large dark blue, box-like cartridges trotted off with two police horses pulling each one.

Mr Huffham walked into his littered and chaotic kitchen and noticed the fine, brown, loose tea strewn all over the floor, resembling a vast ant's nest. With a sad exhale, he then walked to his parlour room and sat down to smoke his pipe.

He held a very concerned look and pondered as to what he would and could do to help. Whilst in deep thought, he looked across at Jonathan's half burnt cigar, which was still balanced on the ashtray. It seemed a little strange that the cigar was still calm, unmoved, and balanced nicely. He took a long, slow breath in a saddening and worried way as he looked forward into thin air, almost in a hypnotized daze.

Chapter 24

It was 10am when Mr Huffham entered his shop two days after Jonathan's arrest. He looked like he had been awake for forty-eight hours. For good reason, he had. His appearance was still excellent, but the bags under his eyes that hung down heavy and sat upon a worried face made him a little less immaculate and joyful than usual.

The previous day and a half, his efforts had consisted of finding out as much as possible about why Jonathan was arrested and where his current location was. The different police stations seldom communicated with each other, so obtaining information from the different districts was not always the easiest of tasks, especially given the fact that the arresting sergeant at the time appeared to act deliberately deaf and dumb when asked for any reasoning, almost relishing in the ignorance he wanted to push on Mr Huffham, Sally, and Jonathan.

Mr Huffham firstly went to Westminster police station and learned that they had never heard of 'Jonathan White', let alone his forceful home invasion and arrest. It was only several hours later that he took knowledge of all the facts, including the accusation that Jonathan was Jack the Ripper and that he was being held in Whitechapel.

His first and foremost course of action to learn of his whereabouts was to go to Whitechapel station in order to talk to anyone in charge of the case. His wish to do such came to only the desk sergeant. No matter how much he insisted, the police did not want to hear a single word. Furthermore, any other attempt that day to step further into the station would result in either a beating, an arrest, or more likely both. He knew if that were to be the case, then it would render him utterly useless to Jonathan, as well as everyone else. If he himself were behind bars, it would only add to the turmoil of the whole situation.

He carried some serenity and solace in his heart, knowing at least where Jonathan was being held, but the thought of not being able to do much about it was mortifying. He was aware it would have to be a waiting game to see what would occur next. It was somewhat torturous, but his sense of patience was strong and he knew the time would come soon enough to see him.

As he walked into his shop, a 'Good morning' greeting came from Koots and Jessica, his reply was the same in terms of wording, but the tone was a little deflated compared to every other morning.

Koots and Jessica were well aware of Jonathan's arrest and offered their help whenever it was needed.

'Anything we can do, sir, just ask,' Koots offered.

Jessica brought over a steaming cup of tea to help add a tiny piece of comfort. He sat down by the shop counter and drank it slowly, thanking her with his first sip.

'What's going to happen, sir?' she asked.

'I do not know, Jessica, it is out of my hands.'

Koots walked towards him and leaned against the till, which was so large and weighted heavily with gleaming stainless steel and marble, it did not move an inch.

'Don't worry sir, it'll be sorted. We all know he is innocent. He would never do what they are saying.'

Mr Huffham smiled at his kind words, but unfortunately it brought little comfort. 'I wish it were that simple, Koots.'

'But he's innocent, sir,' said Jessica.

'That he is, but I fear it will not be just about innocence and guilt. It should be, but I suspect it will not be as binary as black and white, fact or fiction.'

A melancholic stillness filled the air with trepidation and nerves, with the sense of unknowing.

The shop doorbell rang, the door opening fast to break the silence. They all turned, expecting to see a customer, but instead it was just the paperboy.

'Papers,' he yelled in his high-pitched, young voice as he dropped the rolled-up newspaper on to the floor, only to then leave to do the same with the next shop along and so on.

'Koots, get that will you, please?'

Koots walked over to the newspaper and saw the front page. He read it briefly as he returned back to the counter to join his boss and his work colleague. 'Ah … another murder last night … it's sickening,' said Koots.

Mr Huffham's head turned. 'Had me that, will you?'

He grabbed the paper and read the front page. His eyes narrowed as he took it in and concentrated on every word.

The story was one of dreadful violence. It carried the sordid details of a murder the previous night. The poor victim was called Annie Chapman, a prostitute in Whitechapel who met her demise in a most despicable and gruesome way. Another killing was not uncommon, but the body being dismembered and sliced to pieces was.

He folded up the paper and slid it in his inner pocket and looked up as he immersed himself in deep philosophical thought. Jessica saw the glare in his face that changed with the news the paper held.

'What is it, sir?'

'This Annie Chapman was killed in a very similar way to Mary-Ann, the girl who Jonathan is being accused of killing,' he replied/

'Right ...' she replied in a curious way.

'It happened yesterday. Jonathan has been locked up in the police station for the last two days,' he said as he continued his pondering.

A moment later, the doorbell rang again. He was so lost in thought, he did not even turn his gaze.

He heard the pitter patter of feet and then felt two arms hug him tight from behind. He turned around and saw Lizzie, who could not bring herself to say one word, let alone a coherent sentence. Instead, she just held him with her head nestled in his chest.

'Ah come come, dear,' he said as he held her arms.

'I've only just heard about everything. I was so worried when ... when he didn't turn up to meet me a few days ago ... and now he's been arrested for being the Ripper?' she stuttered. She continued with a pleading, 'He's innocent, sir! I know he's innocent. I was with him when Mary was killed ... and we ... we saw her.'

'Calm ... calm yourself, Lizzie. I know of this. You have not got to plead his case to me,' he replied in his placid voice.

'What are we to do?'

Mr Huffham took out the newspaper and showed her the front page.

'How awful,' she said as she read the first couple of lines.

'Have you heard of this Annie?' he asked.

She took a moment to think, her eyes looking up and to the right to try to retain a memory.

'The name sort of rings a bell, but I do not know her. I think I remember her being a lady of the night in my area, but there are so many. This paper tells more than I could.'

Mr Huffham took the paper off her and said, 'I am going to Whitechapel Police Station, and this time, I will not be cast off.'

Lizzie, without being asked, insisted that she come along, to which he agreed, although with her determination, it appeared even a lion at full charge could not stop her.

'Koots!'

'Yes, sir?'

'You are in charge of the shop. Do you know your next job?'

'Yes, sir, just got to paint the train master's safe.'

'Well done. Carry on.'

Mr Huffham and Lizzie walked with haste towards the shop door, like they were on an important mission. He reached for the door handle when he heard from Koots.

'Oh and sir?'

'Yes?'

'What colour?'

'Pardon?' said Mr Huffham in a confused tone.

'What colour shall I paint the safe? Lime green or dark blue?'

He did not answer. Instead, he just looked at him with stare of impatience.

'Don't worry sir, I'll figure it out.'

'Yes, you do that, Koots. Jessica, look after him will you, please?'

Jessica nodded with a smile as Mr Huffham and Lizzie left the shop.

They stood on the pavement next to each other, looking left and right for an empty cab.

'I would in jest say neon pink, but I fear he would do just that,' he said.

Lizzie giggled, which was quite a feat, seeing how sad she was. Maybe it was a half giggle for a polite reply, but it was a change to her current state, even for a brief moment.

They scanned the road up and down, their eyes cast upon tradesmen operating in their blacksmith and cooper yards, street sellers haggling with their customers, shop keepers tending to their tills, window cleaners, dog walkers, shoppers, and the occasional young man riding his penny farthing. However, a cab was nowhere to be seen.

'Always the same; dozens around when you don't need one, but the minute you do, there are none to be seen.'

'Sod's law,' she replied in agreement.

Minute after minute drifted by with still no cab in sight. Mr Huffham's blood pressure began to rise as Lizzie's state turned evermore on edge. Every time they heard hooves clattering from the distance, a ray of hope would come, only to be taken away again when they realised it was a horse in another occupation.

Ten minutes had passed, which felt like thirty, and still nothing. 'Right ... follow me, my girl,' he said as he turned to walk up the pavement.

She followed his steps with curiosity. He did not run as that would not be refined, but his pace did possess a certain urgency.

Just fifty yards of travel was covered when they arrived at the local blacksmiths. A long, wide side alley that was flanked by two grey stone walls made the entrance to the large square yard. The heat from the furnaces blew out with power and was quite overwhelming at first. The furnaces were small in stature but they were many, with smoke and steam bellowing high and far. Mr Huffham caught the attention of the lead smith, who greeted them in a friendly manner as they walked in.

'Yes, sir ... and ma'am. How can I help? Horseshoes needed?' the smith asked as he wiped his hefty black hands on his brown leather apron.

'Ah, my good man, yes, we are in need of four horseshoes.'

Lizzie looked at him with a muddled look of confusion and vaguenesss.

Mr Huffham continued with, 'And a horse to wear them, along with a cart, if you please ... only on loan. They will be returned to you later.'

The smith held an empty gaze for he did not fully understand.

'Sir, we do not sell or rent horses, we are just a humble blacksmiths. Ironwork is our trade.'

Mr Huffham pointed out that he was aware of his trade and what it included.

He could see three horses standing at the rear of the yard, secure with their reins, tied to hooks that lined the wall. Another observation of his was the pile of goods at the back, which on first appearance had the resemblance of a scrapyard. It was a pile of clutter. Carts, wagon wheels, grates, large iron tires, barrels, broken railings, and gates, some of which were beyond repair, and some with life still in them.

'I'm sorry, sir, you have come to the wrong place,' the smith regrettably muttered.

Mr Huffham opened his wallet to produce a crisp ten-pound note. He offered it to the smith with a point of his finger and said, 'That horse and that cart?'

The smith's eyes lit up as he snatched the money, and it crunched as he grabbed it.

'Yes, sir, no problem at all, help yourself. Will need the horse back by nightfall at the latest, though.'

'Splendid, you are most kind,' said Mr Huffham as he walked to the backyard to untie the horse.

The smith ran back to help pull out the small two-seater cart, to then attach it accordingly to the horse.

The whole job was completed in just a couple of minutes, as Mr Huffham climbed on one side of the seat, to then take the reins to command the horse out of the yard. Lizzie was taken back as she too climbed onto the seat to sit next to him.

They left the yard and waved goodbye to the blacksmith as he stood still with his hands on his hips, not totally sure what had just happened. After a few seconds, ten pound note, which was now in his pocket, helped him comprehend the situation.

Even Mr Huffham was rather pleased and gave himself a ten out of ten for his initiative and unconventional feat. They were on the road and in high spirits with their little victory, with Lizzie saying, 'Course, you know what we'll see now, don't you?'

'Yes ... an empty cab going right past us. I know,' he replied in a hushed tone. H 'Another funny thing, I have Tammylan, my horse, and a suitable cart at home. Still, too late now. We are on the move and that is the main thing.'

She smiled and agreed that it did not matter, for they were on their way to Whitechapel and hopefully Jonathan. They were moving with more velocity than the everyday, professional cab, so in her mind, that only strengthened the feeling that his idea had worked out for the best, even though it was costly and unorthodox.

They raced through the centre of Westminster in only a couple of minutes, before leaving the area to make their way to their destination. The cart was bobbing up and down with the sheer speed and power of the horse, the sounds of old wood cracking and contorting as the thin wheels rolled over the road. The horse was much more virile and energetic than any other they had come across before. They could not sit still even for a few seconds as their bodies would rise and then fall again, flung left and right, with the rough and very uncomfortable ride.. Lizzie's long hair blew out behind her, so much so it looked like an invisible man was pulling her hair from behind. They cut through the air like a speeding bullet with the horse showing no signs of letting up.

'Assay! ... Assay!' Mr Huffham commanded to the horse as he franticly held onto the reins, whilst at the same time trying to hold his top hat in one place.

They could feel the moment they reached Whitechapel, for the roads and cobbles were rougher and much bumpier than in Westminster. Just a couple more roads to go and the bone rattling, teeth shaking, fearsome ride would come to an end.

With a very hard pull on the reins, the horse managed to stop directly outside the police station. They stopped so suddenly, it made them fall forward as the wooden wheels skidded to a halt.

They both managed to take composure and tidy themselves up, with a large deep breath from each of them, and fully appreciate finally being on solid ground.

'That horse is not right in the head!' said Mr Huffham.

'Gosh! I've never gone so fast in my life. I'm still shaking,' Lizzie said, then raised her arm up to show her quaking hand. She continued with, 'What was that word you were saying? Assay? It certainly made the horse bolt. What does it mean exactly?'

'It's an old Indian word … it means, 'stop.''

She smiled and gave a little laugh when he looked at the horse as if he was about to tell it off. He arched his back in order to stretch out, and Lizzie had to do the same. He took out his gold pocket watch with one hand and flicked the outer case open, using nothing more than the edge of his thumb.

'By Jove … eighteen minutes flat. Splendid.'

The same journey in more usual circumstances would take around thirty minutes, so he held a certain amount of pride in what could easily be the fastest time anyone had ever taken that same journey.

He looked at the underside of the horse, which made his eyes widen when he saw the horse's member.

'That bastard horse has not been castrated, that's for sure Look at the size of its thing!' Lizzie looked at Mr Huffham with an impatient glare. 'Almost scraping the ground. Mind you, that's one way to get him circumcised,' he continued in almost disbelief.

'Come on,' said Lizzie.

They walked side by side up the grey, flat stone steps that lead to the entrance hall. He turned the polished brass knob and pushed open one of the two large oak doors to enter the station.

The first thing they saw was a huge dark brown solid wooden desk, which sat in front of the same desk sergeant Mr Huffham had dealings with the day before, with a regrettable and unhelpful conclusion.

The desk sergeant was a mean, intolerant man who would always hold the notion that he was better and more deserving than the role in which he stood, which made him bitter and cruel. He looked up from his paperwork and noticed them as they walked towards him. He sighed deeply, for he could not be bothered with the repeated insistence and debate he was expecting from Mr Huffham.

'Ah, you again,' the desk sergeant said with a huff.

'Yes, it is I again,' replied Mr Huffham in a strong and forthright way.

He kindly asked to see the police chief and said it was a matter of urgency and great importance. But the request fell on deaf ears with a reply he did not want to hear.

'Is he in at the moment or not?' he asked.

Any easy answer, albeit a lie, would be to say the chief is out. However, the sergeant was so cruel, he took delight in saying that the chief was available and in the building, but the answer was still a stern 'NO.'

When asked why he would not see them, the sergeant just shrugged his shoulders like a petulant child, which only served to push Mr Huffham's temper to its limits. He walked round to the side of the desk and demanded he have just five minutes with the chief. The response was the same as before, but this time the word was also supported by the sergeant holding his truncheon with a firm grip.

'Listen to me. You are holding an innocent man back there. Five minutes is all I ask. If he is busy or in a meeting, we can wait.'

The sergeant left his desk and stood toe to toe with him and said, 'How about you hop it! You can leave your female companion, though, and after I'm done with her, I'll throw her in the cells with the men. What do you think will happen to her? They'll tear her apart.'

Mr Huffham's blood boiled, and he struck the sergeant clean on his jaw with a single hard punch.

The sergeant's body spun round with the impact and he fell to the floor.

Mr Huffham stood over him and said, 'Do I make myself clear?'

The sergeant rolled over and looked up whilst holding the side of his face. 'I'll have you for that! It's a five pound fine for assaulting a policeman!'

Mr Huffham threw down a one-pound note onto the sergeant's chest and said, 'And I could have you dismissed within an instant for threatening a lady. Now take your money and count yourself lucky.'

The sergeant fell silent, still lying on the floor.

'I happen to be personal friends with the London Police Commissioner. This is his niece,' Mr Huffham lied as he pointed to Lizzie.

He then offered his hand out to help the man up from the floor. 'We understand one another?'

The sergeant nodded and then pointed to the chief's office door.

Mr Huffham was not in the habit of striking police officers, this being his first time, and he had been very tempted to bribe the sergeant almost any amount, for losing coin was much better than losing one's morals. However, the threat and thought of Lizzie being set upon by a cell full of male criminals was a step too far. His first act had to be to eradicate such words as soon as possible. He could not allow such vile speech to go unpunished.

They walked to the police chief's office door and knocked sedately.

'Come!' the voice came from the other side.

They entered and kept a tranquil state at first in order to simply talk, which was what they thought would be the best approach. Storming in, demanding this and that, would not bode well, especially seeing as they were in a building with at least forty policemen.

Mr Huffham introduced himself and Lizzie to the chief and ascertained that they were talking to the right man in the building who held the authority. He told the chief all about Jonathan and that they were holding the wrong man. They asked for him to be released, even if it were only temporarily, until any decent evidence could be brought to light.

Mr Dallyard leaned back in his chair and heard all that was said to him. 'I'm afraid that would not be possible. I believe we have the right suspect, and that monster would not be leaving with you today, or indeed any day if it was solely up to me.'

'But I was with him the night of Mary-Ann's death. You have the wrong man!' cried Lizzie.

'I have been tasked to catch Jack the Ripper, and that is exactly I have done,' he said proudly.

Mr Huffham reached into his coat pocket and pulled out the newspaper, which he then threw on the desk.

'There is your so-called 'Ripper'. He has struck again. Can't you see you have the wrong man, dammit!'

'Nonsense, just another madman there, another body of a whore is all. The Ripper case has made many a man into a copycat. Look what came only this morning.'

Mr Dallyard opened his desk drawer and pulled out a white handkerchief stained with blood. He opened it up and showed them the contents. Mr Huffham and Lizzie leaned forward and saw two human ears.

''Tis but a sick man's joke. We have been inundated with this sort of thing, as well as letters.'

'You are blind, sir, to words written in black and white right in front of you! You have no evidence at all, or at least none of worth.'

Mr Dallyard's moustache began to twitch. He stood up and swiped the paper from his desk.

'Look here, You came into my office! I am a busy man. Do you realise the landlord of the house next door was shot only last week? Crime continues and you are delaying me from doing my job!'

'You are not doing your job in the correct way. If you are a detective, then go and detect! For every hour you keep Jonathan, the real Ripper is still out there!' yelled Mr Huffham.

'Your Jonathan will be in court in due course. It is not up to me. Now leave before I have you both arrested!'

Mr Huffham took a deflated breath and opened the door.

'You are a fool, sir. There are none so blind as those who refuse to see.'

'Get out of my office at once!'

He left the office with Lizzie, and realised for now nothing could be done to help Jonathan. Neither a strong word, a lie, a bribe, nor a huge favour could change the current situation.

Mr Dallyard stayed in his office as he heard his door being slammed shut. His pompousness was as strong as ever. When it came to true justice, it would be his Achilles heel later in life.

Mr Huffham and Lizzie stood on the pavement outside the station with a sadness in their eyes.

'What are we to do?' she asked.

'We shall attend court. For now, that is all we can do.'

He reached out to offer a hug, which was taken up within a second.

'Come … join me for a late breakfast'

'Oh no, sir, I can't eat, I am too worried.'

'Lizzie, dear, you are thin and must eat. Your empty stomach will not help our friend.

She nodded slowly.

'Justice will finds its path, I'm sure. We will be there for him in court. Have no fear of that, my dear.'

Chapter 25

Two whole weeks later and it was the day of the court case. Every one of those fourteen days was full of desperate worry for Lizzie and Mr Huffham, with minutes feeling like hours and hours feeling like days. The waiting was unbearable for them both. The unknown about what it was exactly like for Jonathan being locked up in the police cells was hellish, but they knew it would be hell itself for him. They both went through the despair with him, but without being able to be by his side in person, it was impossible to fully realise the monstrous burden that had been forced upon him.

During the previous two weeks, they were not allowed a single visitation, not even for five minutes. With letters and telegrams of love, hope, and thoughts not venturing further than the desk sergeant, it was impossible to know anything that was going on, except that he was being held in chains in the cold and odious cells.

The lack of any knowledge played dirty tricks on Lizzie's psyche. The nights were the worst for her as paranoid thoughts ran through her mind all night, imagining Jonathan being starved, beaten, and shamed. Every now and then, she would force herself to snap out of it, wiping away her tears.

'Pull yourself together, girl. He's all right. The mistreatment of prisoners awaiting sentence doesn't happen that much, it's rare.'

But deep down in her heart, she knew that there was a strong possibility that cruelty was being thrust upon him.

Being only a police cell, as opposed to a prison, there was no formal punishment or rule system in place for chastisement. No working the hand crank for hours on end or walking the penal treadmill, but secret street justice, or cell justice. Some officers who had the comfort of privacy, away from the public gaze, would turn a blind eye and order beatings to whomever they saw fit whilst in their detention.

Many a man died whilst in the so-called protective custody of the cells, with some attacks being so inhuman it could be just to save the court's time and money or to free up some much needed space. With a backlog of cases, each one costing a pretty penny, it would be rather convenient and beneficial to the local constituency if some of the accused men were to 'disappear'.

Wicked games would be played by exceptionally heinous officers who had a certain grievance, merely for their amusement and misuse of power. An order for one prisoner to fight or maim another would be given often, or the offer of an extra crust of bread as a reward to act out vicious deeds. Prisoners harming others due to the commands of their keepers would be entertainment for the officers, just as cruel as it had been for the ancient Roman Gladiators. The vile cells would take the place of the Colosseum, but instead of the blood-soaked sands of Rome, it would be the blood-soaked stone floors of the iron cage. The surroundings of two thousand years ago may have changed, but the brutish principle did not. The prisoners, even before their sentence, were seen and treated by some as no higher than a hound. The wicked games were nothing more than a public dog fight, with some even placing bets to add to their entertainment.

Be that as it may, with all the dread, there were two more pleasant thoughts that circulated through Lizzie's system the closer the court date came. Lizzie pictured the somewhat foreboding court case as the opportunity to give Jonathan a change of scene, knowing that he would at last be out of the police station. She would also finally be able to see him in the flesh. It would be torturous not being able to touch him, but even a smile whenever she could would hopefully give him a ray of optimism. A blown kiss or a quite word of affection could mean the world when that was all she could do.

Mr Huffham met Lizzie outside the large courtroom, which situated itself on the edge of Whitechapel. He greeted her at ten in the morning with plenty of time for the eleven o'clock hearing. He was dressed in his finest, with a sharply pressed black suit, the shade being broken up by details of smooth gold from his watch chain, tie pin, and cufflinks, alongside a top hat that gleamed in the shine to reflect his highly polished, shimmering black shoes.

They looked up at the once magnificent building that presented hand-carved stone figurines in the masonry, with engraved Latin scripture on small, curved banners showing principle figures immortalised in the stone work. If a passerby did not know any better, he or she could be forgiven for thinking it was a small cathedral at first glance.

It was built many years ago, and if the walls had the ability to talk, they could tell thousands upon thousands of tales, with its rich history and tales of happiness and horror. Stories of terror in its highest and most graphic form sat alongside tales of justice and decency.

Twenty dark grey steps lay at the base as an attractive front for all the public to see and use. However, it was another case for a small, secluded part of the rear of the building. A narrow tunnel, tall enough for a horse and cart, with two large iron gates, fed through the underbelly of the court. Only the condemned would pass through here if the judge were to give the verdict of guilt. The outer gate, with its long, ornate, curved hinges and black iron bars that made up the entrance of the tunnel, looked macabre and gothic and would be more befitting in Dracula's castle with its haunting presence, especially as it services only one purpose for a very unfortunate soul. Over time, it was nicknamed 'Traitor's Gate', with an admiring nod to the same name at the Tower of London.

'He who passed Traitor's Gate will meet his death in dreadful state.'

This was the wretched epigraph that was etched in the top shaft of the gate and was chillingly muttered by guards and law enforcement.

Mr Huffham was aware of this place, mainly through rumour, whispers, and hearsay, but he wished more than anything that it would not be used this day.

They struggled their way up the steps, as if every step was a miniature Everest, full of trepidation and hope for Jonathan.

They entered the lobby of the large court, only to be ushered into the upper viewing gallery. Their seating area had two slightly curved wooden benches, one behind the other, long enough to hold fifteen people each. It was similar to the upper dress circle in a theatre, although what would hold their attention was not a show of song and dance, or lights and magic. Today, real life itself was in the balance.

They would have favoured being the only occupants of the gallery, but with this case being as high profile as what it was, their preference and wishes were not met.

They found themselves surrounded by many others, not one seat being vacant. There was a varied concoction of citizens sat next to them and behind. It was an audience of amateur criminologists, a doctor, a distant relative of Mary-Ann's, who even Lizzie had not made a previous acquaintance with, six journalists, and a myriad of curious civilians who indulged in a general interest of how a court of law functions and unfolds.

The viewing gallery was approximately thirty feet from the court floor below and was quite unnerving at first for Mr Huffham, who was not one for heights. He'd look over the barrier to glance down with a slight agitated look on his face.

'You're scared of heights?' asked Lizzie.

'My dear, it is not heights that bother me so. I can look up at a high structure and my heartbeat would remain steadfast. It's depths I am not agreeable with.'

As they sat there next to each other, awaiting the case to begin, they did not talk much, for inner feelings and thoughts took over the desire for speech. Lizzie leaned forward, rested on the wooden panelled barrier, and looked down at the considerably large room.

The court was square with the judge's bench at one end and the witness stand raised a little beside it. The prisoner's dock lay at the opposite end, and that too was raised off the floor with two wooden steps in front and behind. At the far end to stood the jury benches, which, with the exception of the judge's chair, looked to be the most comfortable seats in the building, with their soft, worn leather upholstery and velvet backing. Most of the floor was made up of an array of chairs and tables for all the officials and court staff to use, while the were thin oak panelling, marked sporadically through the years of time.

As time ticked on, the floor became more and more busy as it slowly filled up with clerks, the defence and prosecution, and the judicial power. Lizzie looked around and saw five police constables acting as security. The security roles here were not specialized careers, as they were the same policemen as any from the Metropolitan. She had never been inside such a building before, of which she had no knowledge, but it was clear when looking at the uniforms that these constables were of the same level as any bobby on the beat. They were there mainly for a precaution. If and when the accused would dare try to make a break for it, or act out his own justice and revenge on a magistrate, they would be there to quell any attempt at violence. They were also there to aid in any transportation of the prisoner, as well as the safety of everyone in the room.

With the distance between the judge's chair and the prisoner's dock being at least fifty feet, and taking into account the accused was in chains, it would be easy to think that no one would be foolhardy enough to attempt such an attack on a judge. But a desperate man in desperate times, fuelled with hate in a criminal mind, would, on the rare occasion, try such a deed. If it was not for the police presence, the position for a new judge would be advertised in the paper almost every week, for the life expectancy would be rather short.

She continued to look at all the people in their varied and official capacities.

She heard the dull sound of chitter-chatter from close to thirty souls that were in the room, only to be raised a few octaves when the twelve men of the jury entered from a side door.

The jury, including the foreman, sat down on the two benches and muttered to each other. Lizzie could not hear what they were saying, which only heightened her tense state. She focused her gaze on each and every one of their faces to try to deduct some sort of analysis as to their personality. She hoped to see at least a glimmer of fairness, mercy, and kindness in their eyes and mannerisms. Unfortunately, she could tell nothing concrete from this distance, each of them looking somewhat alike. The only traits she could establish from their demeanour and faces were not pleasant, as each jury member carried a look of sternness, with strict expressions. She prayed that those traits did not reflect their hearts but were only present due to the nature of them carrying such a responsibility and knowing the gravity of their surroundings. It was her hope that these twelve gentlemen were soft and fair inside, with just the outer appearance being a falsehood for show.

The chit-chat was silenced in a second when a voice rang out.

'All rise.'

The sound of dozens of wooden chairs being pushed back a few inches over the floor echoed around the room, every seated person rising to their feet. Then, nothing but absolute quiet. The silence was deafening, as if Lizzie and Mr Huffham could hear a pin drop. The only sound they could hear was their own beating hearts. A few seconds later, a door that stood behind the judge's bench opened.

The judge entered the room to then walk the few paces to reach his chair. He stood in front of it and said, 'I, Judge Cornelius Barnaby William Montague, will take the chair.'

Everyone in the court proceeded to sit down after him, the sounds of the chairs being dragged to their original positions, and await the first order of business.

If it was not for the sheer magnitude of the situation, Lizzie would most probably have laughed when hearing his name, for it was one of the most peculiar names she had ever heard. However, when she saw his face, she soon felt that there was nothing to take jest at. She looked hard at the judge's face, just as she had done with the members of the jury. Her sentiment carried bitter misgivings as a cold chill shot down her spine.

Judge Montague was old and as mean and intolerant as a man could be. His soul was as black as a bailiff's heart, his guise imitating his beat. He was of slim build, with a face that was gaunt and thin, so much so it appeared to be only one meal away from being a skull. His cheek bones protruded outward as if his skin was too thin as it stretched over the bone. His eye sockets were deep set, with narrow eyes looking hard and callous through rounded glass spectacles.

He was well experienced in dishing out pain and excelled in giving misery to others. His draconian and strict ways stemmed from his younger days when he'd held the rank of Major in the British Army.

He was born seven decades prior and was thrust into a very harsh and cruel world the minute he left his mother's breast. From birth, it was obvious that he had not managed to see the world in any other light. His father, his masters at school, and his army peers were far stricter than the average, which, in the early nineteenth century, was up against some stiff competition.

He detested criminals, the poor, and children and he rejoiced in the thought of casting them aside like cockroaches or vermin. He held the perception of professionalism and took his job very seriously. With his inner cruelty, there were times when his behaviour to others did not mirror his heart. He was well aware he should believe that all who stand accused were innocent until proven guilty. However, inside himself, at times, his belief was of guilt until proven innocent, especially when he did not like the accused.

The door behind the dock opened with a creek as two heavyset constables brought forward Jonathan. They stood either side of him as he took his place on the spot. Lizzie and Mr Huffham looked at him with expressions of positivity and strength to hopefully be passed on. They were sad when they noticed his face and body was much thinner that when they'd last seen him. Nonetheless, they tried their utmost not to show their sadness too much for his sake. The agony and upset in their cores turned deeper when they saw cuts and bruising on his thin face, which was a distinct and plain result of mistreatment whilst in custody.

Jonathan stood still with his wrists bound, while the cold steel cuffs that were locked so tight dug into his flesh, making them bleed. They were so compressed that one twist from the constable would be enough to break his wrists if he so choose.

His expression held emptiness and hopelessness as he was but a shadow of the man he once was. He looked up to the viewing gallery and quickly spotted Lizzie and Mr Huffham. A smile slowly stretched across his face at the vision of them both. It was his first smile in over two weeks but was powerful enough to make up for the lost time.

The judge looked straight ahead at him with his beady eyes and noticed the smile, which only angered him, as he saw it as a personal jibe. Suddenly, a cough came from one of the members of the jury.

'Clerk, get that man a glass of water. I will not have coughing in my ear,' ordered the judge.

The clerk nodded whilst he quickly and nervously filled a glass from a water jug and handed it over to the jury.

The first proceeding was to establish that the accused had opted for a defence from the local area, a public defender who was young and tall, but short on experience.

Jonathan and Mr Huffham looked confused. a Why didn't he have a private attorney?

'Yes m'lud, the accused did not have the funds to hire a defence of his choosing,' said the defence.

Jonathan and Mr Huffham looked at each other in disbelief and soon realised that something was not quite right. The judge ordered Jonathan to state his name.

He answered, 'Jonathan White' and began to explain that the young defender was not who he wanted to represent him. Just a couple of his words left his mouth when he was ordered to shut up, as he was only to state his name at this point in time.

'Mr White, you stand here accused of the murder of a Mary-Ann Nichols, also known as Polly, and you are accused of being the infamous Jack the Ripper. How do you plead?'

He entered a plea of not guilty, to which the judge smiled in a cruel manner. The judge knew that if he was found guilty, he had extra power to inflict a tougher punishment, a feeling and power he viciously adored.

He ordered the defence to begin their opening statement. The lead defender, who could not have

been older than twenty and two, rose to his feet
and said in a somewhat squeaky voice, 'Thank
you, m'lud. This is an open and shut case. My
client stands here an innocent man. Not only
did he not commit this appalling crime, but he
himself is also deeply saddened and distressed
by the loss of Mary-Ann, as he knew her and held
much fondness for her. He had no reason or will
to kill her. I challenge the prosecution to present
any evidence they have, as they cannot have any
of meaningful substance. On the night of the
murder, Mr White was elsewhere. Jonathan White
is not the killer, ergo he is not Jack the Ripper.'

He sat down when the prosecution stood up.
The lead prosecutor was a gentleman and, unfortunately for Jonathan, a close friend of the judge.
He stood slim and passing six feet in height. His
age and experience doubled the defence's.

'The challenge from the defence shall be gladly
accepted,' he replied.

The first piece of evidence involved Jonathan's
alibi that he was not down Buck's Row at the time
of the murder, but out with Lizzie.

The prosecutor reached down at his desk and
checked his paperwork. He then turned to face
Jonathan. 'You were out for a stroll?' he asked.

'Yes.'

'Being the time that it was, you said there were
other people on the street. How can you explain
that not one person can back up your location on
the night in question?'

'They can. The young lady I was with. I told you everything already,' replied Jonathan. The prosecutor told the court there was no such lady present.

Immediately, Lizzie stood up and yelled from the gallery,

'That's a lie! I was there!'

The judge looked over at her with an angry look on his face.

'Quiet up there! The viewing gallery is for … viewing and not speaking!'

She sat down and repeated in a sorrowful manner, 'But it's a lie.'

The judge leaned forward and took off his spectacles.

'I said quiet, woman! One more word and I shall have you thrown out and held in contempt of court!'

With huge reluctance and a nod of advice from Mr Huffham by her side, she stayed seated and did not interrupt or say anything else.

The judge ordered the prosecution to continue.

'So you were out for a stroll, and no person or persons who you passed that night saw you? How convenient.'

'Looking at the situation I am in now, I would say it was very *in*convenient.' Jonathan said in a moody tone.

The prosecution moved on to their next piece of evidence, which took the form of a pair of blood-soaked trousers.

'These are yours, are they not?'

Jonathan nodded.

The prosecution showed the bloodied trousers to the jury for closer inspection.

The defence suddenly stood up and said, 'M'lud, that is circumstantial. There is no way to say that is the blood of the deceased in question.'

The judge told the defence that his interjection was sustained. He then allowed the prosecution to carry on.

'How do you explain the blood, Mr White? Cut yourself shaving, perhaps?'

A quiet laughter filled the room from everyone, including the judge. Everyone except Lizzie, Mr Huffham, and Jonathan that is.

Jonathan said that the blood was Mary-Ann's, which made the jury gasp.

He continued, 'I knelt down by Mary's body when we laid eyes on her.'

'The police have no mention of this in their reports,' the prosecutor claimed.

Jonathan gripped the waist-high railings that stood in front of him and replied, 'I do not care what their report says. I am telling you the truth. Would I say it was Mary's blood if I were lying? My knees were covered in blood as I was kneeling down. There must be a constable who can tell you.'

The prosecution smiled and said, 'We have asked, and there is not.'

Jonathan looked down and shook his head as the prosecutor, who held a smug look whilst gripping his own lapels, strutted left and right in front of the jury.

'Moving on … the surgeon's report states that the killer is a man with a high skill and knowledge of bladed articles, would you agree?'

'I guess so,' replied Jonathan.

'You 'guess so'. Well, during the police investigation, they discovered that you are not a stranger when handling a blade and even have a skill in knife throwing.'

'I enjoy knife throwing, as does many a man I know.'

The prosecutor stopped his strutting and turned to face Jonathan, but kept his confident hands resting on his suit lapels and asked, 'So where did this morbid fascination of blades stem from?'

"Tis no morbid fascination. It is a fine art and very hard to accomplish. I bet you couldn't do it,' said Jonathan with a half-smile and with a quick nod up to the viewing gallery.

The jury members laughed out loud.

The judge turned his gaze and aimed it at the jury bench and bellowed, 'Silence!'

When the laughter ceased, the prosecution called their witness.

The clerk of the court opened the door that stood behind the witness stand.

'Call the witness,' a voice rang out from the dark, coming from the other side of the open door.

From the darkness came a man walking from the waiting room and into the court.

Scarface was the figure that entered the room, to then take his place on the witness stand. He stood there with a devious smile on his face and held his evil stare straight at the prisoner's dock. Jonathan tilted his head and realised who it was, standing dead ahead in the stand.

'You!'

The judge stood up and addressed him directly. 'Mr White! You will speak when spoken to. Another outburst like that in my court I shall have you gagged!'

Jonathan took a deep breath through shear frustration but kept quiet.

The prosecutor spoke to Scarface and asked for his account on what he reported to see. He responded with a pack of lies, as well as some truth, as he told the court that he'd seen Jonathan kill Mary-Ann. He went into great detail about slicing flesh with wanton violence and bloodshed. Of course, his account as to the wounds on the body was one hundred per cent correct. Not only was his story false as to who committed the crime, but the manner he told it carried more lies, by saying how terrible and scared he was when he saw what had happened, only to receive sympathy from the people in the room.

'Must have been dreadful for you. You are very brave for coming here today,' said the prosecutor.

The judge asked the defence if he wished to cross examine the witness, to which the response was, 'No, m'lud'

Mr Huffham stood up, for he could not help but say out loud, 'This is a farce!'

The judge's temper quickly matched his and he replied with, 'Quiet! Clerk of the court, you will take that man's name. You, sir, will be charged ten pounds for that disgraceful outburst!'

Just as Lizzie had been told off and sat down, he had to do follow suit, but his expression showed great discontent. Lizzie held his hand for support and to reassure him that his outburst was valid and the right thing to say.

The judge allowed Scarface to leave the stand. He turned and left the room through the same door he'd come through earlier. Just before leaving the courtroom, he turned round and gave a smirk at Jonathan.

The case carried on, it being very much one-sided and in favour of the confident and more powerful prosecution, with other so-called evidence, including the letter to the police.

After a couple of hours, the judge ordered the closing statements from both defence and prosecution, with the defence going first. The judge knew that even the order to which they presented their statements could carry an advantage, with the latter words in the second statement being the freshest in the juror's minds.

The defence stood up and addressed the jury directly.

'Gentlemen of the jury. My client is no Jack the Ripper. All the so-called evidence that was brought before you Mr White has a valid explanation for. If you are in any reasonable doubt, then you must not find him guilty, but innocent of the charge.

The prosecution has one man's word, that is all. If you are to listen to just one man, then listen to Mr White. I ask you to search your hearts and your minds and find my client innocent. Thank you.'

The prosecution then stood for their turn to address the jury for the final time.

'Gentlemen of the jury. You have seen and heard not one, not two, but four pieces of hard evidence that puts Mr White as the sole murderer. Why exactly he committed these crimes we do not know. The fact, not belief, gentlemen, t that they have been committed by him is enough. His hands are stained with the blood of a sweet, innocent woman, as his clothing is stained with such. Thank you.

The judge looked at the jury and ordered them to leave for deliberation. 'We shall break and return in two hours,' said the judge.

Jonathan looked up and desperately said, 'Two hours! Give them longer than that, for God's sake!'

'Constable, gag Mr White at once!' The judge demanded, and continued with, 'I will not have this place turned into a free-for-all with the accused and his viewing party behaving in such a manner!'

Jonathan struggled with the two officers as they gagged him tight with a piece of narrow cloth. He continued struggling when one of the officers punched him in the face. Lizzie and Mr Huffham looked on in powerless grief and heartache.

The hearing took its break whilst the jury deliberated. Jonathan was pulled from the dock at the same time when everyone left to await the verdict.

Lizzie and Mr Huffham made their way out and sat on the stone steps outside the court building entrance. It was quite literately a breath of fresh air when they took deep breaths from the cold outside. The courtroom was large and very airy, but with the amount of people in it, coupled with the heightened distress they had, it felt horrible, claustrophobic, and very stuffy.

Mr Huffham's face could not shake off a very worried look as his eyebrows lowered. They sat in silence at first as their minds tried to fully digest what had just happened. He took out his trusted old pipe and began to smoke to try and regain some sense of calm.

'Mr Huffham?' asked Lizzie.

His reply was one she did not expect when he slowly said, 'Call me John'

'May I have a puff on your pipe please?' she asked.

He turned towards her with a surprised look. 'As you wish. Not exactly an attractive sight, a lady with a pipe in hand, but I guess at the moment it matters not.'

He handed over his pipe without argument and continued with, 'That was a farce if ever I saw one. A miscarriage of justice, and the defence was an ass.'

'What did you expect? It is Whitechapel,' she replied, only to then cough on the pipe.

'That is no excuse. It is a court of the land.' . Mr Huffham faced her and said, 'My knowledge of the courts and barristers, although somewhat limited, I might add, seldom involves the application of law, but more the manipulation of people.'

Her eyes welled up. He placed his hand on her knee and continued with, 'There is no verdict yet. Let us wait without thought of prediction.'

She sniffed and nodded as she handed back his pipe. 'Why wasn't I called as a witness?' she asked.

'One cannot say. Could be a multitude of ill reasons. The defence's first case, bribery, the judge being a nasty piece of work; the list is endless. Let us just wait and see what happens.'

Ninety minutes had passed when the sound from a loud hand bell rang as the request for all to return to the courtroom.

Lizzie and Mr Huffham, sat in the same place in the viewing gallery, were full of nerves as they waited for Jonathan and the jury to return to court.

Ten minutes of being on tenterhooks passed, when suddenly the jurors entered at the same time as Jonathan was pushed forward into the dock. The judge asked the foreman of the jury if they had deliberated and all fully come to an agreeable conclusion.

'Yes, your honour,' replied the foreman as he stood up and continued with, 'We, the jury of this case, find the accused. Jonathan White, guilty.'

'Say you one, say you all?' asked the judge.

'Yes, your honour,' said the foreman who then nodded in respect.

With the order from the judge, the twelve jurors left the courtroom.

Lizzie started to cry at the same time as Mr Huffham's head dropped. The sound of her cries angered the judge.

'Shut up, up there! Muffle your emotions in your handkerchiefs!' He followed this with an order for one of the constables to remove Jonathan's gag.

'Mr White, before I pass sentence, indulge me as to the reason why you teased the police force with your letters.'

Jonathan looked up and stared at the judge and said in an angry voice, 'I know not of any letters. They were not written by my hand. My hands held no quill and no knife that very night!'

'Do you have anything else to say?' asked the judge.

'Yes, fuck you,' he replied.

Whether it was bravery or sheer stupidity, those words made Mr Huffham smile. The remaining people in the courtroom were shocked at Jonathan's words, and whispers and giggles spread through the room expeditiously.

The judge was furious and livid, more so than ever before. He yelled, 'Order! Order! I will have order here!'

He smashed his gavel down hard again and again. The sound of the wood thudding silenced the people. He looked at Jonathan in a vicious way and said,

'Jonathan White, in usual circumstances, I am recommended to pass sentence of no less than twenty years of hard labour, working the crank at her majesty's pleasure. However, given the viciousness of the crime and your wanton lack of personal responsibility in your attitude, and plea of 'not guilty', I sentence you to death! You shall be taken from this court to Newgate Prison. Three days hence you shall be hanged by the neck until you are dead!'

The gavel hit the bench with one final BANG, the sound of which echoed in Lizzie's and Mr Huffham's hearts forever, akin to the sound of a gunshot and felt just as devastating.

Chapter 26

The following night, Mr Huffham was sat at his dining table. The walnut, polished wooden top held a variety of delicious foods and red wine. It was a spread of roast chicken, roast goose, crispy potatoes, and a variety of vegetables, with thick cut bread smeared with butter. The yellow flare from the gaslight reflected the shine of the silver gravy boat, meat dish, and cutlery, the glaze from the chicken skin combined made a warm and homely sight.

Usually, the evening meal that he cast his eyes on would give an agreeable and cosy feeling inside, a simple pleasure that he experienced every night, with the familiarity and routine never being taken for granted and never becoming boring or repetitive. Sally excelled in her duties and on no account was guilty of dereliction, her having the remarkable talent to turn a house into a home. It came naturally to her and not just for a wage. She was as good as any wife, mother, or maid, but this evening carried a sadness that was a rarity to say the least.

She was allowed to cook whatever she pleased, as for some time now, she had learned what Mr Huffham's tastes were, and over the past few years, each and every meal she prepared was more than satisfactory for the whole household. Every day, when the last mouthful was washed down with drink, Mr Huffham and Jonathan would be thankful and acknowledged her efforts, each meal receiving more distinctive merit than the last.

Every menu, be it a light snack or full spread, contained everything that was desired at that particular moment. The large oval table would sometimes be so festooned with food, there would not be much space in between the plates, bowls, condiments, and other tableware. However, this evening, there was an empty space, in the form of an empty chair, which Sally and her master looked at in a deflated manner. The chair that always seated Jonathan lay bare and used , which they could not get used to. It was a new, dreadful feeling and not one that sat well in their hearts.

Mr Huffham began to eat, but this evening, the chicken and gravy seemed to lose its flavour, serving only as simple fuel for the body. The sound of laughter, intelligent debate, shop talk, and chat that was the normality around that table at mealtimes was now cut dramatically, as life now was sadly not the same.

Sally believed that life would never be the same again, and the thought of laughter emitting from the household was now but a memory and only in the passages of history.

Mr Huffham held his chin up, as did Sally, in order to support one another and get through this dire situation.

Sally was experiencing something she had never witnessed before. Life seemed to be pushing the limits and testing them down to their core, as it does from time to time for every soul on the planet. Every single hardship, problem, dilemma, obstacle, and even disaster that she saw or was party to Mr Huffham had rectified and remedied to restore harmonious peace. Nothing was unfeasible with him, and just like a cloud with a silver lining, he made every negative case end with a positive conclusion. Luckily, with the prosperity he possessed, common worldly worries and troubles were very few and far between in his house. But even he could not change the current unfolding events and the judge's verdict. He was a miracle worker, but going back in time was a task that no wizard, alchemist, sorcerer, genie, god, wish, or belief could ever achieve.

As the second forkful of crisp potato entered Sally's mouth, the doorbell rang. She wiped her lips with the serviette and went to the door, just as Mr Huffham held an expression of dislike and surprise at the rude interruption. He remained sat at the head of his table, just as his facial expression of discontent also remained. He was about to voice rather loudly that whoever it was should 'Sod off', for he was not in the mood to entertain, especially with it being dinnertime.

Sally returned to the dining room a moment later and stated that is was Lizzie at the front door. His face of displeasure quickly changed.

'Shall I ask her to wait for you in the parlour, sir?'

'You will do no such thing. Bring her in, if you please.'

She returned with Lizzie, who felt bad when she saw she had interrupted their dinner.

'Good evening, Lizzie'

'Evening, Mr Huffham – John - I am so sorry for my intrusion. I did not know you were dining,' she said in a high-pitched, awkward tone.

He offered her a chair at the table and asked her to join him as he said, 'Not at all. Anyone other than yourself would have received a closed door tonight. You are the exception, and your company is always welcome here.'

She sat down and looked at the freshly roasted meat. Her eyes closed for a second as she smelt the succulent aroma, taking in a deep, slow breath. He was about to ask Sally to get an extra plate for their guest, but as soon as he opened his mouth to give the friendly order, she already had the plate in her hand and placed it at Lizzie's table place.

'I really am sorry for coming uninvited,' she said.

'Now now, you have apologised twice now, and that is twice too many. I would rather have *you* here as an uninvited guest than the majority of the invited ones I seem to have,' he replied in a reassuring way.

Sally sat down and placed her hand on Lizzie's forearm and said with a smile,

'Count yourself lucky you haven't seen his bed clothes yet?'

She was taken aback a little a looked confused, as Sally continued with one of the many amusing habits Mr Huffham possessed.

'You see, love, when guests come, be it distant family, friends, or business gentlemen, if he gets bored and wishes them to leave, he simply rushes upstairs, gets changed into his night attire, and returns. He then just sits down in front of them in silence.'

Mr Huffham leaned back with a sip of wine and kindly told Sally not to natter about his habits and added, 'A gentleman never rushes.'

Lizzie and Sally gave a little smile to each other.

He gestured for Lizzie to tuck into the meal, but she could not eat a single thing. Her stomach was indeed empty of food, but her mind was full of upset. She was rather dumbfounded at how he seemed able not only to eat, but to enjoy it.

'How can you eat, sir? Are you not worried about Jonathan?'

Sally tapped Lizzie's leg under the table, just as a friendly warning.

'Lizzie, dear, what makes you think I am not racked with worry and that my demeanour, which you have only seen for the last two minutes, is not a mere façade?'

She paused for a brief moment.

He continued, 'I do not speak in riddles.'

She felt guilt from his reaction but was still a little perplexed by his calmness.

'But Jonathan will die!' she exclaimed and continued with, 'We must see him.'

He explained that he had already tried to visit, but the visitation could only take place the following day. At first, she asked to accompany him, but before he had the chance to answer,, she corrected herself and spoke freely by changing her ask to a demand.

For the first time, she did not care if she spoke out of place and turn, and although she would never deliberately offend Mr Huffham, on this occasion, nothing and no one would stop her from being able to see Jonathan, especially as it would be the last time she could see him before his execution.

He recognised her need, for his feeling reflected hers, and accepted it greatly, whilst deep down being pleased with her pertinacity, for it showed him how much she cared.

'You are in love with him, aren't you?' he asked, though it sounded more like a statement.

She nodded with a smile as a tear slid down her cheek to reach the curve of her lips.

"Do you think he loves me too?" she asked.

'I know him better than most. He has been with me for a long time, but my beliefs may not stand as fact, and if you were to hear that splendid word, it is not my place to say. However, I will say that you are what he thinks of daily, and you are one of the most important people to him, as you seem to be the forefront in his mind.'

Her smile stretched further as she held out her hand to grip his. Her heart was full from hearing those words, but it was also full of agony. For the first time in her life, she had someone who truly cared so much, and yet she was about to lose him.

The few weeks they'd had together were simply not enough. She wanted more ... a lifetime more. Sally rubbed her arm softly to then hug her fondly.

After a few minutes of Lizzie trying to regain some calm, she looked across the table and saw a dark blue glass bowl full of fruit. Mr Huffham told her to help herself if she wished. She reached for a banana, and without peeling it, she took a bite off the end, only to pull a face of repugnance. Mr Huffham proceeded to show her how to eat it properly, since she had never even seen one in her life. She was not in the least bit stupid, but it was perfectly understandable to him how that mistake could be made, for only the rich had the luxury of bananas, with the vast majority of people never experiencing the taste.

Nonetheless, his heart had a little flutter of joy with the amusing sight of a person eating a banana for the first time. For now though, the joyful feeling had to be switched to a more sombre note.

'There is one thing you must do when we visit Jonathan tomorrow,' he demanded.

She looked on, hanging onto his next sentence with bated breath. 'Have you ever been to Newgate Prison before?' he asked.

She shook her head.

'Newgate is not nicknamed 'Hellgate' for nothing. You will see some terrible things, and Jonathan may not be at his best. You will stand strong and not break down, no matter how much you want to. Do you understand? No wailing or such will help anybody.'

'You're asking me to hide my true emotions, as if they are controllable? That is almost impossible.'

'That may be, but I ask it nonetheless … for Jonathan.'

She nodded in agreement, with his last words convincing her initial doubt to dissipate. She asked if she could do anything for Jonathan. She'd felt useless at the court case and felt she had to do something now. Money, food, drink, a soft pillow, anything at all.

Whilst soaking up the last piece of chicken in the thick gravy, he said, 'Well, I do have some knowledge of that prison, for I was once briefly a resident and comfort is paramount. I intent to bring him a pair of his shoes. Perhaps you would like to go upstairs and see what takes your fancy?'

She agreed, but she did not expect him to say that at all. He looked at her bewildered face and said, 'Trust me, fine shoes in a place like that are worth their weight in gold.'

She understood that such a simple thing like footwear could be invaluable, even if it were to be used for only one day. In the free, outside world, it was vital enough to have a decent pair, but it was ten-fold in prison, for personal comfort or even to use as a trade.

Mr Huffham doublechecked that she could have the day off for the visit. She swallowed and held the expression of regret on her face. Her answer was, 'Yes,' but it came with unfortunate news.

'Mr Fenchurch sacked me this morning'

'What?'

'He said he didn't want a staff member who was associated with Jonathan or, as he put it, Jack the Ripper,' she said as she squeezed his hand.

He sat back and shook his head, whilst saying to himself, 'Stupid man. I would have thought Fenchurch held a little more intelligence than that.'

Her tear went from a drop to a flow, as she told him she was now absent of a job and a home.

He handed over his napkin to wipe her face and offered his home as hers for the night at least, with the suggestion of her sleeping in Jonathan's bed.

'Thank you, sir. Are you absolutely sure that would be all right?'

'Do not ask if I am sure. If I was not, then one would not offer."

She stood up to go to Jonathan's bedroom to pick a pair of shoes. Just before she left the dining room, she turned to Mr Huffham and asked why he was once in Newgate.

He coughed and replied with a slight stutter.

"Twas ... a tiny misunderstanding, you could say. The folly of youth, which is wasted on the young. I shall tell my tale another time. It is hardly fitting for the dinner table.'

A giggle came from Sally, which broke the sudden, quiet stillness that hovered in the air.

Lizzie smirked with a friendly face as she left the room for Jonathan's bedroom to find what she thought would be the nicest and most comfortable shoes.

Chapter 27

Five o'clock the next day. Just as the first hint of darkness spread its cold touch in the winter air, Lizzie and Mr Huffham were at the notorious Newgate Prison. As they approached, she clutched Jonathan's shoes, which were wrapped in brown paper and tied with string, holding the package close to her chest like a child squeezing a teddy bear for comfort. She looked up at the central front tower that gave her a chilling feeling of true horror. From the outside, it had the appearance of a medieval castle. Its stone walls and spiked port cutlass front gate matched the infrastructure of the dark ages.

The infamous prison, which made even the toughest of men tremble just by hearing the name, was the oldest, hardest, and most cruel in the country. To this day, as it had done since being first erected, it only housed the worst of the worst. It had stood there for many a century, the first foundation having been built in the twelve hundreds. Even after almost a millennium, the acts of the barbaric, medieval ways had not altered that much. The vile secrets that dwelt within were tragically infinite. The torture and cruelty were to remain unknown, forever held in the lifeless walls and silent, unfeeling stone, along with the dead, who could not speak to tell their tales.

They passed through the central arch in the outer wall that towered over them by several feet and held hundreds upon hundreds of thick, razor-sharp iron spikes that the prison staff nicknamed 'dragon's teeth'.

A few more paces forward, with the sound of the screeching rusty front gate being swung closed behind them, they entered the front desk. Only visitors, guards, the warden, and other staff were permitted here. The man at the desk was called Mr Grimshaw, who had worked there for many years. He had started young, keen, and relativity soft, but as the years rolled on, he had become hardened by the darker side of human nature. He had only recently been transferred to this job from being a duty guard, an effort to rein in some of the more vicious sights of crime and punishment. He carried the beginnings of heavy facial hair, trimmed neatly in the hope that it would grow to a full beard.

Not many of the guards had a full beard, for it was against the ruling of the warden. Only staff with very plausible reasons were worthy and seen fit to have such an appearance. The reasoning behind Mr Grimshaw's attempt of a beard was just three weeks ago he was attacked. Whilst working as a guard in the prison, doing a routine 'walkabout', as they called it, he was brutally set upon and received a deep slash across his face from a hand-forged primitive blade. The cut ran so long it, started at his ear and reached down to his chin. As a result, he was allowed to mask the ugly, ragged scar as a form of compensation.

Mr Huffham said why they were there and who they were visiting. Mr Grimshaw pulled out a small drawer that contained record cards of all the visiting information. After a few seconds of flicking through the pocket-sized cards, he came across the appropriate data.

'Ah yes, here we are … Jonathan White, also known as Jack the Ripper. Five o'clock. Perfect,' he said.

Lizzie opened her mouth to voice her dislike for what he'd said, but she kept her silence after a certain look from Mr Huffham. She pouted her lips to scream her emotions inside of her being, for only her mind to hear.

With the order to follow the guard on duty, they passed through the front lobby and ventured in single file towards the dark heart of the prison.

All one million of Lizzie's tiny fair hairs from foot to neck stood on end as they walked deeper and deeper into the underbelly. They followed the guard and stayed close to one another. Step by step, forward down a wide hallway, they then bore left and then right as the passageways slowly became narrower.

They passed cells a-plenty, lined up next to each other, the back and side wall being of thick stone, the fronts barred from floor to ceiling. Her gaze stayed forward as if practicing a focused military march, but her curiosity could not help but stare left and right every now and then at the soulless inmates, some of whom looked almost dead on their beds, others pacing up and down like caged lions, only needing five or six steps to reach from one wall to the other. It was about fifty cells in when she saw ahead two arms slumped through some iron bars. As she got closer, she saw a face almost wedged in between the bars as the prisoner's body leaned against the front of his cell. He appeared completely motionless, as if asleep, but standing with his eyes wide open. She gasped when, after a couple of seconds of looking that the man was dead, only to be discarded like a piece of rubbish.

Mr Huffham tilted his head to encourage her to keep walking. After many more passageways, steps, gates, and cells into the prison, it seemed to only get worse and worse. It became a dungeon with nothing but degradation, misery, and squalor. No natural light and no window, just cold, damp, dreaded atmosphere surrounded them. Every prisoner held a look of utter sadness, with some being chained up to the stone, wearing rags that were once clothes, rotted away as their flesh did the same. Blood-curdling screams from distant inmates pierced her ears as the putrid stink of decay, sewage, and death hit her nose, making her feel sick instantly.

They passed through the suitably named oubliette, coming from the French word 'to forget', which was a large room walled with brick, which held ten prisoners, all chained to circular hoops nailed into the stone floor. With the exception of a mouthful of daily bread, all ten of these prisoners were indeed left to rot and be forgotten.

After five minutes, which felt like five hours, of their journey through hell, they reached the condemned sector. All the men in this area were to be hanged within the week. She knew that Jonathan's cell was in this block.

She tightened her hold on the parcel, which strangely comforted her as she walked closer to his cell. The guard stopped outside the cell and banged his wooden stick on the bars.

'Oi, dead man walking You got visitors.'

'Must you talk in that manner?' she asked.

'Lizzie, hold your tongue,' Mr Huffham quickly said.

They looked at the cage-like structure of Jonathan's cell and saw through the bars that he sat on his bed, his head in his hands. He looked up and ran to Lizzie and Mr Huffham with a desperate expression on his face that accompanied an attempt at a smile.

The guard unlocked the cell door and swung his arm to allow them in. She had just one foot in the cell and was about to embrace Jonathan when she was pulled back by the guard, who noticed her brown paper parcel.

'What's that?' he asked.

'Just a gift is all, a pair of shoes, a shred of comfort for his final hours,' she replied. The guard clicked his fingers to order her to hand it over for an inspection. He ripped the paper open to reveal the pair of laced, black shoes. He looked at the sides, top, and bottom before placing his hand inside to feel for anything out of the ordinary. Mr Huffham stood still with a casual look, knowing that the strict routine was a necessary evil in such an establishment.

The guard handed the shoes back, as he was satisfied they were fine and contained no contraband of any kind. Mr Huffham and Lizzie took a couple steps into the cell as the guard closed the door behind them, which locked itself with a hard slam.

'You got five minutes,' said the guard as he stood inches from the cell door.

They looked at Jonathan in his prison uniform of dark blue shirt and trousers, a tatty pair of shoes and belt. They hugged each other in a way that carried more emphasis than ever before.

Jonathan and Lizzie sat on his bunk bed as Mr Huffham remained standing. They caressed every second and just took in each other's fondness. With a gentle touch, Jonathan swept a hair from Lizzie's cheek to place her locks behind her ears as he kissed her firmly. This kiss was like their first, but it held the knowledge that it would be their last.

They could hardly speak at first, but it did not matter, for there was not much that could be said, but just being able to hold one another was more powerful than a thousand words of feeling or romantic poetry. She did her best not to fall apart, as did Jonathan. They both passed their own tests and held back outcries of sombre emotion. She was so overcome with the heavy situation that even crying was impossible at this stage. All of her energy was so spent that she was too far gone to cry, with the exception of one tear, which in part was due to happiness at being able to hold him again.

Mr Huffham gladly stood still and waited his turn with Jonathan, allowing them to stay in their own little moment for as long as possible.

'We have a gift for you,' she said as she handed over the shoes.

She felt so guilty she could not do more, as handing over the shoes for his final night seemed a little silly, but at least it was something.

With a half smile, he held the shoes and thanked her. The still, powerful feeling in the air was momentarily shattered with a voice from the guard yelling, 'Two minutes!'

She stood up in the cramped cell and let Mr Huffham take her place on the bed. He held Jonathan's arm and carried a strong, stern gaze. His sternness had the same stare as when he would tell off Koots, but at this moment, it was for a very different reason, to hold back his own tears.

He looked towards the bars and kept noticing the beady glare of the ever- present guard, who stood watching and listening to every word.

'It'll be all right, my lad,' he said.

Jonathan tried to smile and wanted to believe his master's words, but his face could only hold a half smile as it also held a look of overbearing dread.

'I'm … I'm scared, sir.'

Mr Huffham gripped his arm tighter and replied in a slow, meaningful way, not being able to bring himself to say the word 'hanging'.

'When it starts … you know, tomorrow morning, I want you to know that you are not alone, for we will be with you.'

His words fell on his ears as he saw Mr Huffham tapping his chest.

They all knew they could be present at the execution, but Jonathan knew exactly what he meant. He continued with, 'A finer friend I have not had.'

He reached his open palm out, as did Jonathan, and they both shook hands with a firm, respectful hold.

No great song, verse, teaching, or outcry of embrace came, for it did not need such. With that handshake among the two gentlemen, nothing else was worthy of note.

His final handshake held his fate, and, hard as it was, he was momentarily at peace. The sound of a key turning in the door clattered as the guard entered, ordering that their time was up. Lizzie ran to Jonathan as he stood up for a hug, which was to be their last.

'I love you and I always will,' she said.

She did not sob, and no sound of whimpering came from her mouth, but tears silently fell from her eyes with no chance of stopping them.

'And I love you ... more than you know,' he replied as he too felt a tear drop on his cheek bone.

Lizzie and Mr Huffham left the cell as the guard immediately slammed the door shut, with a bang from the unnecessary force. The doors did not need to be closed in such a way, but it added to the atmosphere of punishment and despair that the majority of the hardened guards seemed to enjoy.

Jonathan stayed standing as he held the bars with both hands. Lizzie ran her fingers over his before walking off by an order from the guard.

Mr Huffham looked at Jonathan straight in the eye and said in a serious but quite way, 'Don't forget to doublecheck your laces when you wear your shoes.'

Jonathan tilted his head one degree to one side in confusion. Silence drifted between them.

With the guard still only inches away, Mr Huffham stood still and kept his gaze fixated on the epicentre of Jonathan's eyes, both pairs locked and taut, as if trying to convey a silent message.

'Move!' the guard demanded.

He ushered them forward and away from the cell. After a few steps, the guard overtook them in order to lead the way out, back through the candle-lit maze of horror and human suffering.

Not one word was shared between Lizzie and Mr Huffham, as they both held a contrary feeling of wanting to stay with Jonathan and yet wanting to leave. After five minutes of walking though the various blocks and hallways, they finally reached the exit, which was the same opening as the entrance at the front. When the open air hit Lizzie, it was bittersweet. She bent over to the side and was sick. With all the emotion that had built up like a half ton weight, coupled with the shear vileness of what she had seen, smelt, and heard, she could not help but give in to the natural reaction her body felt. Even Mr Huffham, who had quite a strong constitution, had to hold his handkerchief over his nose and mouth on their way out.

After the unpleasant act of vomiting, she apologised profusely.

'That is perfectly all right. If I did not have my handkerchief, I too would have done the same, I'm sure,' he replied. She straightened her body and walked out the tall front gate with him by her side, both with nothing no say, as devastation and disbelief manifested in their hearts.

Both had had their fair share of terrible encounters in life and could easily recollect atrocious tales. However, the last thirty minutes triumphed all other horrors that had passed in their entire lives, a moment that was nothing to be proud of, and if it were possible to be reversed, then heaven and hell would be moved by them in order to do so.

Chapter 28

Later on, as the evening turned into night, Jonathan was in his cell. For the last two days and night, he unfortunately had been forced to call this room of stone and iron home. He sat on his bunk thinking of the following morning and that the prison executioner would have another notch on his tally of hangings. He was angry when he kept thinking that the end of life was not meant to occur in this way. Our last night on earth comes to us all, but life being taken by another before one's prime is an atrocity beyond all else. An old man passing away at peace in his bed, surrounded by loved ones for the final farewell, was not what he would experience.

Thanks to Mr Huffham's teachings, and his library of centuries old wisdom, Johnathan was mentally strong and thought very practically. He was scared of how exactly his hanging would feel. It was the strange case of thousands upon thousands of people meeting the same ill-timed fate by the snap of the neck, but of course not one of them could explain how it felt. Without possessing the so-called magical powers of mediumship, he could not ask a floating spirit. Even if he did have the opportunity to converse with what surely would be a huge number of departed souls, spectres, apparitions, phantoms, and wraiths that haunted Hellgate for the purpose to retrieve advice, he would not believe it, for he considered this practice one of charlatanism, considering ghost stories to be nothing but entertainment and thrilling amusement.

Despite his never-ending fear, he found some solace from Shakespeare which strangely helped him a little. The words he recounted in his head were:

'No man should fear death, but even the bravest fears the manner of his death.'

He would do anything to change the current course of events, but sadly, he realised that nothing could be done. He would chisel his way out with a spoon, if possible. Even using his own fingernails to scrape away the mortar would not be past his abilities. Alas, time and opportunity were not on his side.

Minutes turned into hours and he could think of nothing else. The dreaded feeling of impending death becoming a reality with the next sun rise consumed his soul. He started to think that maybe he would see Wooly and his father in the afterlife, with mixed feelings of happiness and upset.

He leaned back against the stone wall, only to spring forward a second later when an ice-cold droplet of water from the dripping damp fell onto the back of his neck, to then trickle down his spine. With his jolt forward, his feet knocked the new pair of shoes that sat on the floor beside his bed. He looked down and remembered Mr Huffham's words. The sound of his voice in his head made him smile.

Even though it was far past lights out and he would usually be ready for bed at such a late hour, he would not be sleeping, for that was the last thing on his mind on his final night alive. With his intention of being awake all night, to say goodbye to the world, he saw it fit to wear his new shoes. The idea that they came from Mr Huffham and Lizzie made him feel he had their touch with him.

He slid on the shoes and felt they were indeed much more comfortable than his prison issue ones. Whilst tying up the long laces, he felt something was not quite right in one of them. One of the laces did not move as it should. The flexibility it held was just a tiny bit supple and a little less bendy than the other.

He pulled the lace from the holes and studied it as he brought it up close to his eyes. After a few moments of examining with much curiosity, he flicked the end with the tip of his finger and felt a tiny hole. He pealed back the sides of the first inch of lace cloth and found a thin wire. He pulled gently as the wire seemed to grow in length. He pulled more, as if unsheathing a sword from its scabbard, and saw that the wire was the same length as the entire lace. He held it up in front of him and then turned his gaze at the lock on his cell door. A cunning smile came across his face, only to linger further when Mr Huffham's final words hit his mind, as they now made sense.

He quickly looked at the bars that stood either side of his door, to check for any passing guard. Luckily, with great fortune, the passageway on the other side of his cell was clear for now.

He stepped to his door with the foot-long wire in his hand and knelt down to face the lock. He closed one eye to aid his focus on the inner mechanism deep inside the keyhole. The wire was far too flimsy to hold enough solidity to tweak the lock workings, but it was so long, he could fold it many times to double its mass.

After several folds, the wire resembled a paper clip, but contorted and squashed together. The length he needed to pick the lock had to be approximately two inches. With the wire being close to twelve, he had more than enough to work with.

His skillset was exemplary when it came to understanding every piece that made up the lock. He gently pushed the folded wire into the keyhole and started to wiggle it into place. He tried to feel the second spring hook that was embedded deep inside. His hand had to be as steady as a surgeon's performing an operation.

The silence of the dead of night that filled the prison only made each soft clatter of metal on metal feel like a loud bell. Every scrape seemed to amplify the last. The prison was as cold as could be but drops of sweat still managed to run from his temples as his heart pumped harder than ever and his pulse throbbed all over.

He smiled when he felt the curved end of the wire latch on the inner lock hook, a little victory that filled him with elation. However, his happiness was dashed away in a split second when he realised he was in need of another, thicker piece of metal, to twist round a small steal lip that lay inside the lock. He was halfway to opening the door, but it may as well have been a million miles away from being fully picked.

He tapped his torso, thinking about any material that would do for a second skeleton key, but he felt nothing but shirt cloth and buttons as he frantically searched his body. He lowered his hand and felt his belt buckle. With one hand still holding the wire in the lock, he managed to unbuckle his belt to then pull it from his waist with the other.

As gingerly as he could, he released his grip of the wire to leave it poking out but finely balanced on the inner lock hook. With another look through the bars to double check the coast was still clear, he pivoted the central clasp of the buckle. He pulled it back and forth hard and fast. After a couple dozen twists and pulls, he felt the pin weaken. A couple more bends later, he heard the snap of the brass break off from the clasp.

With the two-inch wire in the lock and the similar sized belt buckle pin, he had everything he needed. He returned to the lock to get to work with the hope that he could finish what he'd started. As one hand held the wire, the other wiggled the belt pin, trying to edge it by the steal lip.

After just a couple of minutes of intense concentration, he heard the satisfying click from inside. With two firm twists from his fingers with precise aim, the lock was manipulated free.

The door swung a few inches with a creek, so he grabbed the bars to silence the sound. With another look, checking the absence of a guard, he inched the door further open and tiptoed his way out of the cell. He gently closed the door after him to try to keep the appearance unchanged, if it were to be seen from a distance.

With as much stealth as he could, he silently moved down the dark passageway, passing other cells as he did. Silence surrounded him, as he had to make his footsteps light and soft. He saw the other inmates fast asleep but could not risk waking them. They would either raise the alarm out of shear jealousy or plead for him to take them too. Either way, it was not worth the risk.

He reached the end of the passage and peered round the corner, only one eye showing. He heard the footsteps of a guard in the distance. His heart sank as the steps slowly became louder and louder. He pulled his gaze away and stood as still and as flat to the wall as he could. The steps from the guard got closer and closer as Jonathan stayed against the wall, not moving an inch. The guard stopped on the corner and was within touching distance of him, his eyes half closed to not show the whiteness reflecting the candlelight. He was a shadow, glued to the wall and a still as the lifeless stone itself. From the corner of his eye, he could see the guard hovering.

After a few seconds, of tense stillness, the guard turned around and walked off down a different corridor. Jonathan peaked round the edge of the wall again to watch him walk off. The way was clear, so he was able to edge his way through this part of the prison. He wasn't totally sure of the way out, so he hoped instinct would help guide him. He made his way down another passage and found himself in the large room of the oubliette. He looked around and noticed all ten prisoners were either asleep or dead. He slowly tiptoed down the middle to reach the other side. He did not stop to see if the poor souls were alive or dead, for his goal was to manoeuvre through to the next part of the maze-like prison.

After a few more steps, he found two sets of stairs. One leading down, the other running up. He had no recollection of these stairs, but he did feel that upward was the better route to take. Suddenly, the sound of raised voices came from the lower level. He could not tell how many different voices it was exactly, but it was clear it was more than a couple. He quickly realized he would be in full sight of whoever was walking up. He ran across the open landing and made his way up the other set of steps, just as a small group of prison officers reached the landing where he had stood, just a few seconds prior.

At the top of the stairs, he saw he must have taken a wrong turn, but with the sounds from below, he had nowhere else to go without being found. He looked ahead, only to see a dead end in the form of a solid stone wall. He walked forward and saw a wooden door to his left. The door held a glass panel making up the top half. He looked through and saw the room appeared to be empty. With a slow turn of the rounded doorknob, he opened the door and entered. He looked around and found himself in some sort of locker room. Maybe it was a changing room or an old storage room. With no time to think what the room could be, he searched around for anything of use. Wanting to be as fast but as quiet as possible, for he knew that any minute his cell would be found and the discovery of his empty bed would raise an alarm, he searched every locker for something to aid him. A gun, a stick, a uniform, anything at all.

After a few moments of frantic searching, nothing of worth could be found. Not even a penknife or a pencil lay within. Just dust, cobwebs, and a dozen tall, narrow lockers was what the room had to offer.

In this abandoned room, he saw the walls were made of brick, quite a contrast to the stone walls that seemed to be commonplace within the building. A glimpse of hope came to him when he found a window. He gently unlatched the short metal arm and pulled the window up. The fresh air of the cold night hit him with a cool blast to his face. As he looked out, the sound of heavy rain fell from the dark sky.

The pitch blackness of the night and the constant, dense splash of rainfall would certainly help his chance of escape. He peered out and saw he was one floor up from the ground. He looked ahead and noticed about twenty feet of wet grass, with the large outer wall sitting on the other side. He straddled the window frame and gently slid out. His hands gripped the ledge as his body hung down.

With a look left and right for any guard patrolling the inner perimeter, he saw the ground was clear. It was so dark, he could not see that far either side, but that only made him think, *If I can't see them, then they can't see me.*

He let go of the ledge and dropped ten yards down to the soft, wet grass with the squelch from his feet on his landing. His first thought was to run to the outer wall as soon as possible, but with the clunking sound of his landing, he stood like a statue.

Freedom was now only a short dash across open ground and then one wall to climb. His heart pounded from his chest with the exhilaration of getting as far as he had. However, the constant worry of the alarm ringing at any moment did not allow him to take respite.

He waited a few seconds to pick the right moment. This was possibly the hardest part, for the distance from where he was to the outer wall was not far, but it was totally open, with no place to hide in between. If he was seen now, then all of his achievements would be for nothing, and he would certainly receive a torturous death far worse than a hanging.

Five, four, three, two, one - it was now or never. He sprinted across the grass and reached the perimeter wall. He looked up at his Everest and knew this part would be impossible to climb. An attempt would only cause noise and commotion when he inevitably. He turned his body and held his back close against the wall, keeping himself as flat as possible as he side-stepped along the stone until he reached the corner.

He turned around and looked at the right angle of the two walls. Using the corner of the wall, he carefully climbed up, with his left hand and foot on one wall and his right on the other.

He began to climb with his fingertips, gripping the rough stone, the top edges of his shoes doing the same with only millimetres of space to get a hold of. He climbed and climbed and finally reached the top, just as his muscles were about to snap, for they could not take much more. With his arm reaching out, he grabbed one of the dragon teeth spikes and pulled himself up, to reach the top of the wall.

The rain did not relent its heavy downpour as he carefully lifted himself over the long spikes. This was the moment of truth, and one jump would be the jump to freedom. The height was daunting to say the least, but it was not high enough for death. Even with the high chance of many a broken bone, it was still more appealing than the hangman's noose, or worse. It was something that had to be done and any alternative would just not do.

He lowered himself down over the side and hung his full body, as far as he could, to reduce the distance of the fall. His legs dangled, then he let go of the spikes. He scraped down the stone wall and fell to the outside world. He landed on the pavement with a thud as his knees bent to minimise the chance of a broken angle or leg.

He felt around his lower half with the anticipation of immense pain, but none came. With the exception of a few minor cuts and bruises on his arms and side, he was unharmed.

He looked up through the rain and saw the white of the full moon looking directly back at him, with its strange lunar smile. He took a deep breath, a mouthful of fresh drizzle, and felt the free air fill his lungs.

With one final look left and right, he ran off into the distance like a ghost as he entered the fuzzy haze of the thick, cloudy nighttime mist.

Chapter 29

He ran as fast as his legs could take, with only one feasible destination in his mind. That of his master's house. It was not to be a mere short jaunt, for Mr Huffham's house was close to eight miles away. However, at the forefront of his thinking was that every step took him further from the prison.

He looked back every now and then, expecting to see either a guard or constable giving chase with the sound of the alarm ringing in the distance. For now, every time he turned his head, all he could see was rain, darkness, and the faint outline of the large prison walls through the mist getting smaller and smaller.

It would have been mixed odds for a guard to catch him if there were to be a foot chase. With Jonathan's weakened state, it would appear the guard would have the advantage. However, with Jonathan running to keep his life, it would most probably heighten the stakes for him, with extra energy and determination striking his heart with pure adrenaline.

Luckily at the moment, no such chase seemed to be taking place, as Jonathan was the only man running. He was thrilled when the sound in the air still did not carry an alarm of any sort. Complacency did not enter his being for one moment, for he knew it would only be a matter of time. Even if his barren cell with his vacant bung bed was not discovered by any night guard, sunrise was fast approaching and he would be found out sooner rather than later.

The puddle-ridden square cobbles of the Whitechapel roads felt his light, swift step as he ran and ran.

After twenty minutes, he stopped at a row of iron railings that circled a large park. He grabbed the black iron with both hands for the sole purpose of holding him up. He gasped as his lungs ordered him to rest, even if only for a few seconds. His head dropped as he breathed heavy and deep to restore his efforts to be able to carry on.

The roads and pavements were largely deserted, for all he could see was the early morning 'Knocker-Ups'; the women who had the job of waking people up each morning.

He began to carry on his running after the short but much needed break. He passed half a dozen Knocker-Ups as his steps continued. He was always fascinated with the simplicity of that trade and wondered why anyone would care to do it.

The pea blowers did exactly was their title indicated. The women would be paid a penny to act as a personal early morning alarm clock. They were given the correct address and time of when the customer wished to be woken, and they would blow a dried pea through a short, narrow tube at the bedroom window to help raise a sleepy head, some of whom becoming highly skilled with their aim.

After what felt like an hour, he reached a long avenue. He knew he was getting close to his home. He ran in the middle of the road, right down the avenue that was flanked by rows of leafless winter trees that carried the appearance of dead man's hands, the branches bent and contorted in their jagged way.

After a short time, he finally reached his road, and he briskly walked towards his front door, where he saw through the window a thin strip of yellow light in between the curtains of Mr Huffham's parlour room, a set of eyes peeking out. He could not tell whose face they belonged to, which only added fuel to his paranoia. It crossed his mind that it could be the police, lying in wait, only to pounce on him the moment they could.

He carried on towards the front door regardless, for he had no energy to run anymore. Just as he reached the door, he noticed the parlour curtains twitch in rapid fashion. He thought his game was up and all that he had achieved was for nothing when he looked up and saw the door open right in front of him. His heart skipped a beat when he saw Mr Huffham standing in his hallway, a smile on his face so strong it would make even a professional clown most envious.

He ran into the house as Mr Huffham quickly closed the door after him.

'Oh, sir,' he said in a desperate and exhausted state.

'Well done. I know what you have been through,' replied Mr Huffham as he told him to sit down and have a drink.

Jonathan's energy slowly came back as he sat by the fire, whereupon he saw a large gin and tonic, a cup of tea, and a small blue and white willow pattern plate with three slices of lemon drizzle cake laying side by side. It was as if it had already been there, awaiting him.

'Sally! A change of clothes if you please. He has come,' Mr Huffham ordered with a happy tone to his voice.

Jonathan rested by the warm fire for a few moments as he removed his soaking wet prison shirt.

'It was you, wasn't it? The wire. The shoes,' he asked.

'Quite possibly,' Mr Huffham replied with a smile and a wink. Jonathan smiled back and thanked him greatly.

Sally returned to the entrance of the parlour room holding a set of clean, comfortable clothes, folded nicely in her hands. Jonathan looked up and saw someone standing directly behind her but could not tell who. Sally stepped aside as

Lizzie stood in the door frame. They looked at each other and felt complete. She ran towards him and jumped into his lap to hug him tight, as if she did not want to ever let go.

Jonathan groaned with pain. She loosened her firm hug as she realised he was aching and sore.

'Oh my love, I'm sorry,' she said in a remorseful, caring tone.

He laughed and reassured her everything was fine. He pulled her back towards him and carried on holding her a little longer.

'Sweetheart, I have so much to tell you, but I do not know what to do. I can't stay here,' he said with some sadness.

She told him that Mr Huffham had explained everything to her.

'Yes, I do apologise, my dear, for not telling you my plan before we visited Jonathan, but I could not risk you giving the game away. I needed your reactions to be true. Also, if his demise were to have happened and the plan did not work, it would have been all the more dreadful for you.'

She smiled and understood every word he said and thanked him more than words could express.

Whilst changing his clothes, he turned and repeated that he could not stay, for it would put everyone in danger.

'That is right, my boy. This house is one of the first places they will come for you.' He continued, 'When you have had your food, the both of you will follow me.'

After a few minutes, the plate that held the cake now only held iced sugar crumbs, the glass and cup also void of their original contents, without even leaving a drop. Mr Huffham lead them out to his backyard, where his cart and his beloved horse, Tammylan, lay in wait.

'Take these and go where you can. Do you have a place in mind?' he asked.

Jonathan paused and thought. All he could think of was his childhood home and his mother.

'I have a home, other than here …Lizzie, I know I ask the impossible, but will you come with me?'

She answered within a couple of breaths.

'I do not have to muse or ponder at all. There is nothing else for me here. I will follow you anywhere.'

Jonathan smiled, as did Mr Huffham.

'I have twenty pounds saved,' Jonathan said as he took a step forward to rush upstairs and his fetch his savings.

With a firm hand on his shoulder from Mr Huffham, he was stopped in his tracks.

'You are wrong, my boy.'

Jonathan looked back at him with confusion covering his face. Mr Huffham handed over a small brown leather satchel and said, 'You have one hundred pounds.'

With his confusion not diminishing at all, Jonathan opened up the satchel and saw it was full of pound notes.

'But … but –' he stuttered.

'It is a gift. My eighty to meet your twenty makes a splendid round number, do you not think?' he said in a happy and calm way.

Jonathan was speechless, as was Lizzie, for she had never seen that much money in her entire life.

She turned her gaze from the bag and looked at Mr Huffham in bewilderment and disbelief. 'Are … are you … are you …sure?'

'Do not ask if I am sure.' he interrupted.

Jonathan closed the bag and said. 'No … I … I cannot, sir.'

'You can and you will. That is my last order.'

Jonathan's face looked conflicted as he could only say one word: 'But -'

'Am I not still master of this house? The last time I looked, I believe I was, therefore, you will take it.'

With a huge smile, Jonathan shook his hand firmly.

'Thank you, sir. Thank you for everything. Words cannot express all you have done for me, even what you did when I first came into your service.'

'No words are needed, my boy. Come now, it's getting light. You must go. I'd wager the police will be here within the hour,' he replied.

Jonathan helped Lizzie onto the cart. He then turned to face Mr Huffham. They hugged with sincerity and fondness as the embrace was tremendously heartfelt.

I will see you again … someday,' said Jonathan as a lonely tear dropped from the corner of his eye.

'I know you will, my boy. Good luck and goodbye,' he replied in a calm but sombre voice.

Jonathan jumped on the cart and sat next to Lizzie as he then took charge of the reins. With an order for Tammylan to move, the horse's hooves started to trot forward and leave the yard.

They left the house as Jonathan turned around to see Mr Huffham standing in the middle of the road with a final wave goodbye. He waved back to the man who was not only his saviour, teacher, and master in life, but a true friend and a peerless gentleman, who was as good a father figure beyond all else he knew and one he would never forget for as long as he lived.

Chapter 30

Jonathan and Lizzie were being pulled along the road with the gentle bob and sway as the cartwheels slowly but surely rolled over the gravel. Tammylan was a fine stallion and had almost become a friend to his former master, for over many years he had served him favourably. He was well past his better days and ready for retirement, but the steady walk to leave the city was a task that could still be done with distinction. Fortune would have it, he did not have a heavy load to pull. A small cart, two occupants, and a bag of cash was light enough for this trusty old steed.

As each mile gradually replaced the last, Jonathan had a resting peace within. Discounting a few things, he would not miss London at all. The gallant Mr Huffham, the caring Sally, the harmless, foolhardy Koots, the memory of Wooly, and the locksmith shop itself would always have a special place in his heart. Everything else his last eight years had to offer would gladly just become a memory, to fade little by little as days passed through the sands of time in God's own eternal hourglass.

After two hours of travelling, the sun rose over the lush green landscape of Jonathan's home village. Lizzie took a deep breath as she tilted her beautiful face upward. Her slender body and keen mind felt content when she felt the fresh morning air fill her up, embedding itself through her core.

The air here seemed to feel different to her somehow, as if it was lighter and purer than any she had known before. The atmosphere in her new surroundings felt less of a conflict and intensity.

They rode round a slight bend in the narrow path as they reached the outskirts, passing Mr Pitwick's farm, when a whole host of memories touched his soul. He suddenly carried a weight in his heart. Not through heartbreak or any such sadness, but with excitement knowing he'd see his mother again, wondering how she would fare after all these long years.

His nerves became more brittle as they got closer to Sarah's house. He had a thousand and one doubts and questions on the tip of his tongue. The one that held the most importance, and one he tried to forget about, was if she was even alive. Eight years could feel like twenty for anybody with limited income.

He worked out his dear mother would be approaching the age of fifty and two.

He arched his shoulders, tilted his head left and right, and swallowed to try and eradicate such thoughts and replace them with one vital question. Could he even be forgiven for running away and leaving her with the mess he'd caused?

The guilt he carried then was still with him now, and he did not take for granted that everything would be all right on his return.

With a final pull on the reins, they stopped right outside Sarah's humble house.

He took a moment of stillness, with thoughts buzzing round in his head. Lizzie calmed them in an instant when she placed her hand on his lap and turned to him.

'It'll be all right, I'm sure, my love.'

Her feminine, soft eyes and those words that flew so naturally from her graceful mouth, it was enough to make him smile and give him the courage he needed. He jumped off the cart with his satchel in hand to then help Lizzie down with his arm raised. Her feet rustled as they touched the ground, which was layered with a pale brown blanket of leaves.

With both their hearts pounding, although for different reasons, they walked to the front door and knocked three times. Seconds passed in the tense stillness. His leg bounced and twitched as if his body was fighting his nervous state on its own accord. A few more seconds passed and still no answer.

They remained silent as their nerves took over. He raised his hand to knock again when the door suddenly opened.

He looked at his mother with an adoring, affectionate, but humbling stare. She looked back at her son as her jaw dropped and her eyes widened in shock, questioning what exactly she was seeing. He did not speak but had an apologetic smile on his face.

Her mouth moved as if to say something, but no words could come out. She smiled as tears ran down her face, with immense happiness so powerful it made her drop to her knees.

'Jonathan ... my boy ... it can't be,' she said in a tender, surprised, state.

He knelt down so he could help her up.

'Yes, mother ... it's me,' he said as they both got back to their feet.

She flung her arms around him and hugged him very tight. She could not believe it, but this day was one of the happiest she had ever witnessed.

She took a tissue from her sleeve and wiped away her tears of joy, but her happy face did not leave her.

Jonathan introduced her to Lizzie, and they hugged as if they'd known each other for a long time already. He opened the leather satchel and showed his mum the contents. Her face of ecstasy from the last few minutes still held as another great shock of happy bewilderment was thrust upon her. She let them in her house, which, from this moment on, would be their home too. The door closed and did not open again for many hours, as there was much to say from all. This was now a place where love, happiness, and a sense of belonging dwelled.

Meanwhile, forty-five miles away in Whitechapel, a letter was placed on Police Chief Dallyard's desk. It read:

Dear boss,

Oh what deeds I shall commit. I will take the next whore that I encounter and show her what hell is really like.

You think you know me, but you don't.

You think you know terror, but you don't know Jack!

The End

For Lizzie

Jonathan meeting Wooly

A big thankyou to Nigel Mitchell,
Theresa Loosley and Nicky Prentis
at Biddles Limited